"I'll help you—teach you how to run this place."

Tyler wanted to hug her, his relief was so deep. He put a hand to his heart instead. "Thank you. Seriously. Thank you."

Kit nodded. Then glanced at the sky. "It's getting late. You'd better go get that booze. And this week we'll fill out the order form for the bar together. Maybe we can come up with a form that's less confusing, too."

It was all he could do not to fist-pump the air. She was going to help him. But he kept his voice steady. "That would be great. And we'll get a contract drawn up, with the terms of our partnership, so you can be sure you'll get everything we talked about." He turned toward his truck, then looked back. "See you soon."

He liked saying it. He liked knowing it was true.

Backing his truck down the driveway, he paused for a moment. He felt funny. Lighter. And he realized it was Kit. With her on his side he knew he could do anything. With her help they could make The Dusty Saddle a success. He'd just have to remember not to fall for her, because he was pretty sure he was already partway there.

Dear Reader,

The Sierra Legacy series has been about many things, but overall it's about the legacy left by Nora, Wade and Arch Hoffman's father, his crimes and his abuse. In the first three books of the series, Nora, Wade and Arch all had their chance to come to terms with their past, to discover their purposes in life and to find the loves of their lives.

But there's one person still reeling from everything that's happened: Kit Hayes, the woman who loved Arch, and who has never been able to move on from that love.

His Last Rodeo is Kit's story, her chance to realize her dreams and break free of the past. And it's the story of Tyler Ellis, a man trying to come to terms with his own past as a rodeo champion, as a son and as someone who struggles to overcome a hidden disability.

It was such fun to write their chemistry, humor, friendship and love. I hope you enjoy their journey. And thank you for reading the Sierra Legacy series!

Claire McEwen

CLAIRE McEWEN

—

His Last Rodeo

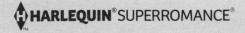
HARLEQUIN®SUPERROMANCE®

Recycling programs
for this product may
not exist in your area.

ISBN-13: 978-0-373-64026-3

His Last Rodeo

Copyright © 2017 by Claire Haiken

Printed in U.S.A.

HARLEQUIN®
www.Harlequin.com

Claire McEwen lives by the ocean in Northern California with her family and a scruffy, mischievous terrier. She loves writing stories where strong heroes and heroines take big, emotional journeys to find their happily-ever-afters. When not dreaming up new books, she can be found digging in her garden with a lot of enthusiasm but, unfortunately, no green thumb. She loves discovering flea-market treasures, walking on the beach, dancing, traveling and reading, of course!

Find Claire on her website, clairemcewen.com, and follow her on Facebook, Facebook.com/cmcewen.writer, Twitter, Twitter.com/clairemcewen1, Pinterest, Pinterest.com/cmcewenwriter, and Instagram, Instagram.com/claire_mcewen_writer.

Books by Claire McEwen

HARLEQUIN SUPERROMANCE

Home Free
Return to Marker Ranch
Wild Horses
Convincing the Rancher
More Than a Rancher
A Ranch to Keep

Other titles by this author available in ebook format.

His Last Rodeo is for all the readers who have embraced the Sierra Legacy series and taken the Hoffmans into their hearts. Thank you for your letters, your encouragement and your enthusiasm!

And for my editor, Karen Reid, whose incredible talent, patience and faith make it all possible.

I couldn't have written *His Last Rodeo* without my son and my husband cheering me on, picking up the slack, and assuring me over and over that I would figure out the best way to tell Kit's story. Arik and Shane, all of my books are for you, but this one really is your achievement as well as mine!

CHAPTER ONE

KIT HAYES STOOD on the steps of the Benson library and watched the love of her life leave town. Again.

Arch Hoffman, duffel bag in the back of his truck, was waiting at the last red light before Main Street turned into highway.

He never used to have a truck. When she'd last seen him a year ago, he was just out of prison and didn't own much.

"That jerk." Kit's best friend, Lila, moved to stand next to her. "Why was he even in town? I though he'd moved to San Francisco."

Kit shrugged. "He must have come to see his family." If he'd been here any longer than a day or two, she'd have been sure to run into him in this tiny California town. It was just a few picturesque roads mushed up against the east side of the Sierras.

"Where'd he get that fancy truck?"

The afternoon sun glinted off the chrome bumper of the red Ford. "He probably has money now," Kit said. "From his sculptures."

"Oh, right. I'd forgotten he's the next big thing in the art world." Lila's tone made it clear she was anything but impressed.

Kit wished she could care so little. A few months ago, there had been a photo of Arch in the *Benson Record*, gorgeous and smiling, taken at an art show in San Diego. She'd stared at the photo for a long time. Years ago—when he'd loved Kit—the only section of the paper Arch would have made was the police blotter. He'd been her charming criminal back then. Neither of them could have imagined he'd become the town's prodigal son.

The light changed and Arch's truck accelerated, oblivious to Kit's scrutiny. Heading back to the city—home to the woman he loved. The pretty, perfect Mandy Allen, who'd swiped Arch's heart just as easily as he used to swipe cars.

Kit shifted, trying to ease the jealousy that squeezed her chest. It may have been over a year since she'd seen Arch, but the feeling still gripped her every time she thought of him and Mandy together.

"You need to let him go," Lila said.

"I'm trying. Trust me, I *hate* feeling like this." Kit held up her stack of books.

Lila glanced at the titles. "More self-help books? You've read about a million of them already and they haven't worked. You need to get back out there. You need a date." She bumped her shoulder gently into Kit's and gave her a sly smile. "You need to get laid."

Kit bumped her right back. "Shush! We're at the library, not the bar."

"No one heard." But Lila lowered her voice. "Seriously, reading about feeling better won't make you feel better. You need to *do* something."

"I've *been* doing stuff." Kit had kept busy at work, trained for a half marathon last summer and gone skiing. "I even took that pole dancing class you talked me into. Which was a disaster, by the way."

Lila grinned. "I didn't realize it was at the seniors' center when I signed us up."

Kit laughed. Which felt good. Seeing Arch drive away left tire marks of regret in her muddy heart. "I'm scarred for life. Images of the seniors getting funky are burned on my brain."

"You laughed so hard after that class. It was better than therapy. Maybe we need to go back. I think their spring session should start any day now."

"No!" Kit didn't know what would help her get out of this black hole of jealousy and loss, but she was sure the cure wasn't pole dancing. She just had to keep reading and keep trying. She'd been working on not loving Arch for almost half her life—she *had* to be successful eventually.

She'd almost managed to unlove him. During the decade after he'd walked away from their four-year relationship, she'd done okay. She'd learned to live without him, had some fun, even had a few boyfriends. All in all, she'd done pretty well, until he showed up again.

The moment she'd seen him, all her old feelings had flooded back, almost as if he'd never left. And they wouldn't go away again.

Stupid, *stupid* feelings.

Meanwhile, Arch had fallen in love and moved to San Francisco, and she *still* didn't feel free of him. Somehow Arch's success as an artist, his happy relationship with Mandy, had made Kit realize how stuck she'd become: living in Benson, looking after her dad, working at a bar. She was thirty-two years old but still living the way she had throughout most of her twenties. It was a depressing thought.

Lila glanced at her phone. "You've got to get to work. Are you okay? Do you want me to take your shift for you?"

Kit shook her head. The last thing she needed was to sit at home and think about Arch. "Work will be good for me. Plus, a shipment was delivered this afternoon and I told Chris I'd check it in."

"I hope Chris is paying you a lot more than he pays me. You're practically running the bar for him."

"I'm glad he gives me a lot of responsibility." Kit took a breath, suddenly ready to say aloud what she'd kept to herself until now. "I've learned a lot and I've saved some money. When he retires, I think I want to buy the place."

"Really?" Lila's green eyes were wide. "That's…that's great." The false enthusiasm in her voice rang too loud in the quiet afternoon.

"What's wrong? You don't think I can do it?"

"No." Lila put her hand on Kit's arm. "No, of course that's not it. You're great at running the bar. It's just…you love reading those travel books and you've been taking those online Spanish classes. I just thought you'd—" The pale skin of her cheeks stained pink. "That's what you want? To stay in Benson and own the Dusty Saddle? I just didn't realize."

Kit inhaled the chill of the early spring evening, hoping it would clear the Arch-induced melancholy from her heart. "What I *want* is to travel. To move to Spain or South America or someplace where I will never have to see or hear about Arch Hoffman again. But I don't get to do that. I have to look after Dad. So owning the Saddle is a pretty good plan B."

"Are you sure you can't fix things for your dad? Did you ever go talk with that ex-boss of his?"

"Mr. Ellis." The evil rancher. "Yes, he finally agreed to meet with me last week. But it didn't help much. He showed me all these papers. Said my dad borrowed money against his pension years ago and never paid it back. So he's only entitled to a hundred dollars a month."

"What about Social Security?"

"It helps a little. But not enough. Even if it did, even if I could travel, Dad's depressed. He's lost without his work. I swear if I didn't stop by his house every day, he'd never get out of bed."

"I'm sorry." Lila's eyes were wide with sympathy. She understood hard times—had seen plenty of her own. "Well, it *is* a good plan B. I can see you owning the bar, and you're certainly a great manager. Almost no one complains ever since you took over the scheduling from Chris."

"*Almost* no one?" Kit teased.

"Well, Tim and I were grousing last week because neither of us wanted to work a Monday. No tips."

"Everyone has to work a Monday sometimes. I'm doing it tonight."

Lila grinned. "We know. It's just fun to complain. But don't worry. Even if we give you a hard time, we still love you."

Kit was suddenly self-conscious. "Well, it might not happen anyway. Who knows if I can save enough? Or if Chris will want to sell it? Or if the bank will give me a loan to do it?"

"It will work out," Lila assured her. "But are

you certain you don't want me to take your shift tonight?"

"I'm fine, thanks." Kit raised an eyebrow. "Why don't you want to go home? Did you and Ethan have a fight?"

Lila sighed. "No. It's the opposite, actually. Ever since we moved in together I've become so…I don't know…attached. He has his veterans' support group tonight and if I'm sitting at home, I'll miss him. And then I'll feel like a lame, dependent girlfriend. I don't want that."

"You mean fiancée," Kit corrected. "And it's *good* that you miss him. It means you like him a lot. Which is great, since you're marrying him."

Lila grinned, just like she did every time Kit mentioned Ethan or marriage. "I guess you're right. It's just a little weird."

"You're not used to being in love yet. You're still getting used to feeling safe and settled." Kit gave Lila a light kiss on the cheek. "It's good to see you so happy. Go cook him a meal or something wifely like that. Or work on your photographs—the show is only a couple months away."

"Don't remind me. I'm so nervous. Which is why I'm probably going to cook. Procrastination is my solace."

"Your photos are gorgeous." Lila took photos of ordinary life around Benson. But somehow she made a simple piece of sagebrush look like a feather, or a high mountain ridge look like it was molded from glistening silver. "Trust me. Every tourist in Mammoth is going to buy one when they walk into that gallery."

"I hope so." Lila glanced at the stack of books in Kit's arms. "Want me to take those for you?" She tucked her own book under her arm and held out her hands. "You can stop by tomorrow to pick them up."

Kit didn't comment on Lila's change of subject. She was private—probably uncomfortable even admitting she was nervous. "No, thanks. It's Monday night. The bar will be empty, just like you said. If I get my work finished, I might have time to read."

"Call me if you get bored with your self-help. We can chat."

"Will do," Kit promised.

They started down the steps. Lila's white Jeep was parked behind Kit's red one. When they'd first met, they'd bonded over their almost-identical cars.

Kit shot one last glance at the stoplight, then shook her head. Lila was right. It had been over a year since Arch had gotten out of jail. Over a year since he'd told her he loved another woman. Kit *had* to move on.

Maybe she'd find the magical words she was looking for in these books. Some insight that would end this endless heartache. But she was getting the feeling that the words she needed to hear hadn't been written yet.

Or maybe there was no cure for a love like hers. Sometimes she wondered if she'd missed Arch so much, for so long, that missing him had become another part of her. An extra limb she'd grown, like an obsolete tail, crafted from layers of her own stupidity, slowing her down as it dragged along the ground.

Kit climbed into her Jeep and dumped the books on the passenger seat. It was a short drive to the Dusty Saddle. She rolled down her windows, hoping that the rain-tossed breeze would blow some sense of hope in along with it. A promise of something new to help her get over this musty old heartache.

THE HANDS OF the old Budweiser clock above the bar were moving backward. Kit was sure of it. As she watched, it paused, then the minute hand lurched backward, like it was trying to gather the momentum to go forward. But it never did.

Kind of like her life, Kit thought. She definitely lacked momentum. Arch's moving on, Lila's getting married, had made that pretty clear.

She wiped a tiny smudge on the bar. The Dusty Saddle was never busy on Mondays, but tonight it was completely empty. The regulars must be home nursing their weekend hangovers. The younger crowd was probably at the High Country Sports Bar, which offered all the games on its multiple TV screens, and drink promotions to go with them.

She'd hoped to keep busy tonight, but she'd unpacked the order in the first hour of her shift. Finished the inventory in the second hour. Then she'd scrubbed every possible surface during the next three hours. Now she had three hours to go and nothing but silence to keep her company. The Dusty Saddle was located on the edge of town, and since Benson was nestled against the east side of the Sierras, it was eerily quiet. If Kit poked her head out the door, she could probably hear coyotes howl. Or maybe an owl or two.

She went behind the bar to get a glass of ice water. Then she pulled a book off the stack she'd left there. *Healing a Broken Heart* by someone named Dr. Melinda Mellton. The doctor's calm, radiant smile on the cover had pulled Kit in. *She* wanted to look and feel that happy. And even if Dr. Melinda's contented glow was Photoshopped, the word *healing* in the title held some promise.

Kit leafed through the first few pages, stopping at the section called "The Broken Heart Questionnaire." Dr. Melinda wanted to know if she was having trouble eating or sleeping, how long she'd been sad, was she dreaming of the person she'd lost. The questions went on for two pages. Mentally answering yes to almost every one, Kit read the analysis of her results. Melinda informed her that, given the number of times Kit had answered yes, it was clear that she had a broken heart. *Duh*.

She slammed the book on the counter. She didn't need a book to tell her that. Pushing away from the bar, she paced the empty room a few times, pausing to throw a few darts at the dartboard. Bull's-eye. Wandering to the bar, she stared at Dr. Melinda's photo. Maybe the questionnaire was dumb, but Kit was desperate for something, even a few words of wisdom to give her hope that she'd feel better soon. She sat and opened the book again.

Chapter 2 was titled "Surviving." That seemed like a good place to start. Surviving was all she'd been doing lately. She was relieved to realize that Dr. Melinda did actually know what it was like to live with a heart made of lead.

"Can't a guy get a drink around here?"

Kit grabbed the edge of the bar to keep from falling off her stool. She'd been so engrossed in Dr. Melinda's sympathetic descriptions of heartache that she hadn't heard anyone come in.

A man stood a few feet away, his black cowboy hat tilted low over his eyes. But the brim didn't hide the broad shoulders or the muscular arms bulging out of his tight black T-shirt. She slid off her stool and hurried behind the bar. "Sorry about that. You sneaked up on me."

"That must be some book you're reading." The man took a few steps toward where she'd been sitting and glanced at the cover. "*Healing a Broken Heart*? Really? *You* were always the one breaking hearts, if I remember it right." He tipped up the brim of his hat and she saw the face of an old friend.

"Tyler Ellis! I didn't recognize you under that grown-up hat of yours."

His lazy grin could melt an iceberg. "All grown up and ready for a beer."

Kit reached for a glass to give herself a moment to regroup. Tyler wasn't just grown up. He was *gorgeous*. She'd known that, of course. He was a world champion bull rider, and his wide, cocky smile was a common sight in the local paper, which covered his successes religiously.

But the photos hadn't done him justice. He smiled at her with a confidence that must work magic with rodeo fans, because it was making even her jaded knees feel wobbly.

She straightened her spine. The last guy she'd felt wobbly for was Arch, and look how *that* turned out. She gestured toward him with the empty glass. "What are you drinking?"

He glanced at the taps. "Pale ale, please."

Kit poured the local ale. Watching it foam was

far more relaxing than watching Tyler. She stole a quick glance. Yup, he was gorgeous. He always had been, even in high school. Back when they'd been best friends.

Back before Kit had fallen head over heels for Arch Hoffman. And gotten herself involved in stuff she shouldn't have.

Back before Tyler had worried about her, and told her to leave Arch, and they'd had the fight that ended their friendship.

Back before Tyler had quit high school and left town.

Kit had managed to avoid him every time he'd come to Benson since then.

"It's been a while," Tyler said quietly, as if reading her thoughts.

"It sure has." Kit slid the pint across the bar, a small peace offering. "It's on me."

"What have you been up to all this time?" He sat heavily on a bar stool and took a gulp of the ale.

"Not too much." What could she possibly tell him? He'd joined the army. Then joined the rodeo, started winning, become one of the Professional Bull Riders big stars. His looks had gotten him product endorsements and modeling contracts. He'd been in magazines, commercials, on billboards even. And all she could say about the past fifteen years was *not much*. "I've worked here, mostly."

"You must like this place." He paused, like he wanted to say something about that. Instead, he picked up her book. "So why *are* you reading this?"

No way would she tell him she was still hung up on Arch Hoffman. Not when he'd lived this incredible life while she'd stayed stuck right here in Benson. She made a grab for the book, but he held it out of reach. Just like they were kids again, growing up on his family's ranch, with her daddy working for his.

The warmth she'd felt at seeing him seeped away slowly at that thought, leaving a hollow anxiety behind. Her dad had been so good to Tyler. He'd been a mentor and a friend. He'd taught Tyler how to ride bulls. Did Tyler know that his father had fired Kit's? Was he complicit in it?

She could feel anger rising. "It's a library book—don't mess it up." She reached for it again, but she was short and he stood, so she didn't have a chance.

His grin dimpled wide and he took a few steps back from the bar. Wobbly steps.

Kit froze, taking in, for the first time, the slight flush to Tyler's face, his untucked shirt. "Hey. Are you okay?" She crooked a practiced finger, summoning him closer, in full bossy-bartender mode now. He obeyed, moving unsteadily to the bar.

Studying his green eyes, she noticed a lack of focus there. He'd always had a sharp gaze. Piercing, even. "You've drunk a lot already."

His answering nod was somber, as if they were sharing a profound moment. "Yes. I have."

"Good to know." She pulled the pint off the bar and set it on the counter behind her, out of his reach.

"Hey! I was enjoying that."

"Great. You can enjoy it another night, when you're not stumbling drunk."

He shook his head and swayed a little. *How had she not seen this before?* "I'm not stumbling."

"That's because you're hanging on to the bar stool."

He glanced at his hand, white-knuckling the stool, and looked puzzled. "I *am*. Must have been the shots I had right before I came here."

He set the book on the bar and Kit quickly placed it with her others, safely out of reach. "You need to get home and sleep this off," she told him.

"You'll go with me?" The tilt of his eyebrow might have been seductive if he'd been remotely sober.

"If you're going to be an idiot, don't talk," she snapped.

"Right," he said. "Good advice."

"Smart boy. Now let me call someone to pick you up."

"It's early. And I want to be here." He slid carefully onto the bar stool and folded his forearms on the bar, looking at her quizzically. "I'm just trying to figure out how in the hell you got more beautiful than you were. How is that even possible?"

She didn't hide the roll of her eyes. "Beer goggles make anything possible." She poured a glass of water and set it in front of him. "Drink this. And then let's get you home before you say any more stuff you'll regret later."

"I won't regret saying it. Should have said it years ago." He pulled his hat off his head and set it on the stool next to him. She'd forgotten his hair. Kind of a reddish brown, straight as a board, and he still wore it just a little too long. "I came back here a couple times. To host the Benson Rodeo, make some guest appearances, stuff like that. How come I didn't see you then?"

"Maybe because I don't watch rodeos. Or maybe because you got your drinks elsewhere. Kind of like you did earlier tonight. Were you at the High Country?"

"Yup." He nodded. "Great bar."

"Sure, if you like cocktails and big-screen TVs."

"And you don't?"

"I prefer the basics. Good beer. Good customers." She couldn't contain her curiosity. "What are you doing in town, so messed up on a Monday night, anyway?"

"A few of my buddies threw me a party. A celebration."

"What are you celebrating?"

He hesitated a fraction. "Moving home."

She'd been expecting him to say another rodeo win or another endorsement deal. Certainly not this. "You're moving to Benson? No more rodeo?"

His head moved in one emphatic shake. "Nope."

He'd lived and breathed bull riding since he was a kid. "Tyler, that's a big deal. How come you quit?"

"A lot of reasons." He took a sip of water then swirled the glass, watching as if it was actually interesting.

"Suddenly you don't want to talk, when we're talking about you."

He shrugged. "Not much to say. I had a great run. I won some titles and made a bunch of money. And I was lucky that I did all that and didn't get hurt much. But I saw a lot of friends get pretty torn up. Figured I'd quit while I was still in one piece."

"But you'll miss it." It was a guess, but she saw the way his eyes widened a little.

Then he hiccuped and blinked a few extra

times. "Excuse me. It's possible that I may have celebrated a little too much."

"Yeah. Which is why I'm suggesting, again, that you get home to sober up."

"Don't really want to do that." His arms folded across his chest in a three-year-old's version of stubborn.

"Fine. Have it your way." She grabbed a clean cloth to start polishing glasses.

Tyler was quiet for a few moments. Unfortunately, his attempt at restraint was no match for the alcohol in his system. "You know those self-help books you're reading are a con, right?"

She glared at him. "They're just books. Maybe I'll learn something, maybe I won't."

"They won't cure what's hurting you." He leaned forward, as if he was about to share a secret. "The only cure for heartache is a good beer and a good lay. I'd be happy to help…"

"Stop!" He might be an old friend and a local hero, but she didn't tolerate harassment. Ever. "You need to get the hell out of my bar if you're going to be a jerk." She moved toward him, grabbed his hat and clapped it on his head. And if she was a little rough, well, maybe he deserved it. She yanked him off his stool. He staggered into her, throwing an arm around her shoulders for balance.

She took a few steps to counter his weight and

regained her footing. Dealing with drunks came with the territory. But dealing with Tyler felt a little different. Because he'd been a friend, she reminded herself. It was that old familiarity that had her noticing the way his body pressed warm and hard against hers. "Please tell me you didn't drive here."

"No car," he told her. "My buddy took the keys."

"He's a good friend. You should thank him tomorrow." She walked Tyler across the room, then shoved open the door so they both stumbled out into the cool night air. "You can walk home. It will do you good. Or sing really loud and the sheriff will pick you up and give you a ride. Of course, he might cite you for disturbing the peace, but I hear the fines are pretty small."

"You're the best, Kit." He pulled her in closer, leaning down as if to plant a kiss on her mouth. She ducked out from under his arm and instinctively stuck her foot behind his. A quick shove on the shoulder and he was flat on his back in the gravel.

He stared at her, and she almost laughed at the shocked expression on his face. "Don't kiss me," she told him. "I'm not part of your celebration."

His smile returned, slow and wide. He sat up and grabbed his hat from where it had fallen, setting it on his head. Then he shoved himself up and staggered a few steps to get vertical. "You haven't even asked what I'm celebrating."

"Your retirement. You told me, remember?"

"Nah… Not sure if I want to celebrate that. There's more. A new business venture."

"Well, I'm pretty sure I don't care," she told him.

"Sure you do."

"Fine," she said, packing as much sarcasm as she could into her tone. "What venture would that be? Something on your daddy's ranch?"

He laughed as if she'd said something truly funny. "Nah, my brothers have that covered." He took a few uneven steps, grinning at her in the faint glow of the outside lights. "You, Kit Hayes, are looking at the new owner of the Dusty Saddle."

He took a few more steps, tipped his hat, then turned, stumbling down the street toward the center of town.

She stared after him, trying to absorb his words. As he walked away, he took her advice and broke into an off-key rendition of "Rhinestone Cowboy." Then he disappeared around the corner.

Kit closed her gaping mouth and sank onto the cracked cement steps. Tyler had bought the bar? Kit hadn't even known it was for sale. Chris had never mentioned it. Which stung, since Kit had been bartending for him for the past nine years.

She shoved her head into her hands. For a moment she relished the darkness there, the shutting out of everything. She'd clung to this idea of owning the Dusty Saddle for the past year. Using it as something to focus on besides Arch. Setting it as a goal to keep her satisfied with living in this town and looking after her dad. And now, in a few heartbeats, that goal had vanished.

This sucked. Just like everything had sucked since Arch got out of prison. She shoved off the step, not willing to sit crumpled and defeated. She walked to the edge of the parking lot. When she faced this direction, there were no lights from town to diminish the night sky. The stars exploded across the darkness, layer upon layer of cosmic insanity.

Usually the sky out here took her breath away. Tonight it just made her nervous. Because it reminded her, the way Tyler had, that in the grand scheme of things, she was nothing.

When Arch told her he didn't want her after all, he'd broken her heart. But at least she'd had her work. A place where she felt she mattered. Now she knew that wasn't true. The boss she'd worked so hard for had sold the business without a word to her. Under this vastness of stars she was a speck of dust, adrift and floating around this piece of the planet that once felt like home.

Stuck here, belonging nowhere.

Jealousy hit hot despite the cool air. What was it like to be Tyler Ellis? Born and raised in a wealthy ranching family, talented enough to achieve the highest level of his chosen sport. Now sauntering into town with enough money to buy a business that should have been *her* business.

Ha. Her business in another world, maybe. She was a Hayes. Permanently poor. Born and raised to work for the Ellis family, just like her daddy had.

If she worked for Tyler, would he screw her over, too? Like his father had cheated hers? Probably. Only he'd do it with a sugar coating of cowboy grin and flattering words, because people like Tyler thought the whole world was there just for them.

And why not? Because it *was* right there for them, waiting at their fingertips. While people like Kit were destined to watch their dreams, slippery as trout in a Sierra stream, wriggle right out of their grasping hands.

CHAPTER TWO

KIT PARKED HER Jeep in the lot in front of the Dusty Saddle. It was early on Tuesday morning, but Chris usually came in about now. She walked to the bar door, shoving it open. "Anybody here?" she called out in the quiet bar.

"We're closed!" Her boss's voice came from the small office to her left.

"It's Kit," she replied.

"Kitto! What's up?" Chris appeared, his sweatpants and I'd Rather Be Fishing T-shirt advertising his readiness for retirement. "You're not on today, right? Did I misread the schedule?"

"It's my day off, but I was hoping you'd have a minute to talk."

"Sure. Grab a seat." He indicated the empty tables she'd polished last night.

Kit picked the closest one and sat, trying to ignore the way her heart seemed to rise and stick like a lump of dough in her throat. They'd worked together for almost a decade, and it hit her that she wasn't just losing the chance to own the Dusty Saddle. She was losing a boss she'd loved. She cleared her throat. "I heard the news. About you selling the bar."

Chris plopped down heavily, his bulky frame dwarfing the chair. "How? I meant to tell you myself."

"Tyler came in last night. Drunk. He told me."

Chris folded his worn hands on the table and huffed out a sigh. "I'm sorry you found out that way. I figured he'd have the sense to check with me before talking to any of my employees."

"Well, he was beyond sense last night. Celebrating his purchase, I guess. I threw him out."

That gave Chris pause. "You threw out the new owner?"

"He hadn't told me he was the new owner yet. And he was giving me a hard time." Seeing the look of alarm on Chris's face, she tried to reassure him. "We knew each other really well growing up. I don't think he'll be too upset about it. Plus, he deserved it."

The relief on his ruddy face showed how much Chris wanted this deal to go through. But maybe it hadn't gone through yet, which meant there might still be hope for her. Kit remembered the opening she'd practiced earlier. "So you're retiring?"

His shy smile was a surprise. "Yup. I'm finally doing it. Gonna spend my days fishing and my nights watching the stars. I've had a good run here—owned this bar for over twenty years. I've enjoyed it, but I don't want to spend another minute of my life behind the bar."

"Congratulations," Kit said. And wanted to mean it. He owed her nothing, so why did she feel betrayed? "Is it a done deal? I mean, are the papers signed and all that?"

"Yup, they are," Chris said. "About a month ago."

"A month ago," she repeated. Her disappointment was edged in nausea.

He must have seen her distress because he leaned forward to take her hand. "Hey, it'll be fine. Tyler will do a great job."

"But why didn't you tell me this was going on?" She wouldn't cry, even though tears were hot under her eyes.

"I didn't want some big fuss. I didn't think you'd be this upset." He let go of her hand and leaned back, suddenly looking all of his sixty-something years. "I'm out of here at the end of the week."

"You mean—" she somehow resisted the urge to whack him upside the head "—you're only giving us a few days' notice?"

"I know you." Chris grinned suddenly, as if delighted with this part of his deception. "You'd want to throw me some big old party where the regulars would get all drunk and weepy on me.

And that's not my style. I'd rather just grab my tackle box and go."

Kit studied him, making sure he meant it. "Fine. Though you're missing out. I plan good parties."

"So I've heard. And seen, when my staff stumbled in the next day."

Disappointment and loss combined, overriding her efforts to hold back her tears. "We're going to miss you so much."

Chris brushed the sentiment off, of course. "Hell, he's Tyler Ellis. Big rodeo champion. I figured you'd all be over the moon to work for a guy like that."

"I guess I'd been hoping to buy the bar myself, if you retired," she admitted.

He looked at her sharply. "You never said."

"You never said you were planning on retiring anytime soon." There it was, that note of accusation she'd planned to avoid.

"I guess I assumed you wouldn't be interested. Because…" Chris stopped, so she finished for him.

"Because I wouldn't have the money?"

"Well, I know you've been taking care of your daddy lately. It's a big responsibility."

"I've been saving. And maybe the bank would have helped me."

"Maybe," Chris said, but she could hear the

doubt. She must seem like an idiot. Like she'd been hoping for a handout.

Her voice came out small. "Can I ask what it sold for? Just so I know if I was even close?"

His gaze went to the table. "Almost a million dollars."

Her gasp burst out before she could bite it back. That much money stole her breath.

He leaned forward, meeting her shock with concern. "You might not realize it, but this bar is on a huge piece of property. I inherited it all, but I only use this building. There's a bunch of barns, outbuildings, all kinds of acreage for ranching. And Tyler wanted it all."

"What's he going to do? Tear the bar down and stick cows on the land?"

"Nah. I think he wants to expand. Maybe even add a restaurant. He's got some big dreams."

A million dollars. Kit might laugh if it didn't sting so badly. She may as well have been saving pennies in a piggy bank.

"Wait until you talk to him," Chris went on. "I'm sure he'll call a meeting with the staff soon and fill you in on his plans. It's gonna be exciting to see what he does. You might find that me heading out to pasture is a good thing for everyone."

"Maybe." He was trying to make her feel better so Kit found a smile, but it felt like a grimace. "But I doubt it. We'll miss you."

"Likewise. It's been a pleasure working with you. You've been a bit like the daughter I never had."

"Well, don't be a stranger then." Her voice was husky. "Take me fishing with you or something."

There was a suspicious shimmer in Chris's eyes. "I'd like that."

"And when will the rodeo star take over?"

Chris chuckled. "Don't give him *too* much of a hard time. I know you've got a disdain for cowboys, but Tyler is a champion for a reason. He worked his butt off to get where he did. You might find he's made of better stuff than you imagine."

His words wormed guilt into her conscience. She'd been cursing Tyler three ways to hell since yesterday. Letting her jealousy and her disappointment make him the villain. He may have been drunk and obnoxious last night, but he'd been her friend when they were kids. He'd stuck by her, stuck up for her, and she'd kicked him out of her life the moment Arch Hoffman tilted a badass eyebrow her way.

"You're right," she admitted. "I might find that out. Or I might already be fired for throwing him out of his own bar."

"He shouldn't have come in here drunk like that." His eye crinkled into a Santa Claus wink. "Though I wouldn't have minded seeing you send him out the door. I'll say something to him.

Make sure he knows who's really been running this place for the past few years."

"Thanks, Chris." His praise didn't warm her the way he meant it to. She'd been running the bar, but now she'd just be one more employee of Tyler Ellis. Just like her dad had been one more employee of Ken Ellis. And look where that had landed him. Broke. Cast off like some old ranch horse. Except the Ellis horses were given nice pastures and good food.

"Now you go enjoy your day off," Chris said, shoving up from his chair. "I've got to open this place up. Strange to think it's one of the last times I'll ever do it."

"Yeah, strange," Kit echoed as she stood on numb limbs. Everything had felt surreal since Tyler showed up last night.

Maybe owning the Dusty Saddle had been a pipe dream, but it had also been her lifeline. The thing that made her feel like she could survive staying in this town. And now Chris had hauled up that line and tossed it to someone else.

She gave Chris a vague wave and left, furious at the traitor tears that kept pooling in her eyes. She had to pull herself together. Her next stop was her dad's house, and she didn't want him suspecting anything was wrong. She was *his* lifeline, and no matter how many things were going wrong in her life, she had to show up as strong as ever for him.

TYLER CHASED HIS third aspirin down with his second glass of water and tried to focus his eyes. His father's kitchen looked exactly the same as it had for the past two decades. Clean, quiet and barren of decor. Sometime after Tyler's mom died, his dad had removed all of her homey touches and never replaced them. The only changes were the new cracks in the faded green linoleum and the increasingly battered edges of the white cabinets.

His father and brothers had long since eaten and headed out for chores. He could almost feel his dad's disapproval in the ticking of the clock, in the tidiness, in the plate of eggs and bacon left for him. There was no way he could keep that down.

How the hell had he ended up drinking so much?

It had started simply enough. He'd met a couple friends at the sports bar. They'd shot some pool, knocked back a few beers, caught up. Then he'd told them about his business plans. How the papers were signed, the money paid. How he was going to turn the Dusty Saddle into the finest bar this side of the Sierras.

And his friends had ordered shots to celebrate.

They didn't know that Tyler was a lightweight. Anyone looking at him could see almost six feet of solid guy. But it took training to ride rodeo as well as Tyler did. As well as he *had*. It took a good diet and hours clocked in the gym. To stay in top form, he didn't drink much.

Until last night.

There'd been some dancing at the High Country. He vaguely remembered a pretty blonde draping her arms around him. Then someone had mentioned how Kit Hayes worked at the Dusty Saddle. Which got his attention. And held it until he didn't care about what the blonde was offering. He'd had to see Kit.

Because she'd haunted him. Was someone he'd always thought about, even when his life had taken him to the biggest arenas in the country. He'd been crazy about her when they were young. But they'd been friends. He hadn't known what to do about his crush. Then she'd fallen hard for Arch Hoffman and that was that.

Going to see her hadn't been such a great idea. But knowing she was a few blocks away, working in the bar he'd just purchased, had been a siren call he couldn't ignore. Seeing her again, it was clear he still had that thing for her. Had it so bad he'd stayed awake last night remembering the way her dark brown eyes—huge already, but totally exotic under the heavy makeup she wore—had flashed at him. How her long black hair gleamed as it swirled to her elbows. How her sweater slipped off her shoulder and revealed a fraction of a tattoo that left him wanting to see the whole picture. Then there was the way she'd felt, pressed against him, when she'd walked him so sternly out of the bar.

And her surprising strength when she sent him sprawling to the ground.

A thumping on the kitchen steps had him turning in time to see his dad come through the door, tall, iron-haired, with shoulders broad from years of work and upright responsibility. He had a binder under his arm and moved like a man in a hurry, but he stopped when he saw Tyler.

"You're up." Tyler could hear the subtext: *The rest of us were up hours ago.*

"Yes, I am." He resorted to the good manners that had been drilled into them. "I appreciate you saving me some breakfast."

"It might be spoiled now. Didn't know it would sit out for so long."

"Right." Not much of an answer but all he could think of in the face of the loud and clear message. He was slacking off.

"You were out drinking last night?"

"Yes, I was."

"I don't appreciate you stumbling in drunk, you hear me?"

"Yes, I do." He was a kid again. Being chastised for his bad grades, his lack of brains, his inability to be what his dad felt he should be. A dull pounding kicked up a rhythm at the base of his skull. Last night was too much to drink, but all this was too much to come home to. What the hell had he been thinking? He could have bought a bar anywhere. Why'd he choose his hometown?

"Your brothers are down on the southern end of the ranch. We're redoing that old border fence. Why don't you go help them out?"

Tyler braced himself for more disapproval. "I was hoping to work on my business plan today."

"Your plan for what?"

"Remember the bar I told you about? That I bought?"

"You don't start working there for a few days. You can help around here until then."

Tyler tried to summon patience through the fog of his hangover. "I can help out today. But I also have my own work to do. I need to be ready when I take the reins."

"You need to be ready? To pour beer?" His dad let out a breath of disgust. "I still can't figure out why you bought that thing, anyway."

"It's a business, Dad."

"This ranch is good business."

Tyler laughed out loud before he could stop himself. He and his father working together would be a disaster resulting in fists or worse. "My brothers have that covered. You don't need me on the ranch."

"You have enough money, you could get your own place."

"I *did* get my own place." He'd explained it all a few times now, but he tried again. "There's a lot of land behind the bar. Maybe I'll raise bulls on it, eventually. But ranching isn't all I want." Tyler cast around for the words to explain. The restless feeling. The need to connect with others after years of hotel rooms and training. "I think ranching's a little too solitary for me. I like being around people."

"Suit yourself." His dad shrugged, looking as mystified as he always had when it came to all things Tyler.

"Trust me, Dad, it's gonna be good."

His dad squinted, as if by changing his vision he could somehow change his son as well. "Well, we aren't a hotel, son. We expect you to earn your keep around here."

Tyler felt his dreams shrink so small they'd fit in his jeans pocket. "Which is why I'm looking for a new place to live. I appreciate you letting me stay a few days, but we both know that won't work out so well in the long run. I've got a few leads on some rentals in town."

"If you say so."

"I do."

His dad nodded and turned away, striding toward his office. Hurrying away from the one son who made no sense to him. Who never had. Who probably never would.

Tyler watched him go, wondering what it would take for his dad to see him as a success. A long time ago he'd thought it would be all those junior rodeo trophies. When he grew up, he thought it would be winning the world championship or making good money. When he decided to retire from rodeo, he thought it might be buying a business and a big piece of property. But nothing had changed. In Ken Ellis's eyes, Tyler was just a disappointment. The third son, who didn't fall in line with the first two. A problem he couldn't fix. Same as always.

Tyler glanced at the congealed meal and shuddered. He scraped the food into the garbage and rinsed the plate. He needed coffee and lots of it. He wished he could eat at the café in town, where the food was hot and the waitresses flirted with him. Where he could be reminded that for a few sweet, short rodeo years, he'd been a hell of a lot more than the Ellis family loser. But he had work to do. So he grabbed an apple out of the bowl on the counter and went to find his brothers.

THE CHESTNUT GELDING Tyler had borrowed nickered low at the sight of the two horses tied to the pasture fence. He picked up the pace, eager to be with his buddies.

At the sound of their approach, Tyler's brothers looked up from their work. Parker stopped cranking the wire taut and grinned. "You finally out of bed, princess?"

Miles was kneeling, hammering in a staple to hold the wire to the fence post. He finished, then joined the fun. "Oh, look who decided to join us. I thought celebrity bull riders were too important for ranch work."

Tyler tied his horse near the others and made his way through the thick spring grass. "I doubt I'll ever get too self-important with you two clowns constantly busting my balls."

"We're just glad you got your beauty rest." Miles grinned, not willing to let the joke go. "In case you have any modeling gigs coming up." Older than Tyler by two years, Miles took special pleasure in tormenting him. One time he'd shown up at a rodeo in Reno carrying a giant pink sign with the words I Love Tyler written in rainbow letters. That sign had made national TV and the other bull riders had teased Tyler about it that entire season.

"What's with coming home hammered?" Parker was the oldest and took that role seriously. Maybe losing their mom before any of them were out of junior high had grown him up too fast.

"I went out with Eric and Mitch. They bought shots to celebrate my new bar."

"You're a lightweight," Miles teased. "It's all that granola and kale you eat."

"Gotta keep fit." Tyler's answer was automatic. Followed by the realization that he didn't actually have to keep fit anymore. Not in bull-riding shape, at least. The idea left him a little hollow.

"Well, you stumbling in singing was like nails on a chalkboard for Dad. He was ranting about it this morning," Parker said.

"Yeah, he ranted when I saw him just now." Tyler grabbed his work gloves out of his pocket. "What can I do to help?"

"Bring a few of those posts over, will you?" Miles jutted his chin to indicate the large pile a few yards away. "And we need that bag of concrete out of the truck."

Tyler nodded. "You guys think Dad's going to get over me buying a bar?"

Parker shook his head. "Doubt it. You know Dad. Ranching's the only job that makes any sense to him."

"But I got over it," Miles chimed in. "In case you were worried. I'm looking forward to free beer."

"Come on by and I'll start you a tab," Tyler shot back. "And I'll bill you for it at the end of each month."

"No family discount?" Parker added with uncharacteristic humor. "Cheapskate."

"Not until I'm running in the black. Right now the place is a money pit."

"So why'd you take it on, then?" Parker asked.

"Because I can make it great."

"You and your big goals." Miles grinned. "Isn't it tiring being so ambitious all the time?" He put a gloved finger to the side of his face, as if he was thinking. "Hmm. I think I'll join the army. Boot camp sounds fun. No, maybe I'll become the best bull rider in the world. Now I'm going to buy a dive bar and convince everyone that it's cool. Yeah, that'll be relaxing."

It was such an accurate portrayal that Tyler couldn't help but laugh. "Yeah, well, maybe I find it relaxing to try to meet my goals. I like pushing forward. Nothing wrong with that."

"No, there isn't." Parker sent Miles a strict glance. "In fact, maybe someone around here could use a few more goals."

Miles took the chiding with his usual good nature. "What, you don't think working for you and Dad is the definition of success? Because it sure is fun."

"Fun until a daddy of one of the girls you chase comes out here with a shotgun."

"That's when I hide behind my big brother." Miles shoved Parker on the shoulder. "Hey, Tyler. Can you grab those posts? Or are you worried you'll break a nail?"

"Shut up, Miles." But Tyler walked to the pile and grabbed a couple off the top. "I wanted you guys to help me with something."

"No beer, no help," Miles said and grabbed the handles of the posthole digger.

"What do you need?" Parker asked.

"I plan to fix up the barn at my new place. It's not in such bad shape—should be done in a few weeks. I want to get a few horses. And a couple bulls."

"Bucking bulls?" Parker eyed him shrewdly. "I thought you were done with rodeo."

"I want to offer a class or two. Get some local kids started in rodeo." Tyler set the posts down near Miles.

"I'm sure parents will love you for that. Especially when one of their little darlings breaks a neck."

"Bull riding's the fastest-growing sport in the country."

"Doesn't make it any less crazy," Parker said.

"You don't have to like it. But can you help me get some bulls?" It didn't matter to Tyler that Parker wasn't a great fan of bull riding. His brother had a better eye for cattle than anyone Tyler knew.

"I can ask around to see if anyone has the stock for that. Horses will be a lot easier. You thinking about some trail riding?"

Tyler nodded. "Trail riding, light ranch work. Quarter horses would be nice, but I'd consider other breeds."

"I'll look into it," Parker promised.

"Thanks, Park," Tyler said, clapping him on the shoulder. "I appreciate your help."

"It's good to have you home," Parker said.

"It's good to have you home and owning a bar," Miles added.

"Shut up, Miles," Tyler and Parker said in unison. And they all burst out laughing.

Tyler walked to the pile for a few more posts. It wasn't fun to clash with his dad again. Or to feel his father's disappointment seep into the confidence Tyler had finally developed once he left home. Being home wasn't easy, but it sure was good to be near his brothers again.

KIT CLIMBED THE rickety steps to her father's door, clutching the railing as she avoided the rotten boards. She glanced at the pile of new wood, still stacked where she'd left it a month ago. Cut to size, ready to be nailed on. Losing his life's work had knocked the wind out of her dad. He wouldn't admit it, but he was totally depressed.

His cottage was perched on a small rise at the edge of town, where he could look out over the high desert that rolled on in miles of dry desolation. Kit worried that he was lonely out here. But her dad insisted he was happy. That the open sky was the best friend a guy could have.

Of course, that was before he'd been fired. Now he and the open sky were spending a lot of time together, and Kit suspected the relationship was no longer healthy.

She knocked, faded bits of green paint raining down on the porch. The afternoon winds were fierce out here. They were sandblasting the place. She had to add "find a painter" to her to-do list.

Her dad was watching TV. Kit could hear the perky cadence of some talk show host when she put her ear to the door. She knocked again and was finally rewarded by a shuffling sound. Her dad still wore his blue flannel pajamas and slippers at 11:00 a.m. His gray eyebrows scrunched together, as if he was puzzled at her arrival.

"Hey, Sunshine."

The old endearment had Kit smiling through her worry. It was a ridiculous name and they both knew it. With her black hair, heavy makeup and tattoos, Kit didn't look like anyone's sunshine. "Did you forget I was coming by? Remember we talked about it on Sunday?"

The frown cleared. "I guess I forgot which day we said." Her dad gestured for Kit to enter. "You want some coffee?"

Kit nodded and her dad shuffled toward the kitchen. Kit stayed by the door, taking in the clutter strewn around the living room. A few dirty dishes teetered on the arm of the couch. Laundry sat in a heap waiting to be folded and a pile of newspapers was stacked haphazardly on an end table. Her dad used to be a neatnik.

Thank you, Ken Ellis. Owner of Sierra Canyon Ranch, where Garth Hayes had worked his entire life. Where his hard work had been rewarded with two words. *You're fired.*

Because the Ellis family took what they wanted and ran right over smaller people, like Kit and her dad, in the process.

Like father, like son.

Guilt twinged. Tyler hadn't taken anything from her. He'd bought what was for sale. Bought what Kit couldn't afford. Still, she *felt* run over.

Automatically, Kit reached for the jacket draped over the rocking chair and hung it up in the small hall closet. Then she went into the kitchen, wincing at the dirty counters and piled dishes. "Dad, things are getting pretty messy here." The words were out before she'd realized she was saying them. But hell, they needed to be said.

He sighed. "I was going to clean up today."

"You told me the same thing on Sunday. But I'm pretty sure I'm staring at the same dirty dishes." Kit took a deep breath, forcing herself to say what had been on her mind. "You aren't dressed. You're watching TV. This isn't like you at all. I think you might be depressed."

He looked out the window to the desert he loved. "I've just been busy lately."

"Doing what, Dad?" Kit couldn't hide the worry that sharpened her voice. "I never see you in town. Jed Watkins asked about you the other day. Said he was concerned because you've been missing poker night. *And* you told him you didn't want to judge the Benson Rodeo this year. You *always* judge the rodeo."

He looked weary. It seemed like the past four months since he'd been *let go*, as Ken Ellis had called it, had aged him twenty years. "I didn't much feel like it this year."

"Because you're depressed. Have you seen Dr. Miller?"

"I don't need a doctor. I'm just having a little trouble figuring out what to do with myself all day long. Retirement is an adjustment, right? Isn't that what they say? So I'm adjusting."

"It doesn't seem like you're adjusting very well." She knew she was nagging, but worry wouldn't let her quit. "What about those boards I got for the steps? They've been on the porch a month now. They're cut to size, Dad. All you have to do is yank out the old ones and nail the new ones down." An idea hit. Manual labor wasn't her cup of tea but maybe it would wake her dad up a bit. "What if I grab the tools right now and we do it together?"

Her dad glanced at her suspiciously. "You hate building stuff. You hate it if you so much as break a fingernail."

Kit glanced at her new manicure, the purple polish so dark it was almost black. Twenty bucks and her favorite color, too. "Nah, it's no big deal," she lied. "Get dressed. Let's take our coffee out on the porch and build some steps."

"If you're sure."

"We can pretend each nail is Ken Ellis's head." *Or Tyler's.*

"Kit Hayes, I didn't raise you to be vindictive." He sounded a little like the tough dad she'd known, before he'd lost everything.

"It may be vindictive, but I bet it's also therapeutic," she retorted. Pushing. Wanting him to come back to her. "Maybe it will help you with all that *adjusting* you're doing."

He glared at her. But she'd rather see him mad than beaten down.

"Fine. I'll get changed. You get the tools out of the shed."

"Sure," she said, trying to keep the triumph out of her voice and the hope out of her heart. But she shouldn't hope. Nothing she'd tried for her dad had worked so far.

On the porch, she left her coffee mug on the

railing and jumped the steps to the ground. She found a couple crowbars in the shed and brought them to the stairs, using hers to rip out the first board. It felt good. Actually, it felt great to see the old boards come off. For months it felt like things had been happening *to* her. Arch not loving her. Ken Ellis firing her dad. Tyler Ellis buying the bar she'd been scraping and saving for.

At least in this moment she, Kit Hayes, was ripping up boards. Making something happen. Maybe this could be a turning point for her, too. Because she sure as hell needed one.

The next board splintered, she went at it so hard. Her dad might have lost his way, but she wasn't letting an Ellis, or anyone, bring her down. She'd already let Arch throw her for a loop when he showed up. It was taking her a while to recover from that, but she *was* recovering. So with this new setback she'd keep in mind how far she'd come. She'd keep pushing forward. She'd find a new dream. One that Tyler Ellis couldn't buy out from under her.

CHAPTER THREE

TYLER LOOKED AT the bar staff he'd inherited, trying to ignore the dismay prickling beneath his skin. His employees sprawled in the circle of chairs he'd set up in the middle of the bar. And none of them looked very happy to be at this meeting.

The Dusty Saddle didn't look great, either. It was even more drab than usual in the bright morning light. The stained, scuffed plank floor probably hadn't been refinished since the bar was built in the early 1900s. Stuffing poked out of ripped brown vinyl booths. Tabletops were covered in drink rings that couldn't be scrubbed off anymore.

This Monday-morning staff meeting had seemed like a way better idea when Tyler had planned it. He'd seen it so rosy in his mind's eye. Everyone chatting happily, excited for his first day as owner of the Dusty Saddle.

But there was no excitement. Quite the opposite. Here he was, trying to give an inspirational speech, but he wasn't sure if anyone had heard a single word.

One of the bouncers, Ernie, a hefty brick of a guy, was playing some game on his phone. Loomis, his fellow bouncer, had one leg slung over the other and was studying the sole of his steel-toed boot. Lila, one of the bartenders, was sleepily twisting a lock of her long red hair, clearly not excited about being at work this early. Her bartending colleagues didn't look any more enthusiastic. Maybe they were here just to pick up the fifty bucks Tyler had bribed them with to get them into the bar first thing on a Monday.

Tyler tried not to look at Kit, but his eyes kept straying her way. She barely seemed to see him, her face a mask of studied boredom that did little to hide the anger in her eyes.

She was still pissed at him. Well deserved after his drunken visit a week ago. He'd stopped by a couple times this past week in hopes of catching her alone to apologize. But she'd avoided him each time, disappearing to the stockroom or announcing, suddenly, that it was time for her break. And since it was Chris's last week, Tyler hadn't wanted to stop by the bar too often. The guy surely needed time to say goodbye to his business and his staff without the new owner breathing down his neck.

Tyler tried again to inspire some enthusiasm. "Picture the bar expanded." He pointed north. "This whole wall will be moved out, doubling our seating capacity. Then we'll build a second bar in the new addition—an area especially for sports fans. That way, we can give the High Country a run for their money on weekdays."

Lila's eyes rolled in Kit's direction. Kit's answering shrug was the embodiment of *whatever*.

Yeah, he was really firing them up. Any more enthusiasm and they'd be asleep.

Ernie raised a beefy hand and Tyler nodded to him, relieved that finally someone cared.

"Does this mean we'll get more hours?"

Hallelujah for something he could say yes to. "Once we've renovated and we're up and running, you'll definitely have more hours if you want them."

Mario, one of the part-time bartenders, yawned. So much for wowing them. Tyler's gaze went to Kit with a will of its own. She was staring somewhere over his shoulder. He followed the direction of her gaze. She was watching the clock.

This chat wasn't working, but he didn't know what else to do except keep going. "We'll have a lot to offer once the renovations are complete. I'd like to add a restaurant with an outdoor barbecue area. And a stage and a dance floor. I'm going to restore the barn and build a small arena. I'm hoping to start a rodeo school. Any questions?"

Of course not.

Then a hand came up. Not one he wanted to choose. "Kit?"

She gave him a smile laced with ice. "Are you gonna give us a raise?"

Damn it. Trust her to ask what he couldn't answer. "I'm still going over the figures. I'll know more after I draw up cost projections, revenue estimates, stuff like that."

She gave him a cool look. "It just seems like if you have all this money to transform the Dusty Saddle into a one-stop cowboy experience, you must have enough to compensate the people who'll be doing all the work."

Ouch. Her cutting summation of his plans stung. She was walking a thin line, but he'd be cool about it, for now. "I'll work hard, too. And I won't pay myself until we're profitable. I'll certainly consider raises once we start making some money."

There was a slight stirring among the staff, an exhaled breath of relief. It must have been the right thing to say. Or as close to right as he'd gotten so far. But it was clear he was missing something here. Some chance. He could feel it as sure he knew a bull would shift left or right.

His palms were damp. He wasn't used to talking like this, trying to inspire others. Put him on a bull and he'd inspire. With actions. With stamina. But with words, he was out of his league. "Look, you all probably know I've spent the past few years hitting the rodeos. But I also spent a lot of time with corporate sponsors, doing promotion, stuff like that."

"'Me and my Wranglers,'" Lila purred. "Yeah, we saw the commercial."

Heat crept from his collar to his jaw. In the commercial Lila referred to, the camera had been mainly focused on his ass. "I may not have experience owning a bar. But I learned some stuff about business along the way. I'm no expert, but I have a feeling about this place."

He paused, gratified to see a few nods from the bouncers and Mario. "I've thought my plans through and I know I can make this place profitable. I just need good people around me to do it. I need *you*, if you'll give it a try with me."

"What if we like the Saddle the way it is?" Kit leaned forward, her elbows on the table and, *oh boy*, her neckline had slid down, treating him to an eyeful of what he should not be looking at. When he raised his glance he saw the fierce emotion in her eyes. She wasn't giving him a hard time for the heck of it. For some reason, she loved this place, ripped vinyl, filthy floor and all.

"There's history here. I get that. But let's be honest, most customers don't appreciate it. The bar is empty most weeknights."

"It's a small town. No one's out drinking," Kit shot back.

"It's a growing town, and the High Country is packed. Look, if we can't bring more customers in, this place will go under. Chris knew it. He told me himself when he sold it to me. And Kit, weren't you just asking me about raises?"

She looked at him sharply and he knew he'd hit a nerve.

"You can't have it both ways," he said. "You can't keep the Dusty Saddle the way it's always been and expect a living wage from it. So we're going to need to make changes."

"Don't get all sentimental, Kit." Loomis finally looked up from his boot. "More money sounds pretty good to me."

"Amen," Ernie added, and Tyler saw several other heads nod around the room.

At least he'd gotten one thing right. He didn't need everyone on board—and clearly Kit wasn't signing up for the Tyler Ellis fan club anytime soon—but he needed some of the staff with him. He looked at Kit. "Not all change is bad. It might even be fun."

"Depends on your idea of fun," Kit murmured, ostensibly to Lila but loud enough for him to hear, too.

"Any questions?" Tyler deliberately looked over Kit's head.

"You gonna change the name?" Tim, a bartender, glanced around. "The Dusty Saddle doesn't really fit what you're describing."

"I hadn't thought about it yet."

"How about the Last Rodeo?" Kit asked, fluttering her eyelashes innocently when he glared at her. "I mean, since you just had yours, right?"

"Ouch," Mario murmured.

"Isn't that a little depressing?" Tim nudged Kit with his elbow. "Not sure we'll get people in the party spirit with that one."

"I kind of like it," Lila countered. "It's mysterious. Like Tyler's rodeo days are over and so what comes next?"

"Dance floors and big-screen TVs, apparently," Kit tossed in. "Not very mysterious, really."

"Let's not worry about it now." A weariness crawled up Tyler's spine, threatening to bring on the headaches he sometimes got from too many falls in the arena. "Plenty of time to come up with a name. For now, you'll all pull schedules similar to what you've been doing. If you want to change that, let me know."

He pulled his new business cards—hot off the press—out of his pocket. An old saddle in faded sepia. His name and contact information in bold letters. He handed one to everyone, feeling inexplicably like a tool. "Call me with any questions or concerns. The schedule will be posted Tuesday, like always."

"We post it on Monday," Kit corrected.

He glanced her way to see if she was messing with him again. Her slight smile was unreadable. "Chris said Tuesdays."

"Chris hasn't done it in five years."

"Oh." This was news to him. But there were bound to be surprises. "Okay, so who makes the schedule?"

"Kit," Lila answered. "She does everything around here."

Tyler looked at Kit but she regarded him calmly, not offering any confirmation.

"Well, Kit, maybe you and I could meet and you could bring me up to speed."

"I'm not working today," she said.

"Okay, so when are you working?"

"I'm not sure, since no one made the schedule." At Tyler's exasperated look, she opened her hands in a gesture of innocence. "Hey, I didn't know. I thought, as the new owner, you might want to take it on."

Tyler looked around, feeling a twinge of desperation. "So no one knows when they're working this week?"

Ten heads shook no.

"Right. Call me later today and I'll have your hours. Anyone want to work today?"

Ten pairs of eyes exchanged furtive *you-do-it* glances. He got it. Once a day off was promised, it was hard to let it go. Especially since they'd all given up their morning for a staff meeting.

He'd never thought his first day on the job would be so rocky. Maybe his ego was a little too big. In the arenas, on the road, he was someone special. People wanted his autograph, a handshake, a piece of his attention. But this meeting reminded him that here in Benson, he was still the same screw-up he'd always been.

"Thanks for coming," he said. "Make sure to put this hour on your time card." The last sentence was lost in the sound of scraping chairs. It was the most enthusiasm he'd seen so far from the employees. And it all centered on getting the hell out of there.

Well, at least today would give him some time here. He could practice making a few drinks. Maybe he should have considered, before he bought a bar, that he had no idea how to bartend.

He walked to the office and stared at the blank wipe-off calendar titled Schedule. How did he figure out who went where? The lines seemed to bend and blur.

"Welcome to the world of bar ownership." Kit leaned against the door frame, the position accentuating all the curves defined by her tight black dress.

"Your type of welcome sucks, to be honest. If you want to work for me, don't act like that in a staff meeting again."

"Or what? You'll keep up the family tradition and fire me?"

He tried to process her words. "What are you talking about?"

She straightened, her arms crossed, outraged, across her chest. "Oh, didn't you know? Your dad fired mine. After my father spent his life working on your ranch."

Tyler knew he should say something, but shock wiped out any response. Kit's dad had been Tyler's mentor. Garth had spent countless hours teaching Tyler how to ride bulls. "When did this happen?"

"A few months ago," Kit bit the words out, and he could see the emotion she was holding back, in her too-bright eyes and the pink flush staining her cheekbones.

"I had no idea. I haven't spent a lot of time on the ranch since I came home. I've rented a house in town." It had been a relief to move off the ranch a few days ago. An even bigger relief, now that he had this piece of news to digest. His dad had *fired* Garth? "Is your dad okay? Does he need anything?"

Pride closed down Kit's face. He could see it in the tilt of her chin, the press of her full lips into a rigid line. "He's fine." But it was clear that she was lying.

Tyler could picture exactly what had happened. His cold, logical dad doing the calculations and deciding that Garth Hayes was no longer an economically sound employee.

A sick feeling melted into Tyler's stomach. Garth had toiled on Sierra Canyon Ranch from dawn until past dusk six days a week for as long as Tyler could remember.

"I tried to talk to your dad last week. My dad borrowed against his pension fund, so he's broke now." Kit's voice had tears in it, though she'd never let them show. "I asked your dad to forgive the debt. But he wouldn't bend."

"Why did your dad need that loan?" Tyler put out a hand to stop her. "Never mind. It's not my business."

"It's okay." Kit sighed. "Ask anyone in town and they'll tell you. When I turned eighteen, my mom asked my dad for a divorce. Seems she'd always hated it here. She left and broke my dad's heart."

"I had no idea." Kit's mom had never come around the ranch, but he'd see her in town and at school events. She'd worn long, flowing skirts and a remote expression on her face.

"My dad still loved my mom. He wanted her to be happy. So he took out that loan to help her start a new life and a business. She owns a groovy crystal shop in a little town on the Oregon coast."

"No kidding." Tyler tried to read her mood.

"She even changed her name. She's Starflower Kindness now, owner of Kindness Crystals and Healing. You can look her up. She has an online store, too."

Kit was tough, as always, shrugging like she didn't care. From the tremor in her husky voice, he'd bet she cared a lot.

"Have you seen her?"

"Once or twice. But not lately, because she never paid Dad back. And now he's struggling to get by. I have trouble forgiving her for that."

"Makes sense." It was tragic that her family had fallen apart. Doubly tragic that her dad had sacrificed so much to make sure the woman who'd left him would be okay. "I'll speak to my father. I'll try to make this right. Your dad deserves a hell of a lot better after all he did for my family. And for me."

She nodded, and he realized it wouldn't help to say more now. He'd talk to his dad, and if by some miracle he got anywhere, he could share that with Kit. Anything else would be empty promises. But they had something else between them that needed to be resolved.

"I can see why you're upset at my dad. But I

don't want it to cause trouble with the staff. If you're pissed at me, tell me straight."

She didn't answer right away, but he saw a twist of guilt in her guarded expression. Finally she sighed. "You're right. I shouldn't have been so rude in the meeting. It won't happen again."

"Okay. Good." He wasn't sure what else to say now that he'd finished laying down the law. But he still had his own guilt to assuage. "The other night, when I sprang the news on you about buying the bar... I should never have shown up here drunk. And I have a feeling I said some other things I shouldn't have."

She smiled faintly. "You did. But if I had a problem dealing with drunks, I'd have quit this job a long time ago."

He nodded at the truth there. "Seems to me you're kind of an expert. You had me on the ground faster than a pissed-off bull."

"It comes in handy."

"I could use a great bartender like you. I hope you'll stick around."

She studied him for a long moment, then nodded, as if considering his invitation. "Do you want help with the schedule?"

He didn't recognize all the new hard edges on her, but this was more like the Kit he remembered from childhood. Getting mad, forgiving easily, then moving on. "Sure."

She tossed her thick black hair over her shoulder. "Okay, so…move over." She walked into the tiny office, brushing up against him to get by. She paused, so close to him that her full breasts pressed into his torso. "Hey, boss? Maybe enlarge this office as part of your remodel. Because this isn't going to work."

That was for damn sure. He could barely breathe. His brain had dropped below his belt, making it crystal clear that she was definitely not the same childhood friend he'd known. "The schedule?"

Her derisive smile was back, letting him know she saw the effect she had on him. "Scoot over."

He shuffled out of her way and she grabbed a file out of a cabinet by the desk. "Let's talk at the bar."

He led the way into the empty room, relieved to have more space between them. "Can I get you something to drink?" he asked, conscious that it was his first time offering anyone anything in his new place.

"Just soda water."

Tyler went behind the bar and grabbed two glasses. He set them on the counter, then realized he had no idea how to get her what she'd asked for.

"You need a little help?"

He nodded. "And I bet you're going to give me a hard time about it?"

But she didn't. Just slid off her stool and came around the bar. "Ice is in that cooler," she said, pointing to a built-in compartment. "And soda, tonic, it's all from this gun." She pointed to a black nozzle that was hooked to a metal bracket.

He picked it up. There were different buttons marked with letters.

"*S* for soda water." She put ice in their glasses, then held them out.

He pushed the button and filled the glasses. It was the only easy thing about today so far. He was still absorbing the news about Kit's dad. And trying to contain the anger he felt toward his own.

He put the nozzle back and followed her to sit side by side. Kit pulled the folder toward him so he could see it and her elbow brushed his. Her dress had short sleeves, and he tried not to stare at the inked rattlesnake that wound its way up her arm, highlighting the way every toned muscle rippled under her creamy skin. It wasn't a tattoo he'd have imagined for her, but then again, what did he know? They'd both changed a lot since they were kids.

Pushing those thoughts aside, he directed his attention to the papers she'd laid out.

"Here are the schedule requests," she said. "Everyone fills one out each week, or they get what they get and no griping."

"Okay." He picked one up and read over it. "Loomis only wants weekends?"

"He's full-time at Lone Mountain Ranch during the week."

"Got it."

"So once you've gone through the request sheets and you know what everyone wants, you plug them into the calendar on the office wall."

"It sounds pretty straightforward."

"It is, sometimes. Other times, everyone wants the same thing so you have to be diplomatic. This week, for example, everyone wants to work Saturday night. And, for that matter, so do I."

"Why this Saturday?"

"The Benson Spring Fling. Huge crowd. Good tips."

Tyler remembered the Fling, with its rummage sale, the art walk downtown, horsemanship demos at the fairgrounds. And he remembered one Spring Fling especially. He and Kit had met up as the day became dusk, and ended the night in the back of a cop car.

She might have remembered it, too, because her pale skin tinged pink. Or maybe she wished he'd hurry up and learn the scheduling so she could get out of here.

"So how do I decide?"

"You're the boss. Figure it out."

"But what would you do?"

"Eeny, meeny, miny, mo." Her feral-cat smile gave no guarantee she told the truth.

"Right."

She took a slow slip of her water, regarding him levelly over the glass. "It's a little surreal, you know, that you're going to be my boss."

"So that means you'll stay and be my employee?" He said it lightly, but it was a real question and they both knew it.

She studied him for a moment, as if considering a serious answer. Then all her sass and attitude were back. "If you're really, *really* lucky." She slid off her stool. "I've got to go. Make sure you put me on for Saturday night."

She gave him the opening. Not his fault if he took it. "Eeny, meeny, miny, mo."

Laughing low, she grabbed her bag. "Story of my damn life. See you around, Tyler."

He watched her saunter out of the bar, riveted by the way her hips moved, by the fall of her hair when she shook it down her back, by the brittle note he'd heard in her laugh that made him wonder if she was really laughing at all.

KIT BLINKED, the bright sunlight of the parking lot accosting her after the dim light inside the bar. Round two with Tyler. At least she hadn't knocked him down this time. That was an improvement.

But not a great one. She hated feeling out of

control, but that's how she'd been in that staff meeting. She knew she was being rude, but somehow she'd been unable to stop. She'd been overcome with a fiery resentment that Tyler could walk in and have the power to change the bar she loved. Just because he had money.

Her thoughts stopped her in her tracks and she fumbled for her keys, absorbing the idea. They'd been friends growing up, but he'd always been the rich kid. The one with the horses they rode, with the truck, as they got older. He'd always had so much to offer, and she'd just tagged along behind.

Is that what all of this fury was really about? Whatever the reason, she had to get it under control. Tyler was right to reprimand her. Her behavior at the meeting was childish and rude. If she wanted to keep working at the Dusty Saddle, she'd have to learn to keep her mouth shut.

She located her keys, but instead of opening the Jeep she leaned against it, looking west toward the immense Sierra peaks, as tumbled and jagged as the jealousy that seemed to have taken up permanent residence in her soul. It had been there ever since Arch came to town and fell in love with Mandy. But now the jealousy encompassed the bar, too. Because once again, something she'd wanted had been scooped up by someone else. Someone who couldn't appreciate it the way she did.

She shouldn't keep working here. Not if it ate at her like this. Not if it was going to bring her to this place where she didn't want to be, wishing so badly for what someone else had.

She'd lied to Tyler about not being able to work today. About having something on her calendar. She had nothing. Just a pile of self-help books and a long afternoon in front of her. Maybe she'd make use of it to fill out an application for a job at the High Country Sports Bar. Because clearly it was time for a change.

TYLER PULLED HIS truck alongside his father's cattle barn and cut the engine. A ranch hand had pointed him this way, saying that his father was here looking over a new bull. He closed his eyes for a moment, feeling the spring sunshine on his face. The warmth felt good after all the tension this morning. He still couldn't decide what was worse. His challenging staff meeting, or learning that his dad had fired Garth.

There was also the way he kept thinking about Kit. That wasn't great, either. Because she was beautiful and sexy as hell, and he had no business noticing that. Maybe it was a little twisted, but he'd kind of liked the way she stood up to him. He wasn't used to it. The women he met on the road were drawn to him because they liked rodeo cowboys. They'd flirted with him and fawned on him more with each victory. Kit, on the other hand, seemed totally unimpressed. It was strangely refreshing.

Tyler shoved his shoulder into the door of his truck when he opened it, not because it was stuck shut but because he needed the impact to jar him out of his reverie. Kit was his employee, and hopefully, still his friend. He should just be grateful for her help with the schedule today.

He should be focused on the injustice his dad had done to hers.

"Dad," he called as he stepped into the barn. He paused to let his eyes adjust to the shadows and spotted his dad at the end of the center aisle. He walked toward him, trying to assemble the words he needed to say into some kind of coherent order.

"Tyler." His dad nodded at his approach. "Check out Red Letter."

The Hereford bull was knee-deep in straw, chewing on alfalfa hay. He eyed Tyler balefully, so much calmer than the bulls he'd faced in the arena. "Looks too mellow to get much done with the heifers."

Talking cattle was about the only time Tyler saw his dad smile. "Don't underestimate him. Give him his own herd and no tough Angus bulls to compete with, and he'll do just fine."

"You're cross-breeding. Doesn't that reduce the price when you sell?"

"A little," his dad said. "But it strengthens the herd in the long run." He turned away from the bull and fixed his piercing gaze on Tyler. "You miss the bulls? Is that why you came by?"

"I miss them a little, but it's not why I'm here. I came by to talk about Garth Hayes."

His dad looked startled. Then worried. "Is he okay?"

"Depends on what you mean by okay. According to Kit, you fired him."

His father's face drew into harsher lines. "I did. He wasn't pulling his weight."

"I'm sure he was doing all he could. He's getting older, but the guy can still work."

"If he wants to work, he can. Just not here."

"And who the hell is going to hire him?" Tyler tried to keep his voice steady, but frustration cut through his tone. "He should be allowed to grow old working here, on the ranch he's given everything to. Why don't you want him here anymore? Did he do something wrong?"

"Not really. But now that your brothers are taking on so much responsibility, we just didn't need him anymore."

A deep breath stemmed the fury that threatened to erupt at his father's cold dismissal of a loyal man. Sometimes it seemed like his wife's death had siphoned all the compassion out of Ken's soul.

Tyler willed away the feeling that he was a kid

about to get his ideas shot down by his dad one more time. "He's got no money. He isn't receiving much of his pension."

Annoyance drew his dad's thick gray eyebrows together. "I already told that daughter of his that Garth's pension situation is out of my control. He borrowed against it and never repaid the money. If he has a complaint about that, he has to contact the folks who manage the pension fund."

"You know full well that the pension fund isn't going to help him out. And did it ever occur to you that the reason he never paid back that loan is maybe you didn't pay him enough? When was the last time you gave your ranch hands a raise?"

"They make plenty," his father snapped. "What, you want me to pay off their gambling debts, too? Their bar tabs? I have grown men working for me and I expect them to handle their own finances."

"And I'm sure most of them do. But Garth worked for you almost his entire adult life. He put in twelve-plus hour days, whether the sun was blistering or the snow was piled deep. He was here on Thanksgiving and Christmas, making sure things ran smoothly while we were all inside enjoying our dinner. He took that loan out because he's an honorable man who felt obligated to provide for his wife, even though she left him. Don't you think we should help him out?"

His father's face went pale with a rage Tyler

hadn't seen since the day he told his father he was hitting the road to rodeo full time. "I have fulfilled my obligations to Garth, and to all of my other employees."

Tyler pulled out his last ace. It was just a guess, but it was worth a try. "What do you have against him? What did he do to you? Is this about how he taught me to ride a bull?"

His father flinched and Tyler knew his guess had some merit.

But no way would his father admit it. "I've done nothing wrong. Garth Hayes retired with all the money that was due him. I met my obligation to him."

"You fired him for no good reason. The least you can do is give him a comfortable retirement. You can certainly afford it."

His father shook his head, his entire face drawn into a defensive mask. "You're a businessman now, son. And you've got to learn to keep emotions out of your work if you're going to have any success."

"If success means turning my back on the people who work for me, then I'll take failure any day." Tyler turned away from his father's narrow worldview, shoulders aching from the tension. He started back through the barn, disappointment weighting his steps.

"Tyler," his father called.

A flicker of hope rose in his heart, but sputtered as soon as Tyler saw the bitter line of his dad's mouth.

"You'll see that I'm right." His father clenched his fists at his sides as tightly as he'd clenched the warmth out of his soul. "The best thing you can do for your employees is to run a tight ship. Expect a lot from them, give them what they're due and nothing more. Everyone will benefit."

"What I see is that you and I are different," Tyler said. "And I don't believe your view is one I want to live by."

He headed for his truck, refusing to look back again. He couldn't control his father's choices, but he could make amends. He'd find a way to repay Garth the debt his family owed him. That he personally owed him. And if he made Kit feel a little better about things in the process, well, that would ease his mind, too.

CHAPTER FOUR

TYLER BLINKED AT the inventory list in front of him. The columns of numbers, units, price per unit, net cost, blurred into a gray blob that ached behind his eyes. He glanced around the small office with its battered desk and dusty window. Maybe he needed more light. He'd pick up a desk lamp at the hardware store later on today.

He stood, rubbing his temples. Who was he kidding? He'd been trying to get his mind around the paperwork all week. It was his third day as owner of the Dusty Saddle, and he'd made almost no progress with any of the files Chris had left behind.

It had always been like this for him. Textbooks, manuals, graphs…they all made him dizzy. Words and numbers were tricky things that never seemed to hold their meaning. It's why he'd left school early. Why he'd left the army. Why he'd chosen rodeo. Bull riding might be dangerous, but it wasn't nearly as scary as that moment when someone realized he could barely read.

Laughter rippled into the office and he gave

in to the temptation, following the sound to its source. Kit. She was behind the bar, laughing at something one of their customers had said. It was a quiet Wednesday afternoon and the guys looked like backpackers, decompressing after a trip in the mountains. Their cargo shorts, hiking boots and back-turned caps were trail-dusted. Their eager eyes, fixed on Kit, were way too eager.

How could he blame them? He wanted to plunk himself next to them and stare, too. She was all creamy skin, thick black hair and dark eyes made up even darker, so a guy could lose himself trying to see behind her tough facade.

Or find himself. Because all that confidence surrounding Kit like heady perfume promised that maybe some of that amused poise would infuse you, lift you up and put your demons on the run.

Tyler joined her behind the bar and she fixed him with the baleful glance he was getting used to. It wasn't a welcome, more like an amused tolerance of his presence. "You need anything?" she asked.

"Just wondering if you want me to fill in for a bit," he offered.

She shrugged. "I don't really need a break yet." She shot a flirtatious smile to the backpackers. "Plus, we're having fun here."

He was jealous and lost in his own bar. His own business, which didn't yet feel like his.

"Do you need a job?" Her smile reminded him of the coiled snake tattooed on her arm. "Because I'm sure I can think of something that needs doing."

He jerked his gaze away from her smile. "I saw the order is due in tomorrow. I figured I'd go fill it. Is there a list of what we've kept in stock?"

"On the wall in the storeroom," she said. "I'll do the ordering if you like. I always did it for Chris."

"If I want to learn the business, I figure I'd better do it myself."

She shrugged. "Suit yourself. There are blank order forms on a clipboard on the shelf in there."

"Okay." Tyler felt her eyes on him as he pushed through the door behind the bar that led to the cramped storeroom. Enlarging this space was high on his list of improvements. He unlocked the door that led outside and propped it open, grateful for the infusion of pine-scented air. Picking up the clipboard from the shelf, he took a look at the order form. His eyes crossed.

More rows and columns. Liquor names listed down the left-hand side. The number of bottles they kept in stock listed next to that. All he had to do was fill in the column with the amounts to be ordered. It was simple. He could do this.

He started at the top. Vodka. They generally kept two dozen bottles around. He jumped up on a stool, grateful to do something active. He counted four bottles, but they'd use a couple in the next few days. He jotted twenty-four on the list. Made his way to triple sec...rye...rows and rows that started to slither like snakes on the page so he traced across with his finger to make sure he was writing on the correct line.

Half an hour later he was finished and desperate to escape from any more paperwork. Fortunately, he had errands to do. He was still moving into the house he'd rented a few blocks away from the bar. He needed dishes, cleaning supplies, pretty much everything. As much as he hated shopping, it would be better than more forms or schedules. He set down the clipboard and headed out to the bar.

Kit was still chatting with the hikers. The scruffy bearded guy was telling Kit a story, gesticulating with hands that housed a woven rainbow-colored bracelet and a thick silver ring, while she polished glasses.

"Sorry to interrupt," Tyler said, not sorry at all. "I'm gonna head out for some errands. What time do you want a break?"

"In an hour. Or later is fine, too."

"Okay then." Still, he lingered, glancing toward the guys at the bar and not liking the way the bearded hiker stared at her backside with the rapt expression of a guy in his own personal heaven.

"You've got my cell number," he said in a low voice. "Don't hesitate to call if these clowns try anything."

One raised eyebrow messaged her utter disbelief. "These college boys? Please."

"I don't like the way they look at you."

She laughed at that. "Tyler, I've been doing this job for years. I know how to handle a few hikers. Now go do something useful."

She still saw a kid when she looked at him and Tyler felt that old high-school need rise up. The need for her to see him as more than just a buddy. It grated. Here he was, fifteen years later, still wanting her to see him differently. Some things never changed.

He had to get a grip. Kit Hayes wasn't the reason he was in Benson. He should focus on what really mattered—making a name for himself, right here in his hometown. Showing everyone who'd doubted him that he was more than a bull rider. More than the kid who'd never been anything but trouble in school and regret in his daddy's eyes.

He gave the hikers one last stern look before he headed out the door.

KIT WATCHED TYLER stalk out of the bar and glanced at her phone. Still no message from the High Country Sports Bar, though she'd handed in her application a couple days ago. Lance, a bartender there, had said they might be hiring. But so far, no word.

She resisted the urge to duck into the storeroom to check Tyler's order. It was tough to let go of control, especially when he was doing all the jobs she'd done. But he owned the place now, and if he wanted to order and inventory and schedule, well, that was his right.

She should be happy. She was pulling down the same wages Chris had paid her, but doing a lot less work. All she had to do was chat with customers, make drinks and keep the bar clean.

She leaned against the counter behind the bar. Tapped a restless foot to the nineties mix playing on the speakers. The thing was, she'd never been much good at just hanging out. She had too much energy for that.

The door opened and she recognized a group of field biologists who came through from time to time. Relief had her smiling broadly as they approached the bar. They were studying reptile populations. Not her favorite topic, but she'd take anything over this boredom.

"What can I get you?" she asked. And when the pints were on the counter, "So how's the research been going lately?" And willed herself to be fascinated by the hunting behavior of the long-nosed leopard lizard. And to ignore the unruly part of her mind that kept wondering when Tyler would walk into the bar again.

Because something was different. In all of her mixed-up feelings around him taking over the bar, there was this awareness of him. Of how he moved with an intense power and grace that was probably what kept him on the back of a bull long enough to be called a champion. Of the way his smile slid sideways to reveal a wry humor, as though he'd seen more ups and downs than most people. Of the creases around his eyes that gave his face a lived-in look and roughed up his beauty enough to keep it manly.

How could she not notice it? Every woman did. Even Lila had been talking about Tyler the other night when Kit went to her friend's house for dinner. She'd gushed so much that Ethan, her fiancé, had finally said he was coming to the bar to check this Tyler guy out. He'd said it laughingly, because he and Lila had a bond that was unbreakable. But he was definitely curious.

Kit had to remember that Tyler was her boss now. He wasn't the kid she'd had hay fights with, swam in lakes with and thrown snowballs at. Their past didn't mean much now that he signed her paychecks. And until she heard from the High Country, she needed those paychecks. So she had to ignore these confusing feelings that had her glancing toward the door.

Lizards, she reminded herself, smiling at the biologist who, thankfully, seemed oblivious to her wandering mind. *Focus on the lizards.*

IT WAS TYLER'S first Friday night behind the bar. It didn't matter how many times he reminded himself that he'd spent the past decade riding bulls whose sole desire was to get him off their backs so they could stomp him to death. After that, nothing should make him nervous. But this did.

So he kept himself busy, slicing lemons at the counter behind the bar. Away from the customers so he'd have a chance to observe a bit before he jumped in.

Kit was on the schedule tonight. Apparently she and Lila usually worked Friday nights together, along with Tim. Ernie and Loomis were by the door ready to bounce anyone who got too rowdy.

He'd understood the books enough to see that most of the bar's income was generated on weekend nights. But he also knew how busy the High Country got on the weekends. Benson wasn't a big town, so he was curious to find out who spent so much money at the Dusty Saddle.

The jukebox in the corner was pounding out one country hit after another. It was still light outside, only about six. This time of year, it wouldn't get dark for another hour. But the door of the bar flung open and the first customer came in, and Tyler couldn't help but stare.

The guy looked like something out of a history book. His faded canvas pants and flannel shirt weren't too surprising around Benson, but his beard was down to his belly and the lines in his face spoke of twenty-four hours a day in the elements.

Then the old-timer spotted Kit and his face lit up in a boyish grin. "There's my angel," he called as he strode across the room to shake her hand, which turned into a hearty, across-the-bar hug and a fatherly peck on her cheek. He did the same for Lila, and gave Tim a hearty handshake and clap on the shoulder.

"How's it going, Crater?" Kit pulled a pint glass from the rack above. "Did you have a good week out there?"

"Better than most." The big man parked himself on a stool that looked impossibly small for his frame. "You know mining. One minute you think you're striking it rich, the next you're chipping away at nothing."

Mining? Tyler had forgotten there were still solitary miners out here. Scraping out silver and gold in high desert claims, burrowing into veins the mining companies had deemed too small when they pulled out of the area years ago.

Kit put the glass under the Guinness tap, poured

a perfectly built pint and set it on the counter. "Peanuts?" she asked.

"You betcha." Crater took a long haul of his pint then sighed, swiping the foam off his mustache with his sleeve. "You all are a sight for sore eyes as usual."

"We know the weekend's starting when you show up," Lila said kindly. "It's great to see you, Crater."

The door swung open again and a tall, thin man ambled in. "Evening, Crater," he said in a quiet tone that still carried in the nearly empty bar.

"Stan." Crater held out a meaty paw that encompassed the other man's bony hand. "Good to see you. Good week?"

"Not bad." Stan nodded gravely, shaking hands with the entire bar staff. "Not bad."

Kit placed a pint of lager in front of Stan and set a shot glass down. "Bourbon?"

"Don't mind if I do," Stan said. "Care to join me, Crater?"

"Not for me, my friend. Gonna take it easy tonight."

"Hard to take it easy when it all goes down so easy," Stan replied, lifting his shot glass in a somber salute.

Crater let out a guffaw and slapped Stan on the shoulder. The bourbon sloshed in his glass, but Stan managed to gulp it before it spilled.

Tyler moved on to slicing limes, listening as Stan and Crater discussed the price of silver. A couple other older customers, Doug and Marcus, joined them. When Kit came to the sink to wash some glasses, Tyler grabbed a towel to help dry. He kept his voice low. "Are those guys really miners?"

"Yep." Kit dunked the glasses in the soapy water. "We get all kinds of interesting characters here. Miners, shepherds, rock hounds, UFO hunters." She grinned at him. "All the wild folks who love this part of the desert show up at the Dusty Saddle." She glanced at his towel in horror. "Use the lint-free kind." She handed him a towel from the stack on the shelf over the sink. "Jeez, you are green, aren't you?"

"Green at this," he admitted. "But rumor has it I'm a pretty quick study."

"Well, I guess we'll find out if the rumors are true," she teased. "It's your first Friday night, isn't it?"

"It sure is." He tried to smile, but it felt a little weak. "I'm looking forward to it. But I've got a few nerves."

"You should. You have no idea what you're doing." Her intoxicating combination of sass and mischief had the glass slipping out of his hand, so he had to hustle to catch it.

"Nice reflexes," she murmured. "Maybe there's hope for you yet."

"If you help me out tonight, there is. I can pour a pint—"

"Barely."

"—and measure out a shot. But if I get anything more complicated than that, I'm toast."

"You don't know your cocktails?"

"Don't drink 'em myself. I've been reading recipes, but I'm more of a hands-on learner." A nice way of saying that half the words he read made no sense. He glanced hopefully in her direction. "I just need a good teacher."

"You want me to train you? You won't be embarrassed?"

"When you rodeo, you learn by falling on your ass in front of hundreds of people. This can't be more humiliating than that."

She studied him from underneath her thick black lashes. "What's in it for me?"

"A boss who's not totally incompetent?"

Her slow smile could melt metal. "But that could be kind of fun to watch."

"No shit-show is fun to watch for long. Plus I saw you with those customers. You pretend to be all tough, but you have a soft spot for the lost and lonely. I'm part of that club right now."

"You?" She laughed, soft and bitter. He'd give a lot to know what put that resentment in her soul.

"Not the words I'd ever use to describe someone like you."

"*Someone like me* will pay you a training stipend. A hundred extra bucks each night."

"Now you're trying to buy my help?" She scrubbed the pint glass in her hand with extra vigor. "Not everything can be bought, you know. Loyalty, for example."

"I'm not asking for your loyalty, though that would be nice," Tyler said. "I'm trying to treat you like a professional. You have years of experience. I have none and I need to learn. So I pay you extra to share your expertise with me. It's only right."

"Fine," she said quietly. "I'll do it. But you have to be willing to move fast and do what I say."

"I'm yours to command," he said, liking the flush creeping up her cheeks at the tiny innuendo. "And I appreciate the help."

She grabbed a stack of dry glasses. "Well, let's get going then. It's getting loud out there, which means it's getting busy."

They rounded the corner and Tyler was amazed to see a crowd that stretched almost to the door. A quick scan revealed a collection of some of the most rugged-looking folks he'd ever seen in one place. Bikers in leather, ranch hands in hats, jeans and bowlegs. Women in tight T-shirts and big hair. Kit glanced over her shoulder, her smile a combination of excitement and derision. "Welcome to the Dusty Saddle. Hope you're ready to earn your spurs."

KIT HATED TO admit it, but Tyler was a born bartender—naturally quick, outgoing, throwing friendly insults back at the regulars who were determined to give the new owner a hard time. After an hour or two he was pouring pints almost as fast as she did, leaving the tap on while he switched glasses with a blur of motion.

She watched him out of the corner of her eye as she measured a couple rum and Cokes. He was laughing at one of Crater's lame jokes. She appreciated his interest in the regulars. Some of them lived such lonely lives, on their own out in the high desert that rolled east of the Sierras, eking out a simple and unpredictable living.

They came to the Dusty Saddle for a drink, but they were after much more. A sense of belonging. A chat and the comfort of knowing that someone would miss them if they didn't show up each weekend. And now Tyler wanted to change all that with his clichéd cowboy ideas. Where would Crater and Stan and the rest of them fit into his fancy new bar?

The old resentment had her slamming the drinks in front of two cute twentysomething girls a little too hard. No matter. They were too busy watching Tyler to notice. Kit didn't recognize them. They were obviously here for Tyler's star power, not the ambiance of a dive bar. She'd bet anything that when word got out that hunky Tyler Ellis owned the Dusty Saddle, the clientele would become much younger, much more female and would show up wearing a whole lot more Daisy Dukes and cowboy boots.

Another girl, blond curls cascading from under a pink cowgirl hat, said something to Tyler and he leaned over the bar to listen. She brought her mouth close to speak into his ear, giving him a close-up of her ample cleavage.

He straightened, nodded and walked to the counter behind the bar to start pulling down bottles. He glanced Kit's way, caught her looking and mouthed the word *help*.

Kit set three pints in front of the burly ranch hand who'd ordered them, flashing him a smile when he handed her a twenty-dollar bill and told her to "Keep the change." At the cash register, she kept an eye on Tyler, who was furtively looking something up on his phone. For a second, the resentful part of her considered letting him sweat out whatever order he was trying to fill. But her promise to him earlier wouldn't let her stay away.

She tapped Tim on the shoulder and tipped her head toward a redhead who was waving her money at them. "Card her? If she's twenty-one, I'll buy you a scotch after closing."

Tim glanced the girl's way and grinned. "Another Tyler groupie? They start young."

"Evidently." Kit joined Tyler. "What's up? Besides blondie practically pulling your face into her breasts?"

He grinned. "Yeah, how 'bout that? I think I'm going to like this job."

"I'll bet."

His smile dimmed a little. "They want cosmopolitans. I looked up the recipe, but I don't know how to do this."

"Piece of cake." Then his words sank in. Cosmopolitans? Kit hadn't had an order for a cosmo here in pretty much ever. Change had come to the Dusty Saddle and Tyler hadn't even torn down a wall yet. Glancing at his phone, she reminded herself of the recipe. Then she grabbed three martini glasses and slicked the rims with lime. She showed him how to dip the rims in sugar and add the cherry and lime to each toothpick as garnish.

"You think you're ready for the shaker?" She elbowed him like it was something naughty, trying to inject some humor into the lesson.

"I'm ready for anything," he said with a wink that should not make her skin warm the way it did.

"Since you're making three, use the biggest shaker and make them all at once."

It was getting busier and louder in the bar. Tyler

tipped his head close to hers to hear her. "How am I supposed to measure it all out?"

She pulled away to avoid his spicy scent, which ran soft fingers over her nerves. Rummaging in a drawer to her left, she grabbed a jigger and showed him the marks on it. "Pour into here to measure the alcohol first."

He blinked at the small metal cup. "We're not baking."

"How else are you going to measure it? Have you practiced your pours?"

He looked confused.

"You have to practice pouring water from a liquor bottle before you can go by instinct."

"I've got good instincts," he protested.

"For bull riding, maybe," she countered. "Make your drinks too strong and you'll waste money and have those girls puking in the bathroom. Tomorrow I'll show you how to practice. Tonight, use the jigger."

He nodded. "I'll take it from here. Thanks, Kit."

She headed to the bar, surprised to see Tyler's red-haired groupie with a drink in her hand. Maybe as Kit was getting older, customers were looking younger. Maybe she just wasn't used to all these sweet young things in her bar. *Tyler's* bar, she corrected herself.

She glanced back as Tyler carefully measured

the vodka into the shaker. It was kind of cute, how seriously he was taking this.

What was she doing, thinking he was cute? She wasn't even sure she liked him. He was cocky. He was overly confident. He wanted to change her bar. And he'd shown up on the busiest night to practice his nonexistent bartending skills. No, she didn't like him much. Not even the tiniest bit.

Tyler had said she had a soft spot for the lost and lonely. Well, he was neither of those things, and she needed to keep that in mind when her heart went soft on her, like it was doing now.

TYLER'S BARTENDING CONFIDENCE was rising with every drink he made. So when Crater asked Kit for another pint of Guinness while she was busy with another order, Tyler offered to get it for him.

"No!" Kit and Crater both yelled at the same time. He must have looked surprised because Kit laughed. "Sorry about that," she said through her giggles. "It's just that pouring Guinness is tricky."

"Only Kit pours my pints, usually." Crater eyed Tyler suspiciously.

"We'll do it together," Kit assured him. "And if it's no good, I'll pour you another. Tyler needs the chance to learn."

"Okay then," Crater said, and turned to Stan. "Sure are a lot of changes happening around here."

"Sure are." Stan nodded sagely. "There sure are."

A lot of changes? Tyler glanced at Kit in disbelief. The only change to the Dusty Saddle so far was that he was behind the bar. Kit's eyes sparkled with suppressed laughter. She loved her regulars but she clearly got the joke.

Kit motioned him over to the Guinness tap. "Okay, this is serious stuff. Are you paying attention?"

"Sure." He was, but it was difficult, because she smelled good. He'd noticed it earlier, too. Some sort of sweet, spicy scent that interfered with coherent thought.

"Okay, so with Guinness, use the tulip pint glasses." She pulled one from above the tap. "See how they have a big curve in the side?"

He took the glass and tilted it. "I see it."

"Fill the glass to the bottom of that curve. Then turn the tap off."

"Sounds doable." He put the glass underneath the tap and went to pull it.

"Wait." Kit covered his hand on the tap with hers. "Tilt the glass at a forty-five-degree angle."

He liked how it looked, her small white hand with sexy wine-colored fingernails over his tanned knuckles. How was he supposed to focus?

"Okay, now we're going to pull the tap forward, slowly. Guinness has to slide down the side of the glass. Otherwise it gets too foamy."

He was stuck on the word *slide* and how her husky voice was low for only him to hear. He tried to ignore the feel of her hand on his, that scent surrounding him now, the heat of her as she stood so close to his side. He watched the way the dark liquid moved down the glass, breathed her in and…

"Enough." She brought his hand back so they closed the tap. "Set the glass down right here. Gently."

Together they lowered the Guinness. "Now just let it stand there."

"This is quite a process." Tyler stepped back, needing a little air, a little distance from her and her perfume and the way it made him want to wrap his arms around her lush curves. Which was totally inappropriate. They were at work, and she worked for him.

"It's an art. A lot of bartending is. Whether it's crafting a cocktail or making someone feel a little less alone for a while, it all takes practice and attention to details."

Tyler stared at her. "You're like the guru of bartending," he said, only half teasing.

"I'd prefer princess, thank you very much."

She threw him a wink and turned away, calling, "Don't you dare touch that pint. I'll be right back."

He watched as she approached a couple rugged guys who'd walked up to the bar and leaned across it to give them each a big hug.

Jealousy flared. It was totally irrational.

He stared at the half-poured Guinness, watching the bubbles settle and disappear. Rodeo was one part mind control. Getting on a bull that you knew might kill you was only possible if you blocked out fear. And if he could block that, he could certainly block this inconvenient desire for Kit.

She took the two men their change and blew them a kiss when they raised their glasses to her. They headed for the pool table and she returned to Tyler. "How's the Guinness?" She eyed the pint. "See how it's settled? There's a clear line between the bubbles on top and the liquid underneath."

At his nod, she went on. "This time, hold the glass straight up, and tip the tap backward. The beer should come out very slowly, right into the middle of the glass."

He tried to ignore the thrill that returned when she put her hand over his and guided him on the tap. Guinness trickled and Tyler's pulse kicked up again. "Don't stop until the foam is all the way to the very rim." She brought their hands forward to stop the pour at just the right moment. "And there you have the perfect pint of Guinness. Now, take it to Crater for the final judging." She stepped away and he instantly missed being connected to her.

He shook his head slightly to clear it and set the pint gingerly in front of Crater for his inspection. "Go easy on me, man."

Crater eyed the pint from above and cocked his head to inspect it from below. "That's a good-looking pint," he finally pronounced. He picked it up, took a sip and wiped the foam off his moustache with a satisfied exhale. "Now *that* is a beer. Well done, Tyler. Stick with Kit and she'll make a bartender out of you yet."

"I think you're right about that." He'd be happy to stick with Kit. Though he knew she wouldn't find that idea quite as appealing.

At least she'd helped him tonight. And if he was lucky, she'd help him again. Because he had a feeling that together they could build a lot more than just pints of Guinness. If she could forgive him for what his dad had done to hers.

CHAPTER FIVE

EVERY THURSDAY MORNING Kit restocked the bar. Maybe it wasn't her job anymore, but she hadn't heard of a change in this routine from Tyler. In fact, she had barely seen him all week. The Spring Fling weekend had gone by in a packed-bar blur. Then she'd taken time off to drive Dad to Reno for a few doctor's appointments. He was a Vietnam veteran and still got his services from the VA there.

They'd stayed overnight at a hotel, and it had been nice. She'd treated him to an evening in a casino, given him a roll of quarters to lose at the slots and bought him a steak dinner. He'd smiled more than she'd seen him smile in a long time. As much as she hated casinos, with their stuffy air, flashing lights and jangling slot machine tunes, it had been worth it to see a bit of a spark in her dad again.

Kit moved behind the bar, assessing the shelves, her decisions almost automatic. They were low on vodka and triple sec. Tyler's cosmos had been a huge hit last weekend. It was almost time to change the keg on the pale ale. The cooler that held the bottled beer was practically empty.

Walking into the storeroom, her thoughts were still on her father. He'd been happy on their Reno trip, but he'd been ready to come home after their short visit. He wasn't someone who wanted vast amounts of leisure time. She needed to find him a purpose. Maybe they could do another project around his house. The porch steps had turned out well, and it was a relief not to worry that he might crash through them.

She remembered the chipping paint on his walls. Repainting could be their next project. She'd grab some color samples at the hardware store and take them over.

She didn't relish the idea of spending her free time painting, but hey, it would keep her busy, too. Keep her mind off the aimless feeling her life had taken on ever since Tyler had bought her sense of purpose out from under her.

Luckily this week had brought good news. A job offer from the High Country Sports Bar. Not full-time work, but enough hours to make her consider the position. Maybe it was worth taking a pay cut in order to have a new start. Although last weekend had been kind of fun. Surprisingly, she'd enjoyed working with Tyler. So maybe she didn't really want to leave.

She put sticky notes on the kegs she needed

to bring out. She'd wrestle them onto the hand truck later on. Pausing, she tapped her pencil idly against the paper in her hand. All the fun she'd had with Tyler behind the bar was exactly why she *should* take another job. The guy could charm anyone, and while it was kind of fun to feel that spark of interest, it would be a terrible idea to act on it.

She walked to where the spirits were and pulled the cord on the overhead bulb so she could see what she was doing. She blinked. Swallowed hard. The shelves were practically empty. Tyler must have forgotten to unpack the boxes.

There were boxes near the outside door, and she knelt to skim the labels. Why were there eight cases of white wine? And two cases of fancy tequila? Where was the vodka? The bottles of Budweiser? The bourbon?

Pulling out her cell phone, she hit the number for the distributor and left a message on his voice mail, asking him to call her. She checked around the room with her heart fluttering in panic. It was Thursday—a busy night. The start of the weekend, which would be busier than usual now that Tyler's rodeo fans were showing up.

She glanced around a little wildly. She had enough beer, as long as customers ordered what was on tap. But there was only one bottle of light rum. No dark. Then her phone chimed. Brian, her distributor, told her that what she had on hand was what had been ordered this week.

Tyler. He'd insisted on doing the order himself. *Damn*.

"Kit?" Tim's voice sounded.

She went into the bar to see him standing by the office door. "What's going on?" she asked.

"I'm here for work," he told her.

"It's morning. We only need one person. Are you sure you didn't get mixed up?"

He pointed to the office and she crossed the bar to look. Both their names were on the schedule for this shift. At least, it looked that way. Tyler's handwriting was messy. Names were written at odd angles.

"He spelled my name wrong," Tim said. "I'm Tin now."

"You're the tin man," Kit teased him. "And look. Ernie is Eernie."

Tim laughed. "His ears do stick out."

Kit frowned. There were two names written in for tomorrow morning as well. "Will you watch the bar? I'll go find Tyler and ask him about this. There's something else I need to speak with him about."

"Sure."

She made her way outside, around the back of the building and through the trees to the old barn. Tyler leaned on the wall, his brown cowboy hat tipped down to block the morning sun. He laughed at something Aaron, of Aaron's Mountain Building, said.

Aaron waved when he spotted her. They'd known each other forever. Even dated a few years ago, until she'd called it off because something didn't feel quite right. Luckily, Aaron had been nice about it. And he'd met the love of his life soon after.

His grin was the only bright thing about the morning. "How you doing, hon?" He pulled her in for a quick hug.

"Doing okay." She shot Tyler a glare to let him know otherwise. "How are Charlotte and the baby?"

"Perfect. She wants you to come by when you can." He glanced at her lace top. "Wear something a little less fancy. I love my son, but he drools like a Saint Bernard."

Kit smiled. "I appreciate the warning. Would you mind if I borrowed Tyler for a minute?"

"Sure. Take him for longer. He's given me so much work my head's gonna explode if he fires off any more ideas."

"Yeah, he's got a lot of those." She didn't bother hiding her wry tone. She was too panicky to play nice.

Aaron must have picked up on it because he whistled low. "Hope you had your coffee this morning, Tyler. 'Cause I think you are about to have a whole lot on your plate. Good luck." He clapped Tyler on the shoulder and strolled off. He was a solid guy.

Unlike certain bar owners who had no idea what they were doing.

"Okay," Tyler drawled, tipping his hat back so she could see his eyes. "What's got you so upset? I've been practicing my pours. I can recognize an ounce of vodka from ten miles away."

She ignored his humor. "You put both Tim and me on the schedule today. He's inside now. You've got an extra person scheduled for tomorrow as well. And you messed up the liquor order. Tonight's going to be busy and we don't have what we need." Frustration boiled over. "Why didn't you let me do my job? I *always* do the schedule. *And* the order!"

"Because I need to learn the business," he said. "Tell me what's wrong."

"You ordered eight cases of white wine. We needed three at most."

"Well, wine improves with age, right?"

"Right, but it won't improve your ability to stay within budget."

He nodded, looking a little grim.

"There's no bottled beer, no vodka and way too much tequila. High-end tequila."

"Okay." His tone was mild but she saw frustration in his eyes. "How do we fix it?"

"We can't. It's too late to place a new order."

"Why don't we just grab some stuff from the liquor store to tide us over? And I'll call the distributor and put in a rush order."

"It'll cost you." A mistake like this would have made Chris furious, because money was tight. But Tyler had money. She'd forgotten that. He could pop a bandage on a mistake like this. It must be nice.

"I'll fix it," Tyler promised. "Maybe we can return some of that wine."

"No returns," she retorted. "What happened? The order form is so straightforward."

"I dunno." He shrugged. "Maybe I got distracted. Why don't you go write me a list of everything we need and I'll go to the liquor store. I need to shut the barn first."

He seemed so casual about messing up what she'd had running so well. "I got a job offer," she blurted.

He froze. "What do you mean?"

"I got hired. At the High Country."

The disappointment on his face surprised her. "You don't want to work here anymore?"

"I figure it's a good time for a change."

He looked away for a moment, then back at her. "That first night. That's the problem, right?

When I was drunk? I gave you a hard time. I regret that, Kit. I promise you, nothing like that will ever happen again."

"Good to know. But it's not that. I've worked here a long time. I'm ready for a change." No more messed-up orders. No more watching her dreams become someone else's. "I'll give you two weeks' notice."

"Right. Sure." He turned away, moving slowly to the barn door to pick up the small padlock as if it weighed a ton.

"And I'll have Tim stay today, since you put us both on the schedule. I have stuff I need to do."

Kit returned to the bar and explained to Tim that she was leaving. She grabbed her purse and headed for her Jeep, waiting for the feeling of relief. Relief that she'd told Tyler she was quitting. Relief that she'd found a way out of this impossible situation.

Relief didn't come. Instead she worried. About the order. About Tim and Lila, her closest friends. About Crater and Stan and all the regulars.

But they weren't her problem. Not anymore. She forced her thoughts to focus on the High Country. It had bands, a dance floor and a huge bar. It was packed every night with young people. Good pay. Great tips. A new start.

So where was the relief she'd been looking for? She leaned on the door of her Jeep, looking at the sagebrush and scrub that surrounded the Dusty Saddle. Yellow wildflowers rose from the barren soil like little pieces of hope. The mountains, still topped in snow, were framed by a bright blue sky. Spring was a glorious time of year east of the Sierras. Lately she'd forgotten to notice the beauty around her.

She sighed, got in and put the key in the ignition. But she couldn't bring herself to start the engine. Because the truth was, she didn't really like the High Country Sports Bar. And there was so much that she adored about the Dusty Saddle. It was hard to drive away when she wasn't sure if she was making the right choice. So she sat and wondered what to do.

TYLER LOCKED THE BARN, shoving the old padlock on and jamming it shut. Owning a bar had seemed like fun. He hadn't thought it through—at least, not about the paperwork involved in running a business.

He hadn't counted on how slow and stubborn his brain could be. And how much it hated reading and writing.

And now Kit, his most capable employee, was leaving.

More than just capable. She was the heart of this place. She brought a sparkle to each of her shifts that the customers clearly appreciated. That he appreciated.

The High Country would appreciate that spark, too.

Damn.

He yanked on the lock to make sure it was truly closed. Then he stared out over the vacant pasture in front of him. Land he hoped to turn into amateur rodeo grounds. Though how he'd do that without his best employee at the bar, he had no idea.

The truth hit him. He needed her. Desperately. There was so much he still needed to learn. So much she knew that he didn't. Plus while she might not share his vision, she was so organized, so good at seeing what steps were needed to happen to accomplish a task. He'd hoped he could involve her more in the remodel design. In everything.

He needed to find a way to make her stay. At least until he could get on his feet.

He shoved away from the wall and jogged around the side of the bar. Relief flooded when he saw that Kit's Jeep was still in the parking lot. He had a chance, maybe, to try to change her mind.

"Kit!" he called, his heavy heart losing a pound or two when she stepped out of the Jeep. "Can I talk to you?" He stopped with his hands open at his sides in appeal. "I need you to stay." It was out before he thought about how to finesse it.

She stared at him. "Why?"

He had to lay it all on the line. "I can't do this without you. I don't know how. The bartending, the schedule, everything. We were in school together. You know I quit early. Reading, numbers, it's all screwed up with me."

"What do you mean, screwed up?" Her features softened into concern. This is what he'd learned about her this week. That she might dress tough in her black clothing, she might look tough with her tattoos, but she was a kind person. A woman who listened to Crater's long-winded stories no matter how many times she'd already heard them. Who made sure everyone in the bar was having a good time.

He took a deep breath before he cut open his soul and let his secret spill out. "I mean, when I look at a page, I don't see it right. Even when I think I've understood it, I find out I got it wrong. At school they told me I had dyslexia and put me in a special class for reading. They said I had something called dyscalculia and gave me a special teacher for math, too. But staring at the numbers and words in a smaller classroom didn't solve the problem."

She nodded slowly. "I think I remember you going to those classes."

"The dumb kid."

"No!" She frowned. "You were never that."

"Well, the schedule, the ordering, I clearly got it wrong. I need you to stay. To help me do those things."

"But you could still get help, couldn't you? With your learning problems?"

"What?" He stared at her. "I'm done with school."

"You could hire someone to teach you, right? There must be some kind of expert who knows how to help you."

That had never occurred to him. "Maybe. But I doubt they're hanging out in Benson, and even if they are, they can't help me fast enough to keep this bar running." He'd beg if need be. "I need you, Kit. And I've got a proposal."

One of her dark eyebrows shot up.

"Not *that* kind of proposal." He wished he could make one of those. But she was off-limits and could barely stand him anyway. He tried to give words to the idea he'd had at the barn. "What if you and I had some kind of partnership?"

"What do you mean?"

"Help me come up with a system for ordering and scheduling that works for me. Teach me how to bartend well. And help me get this place renovated."

She shook her head. "You need someone else. Someone who isn't bitter."

He smiled a little. "You're not *that* bitter. You've helped me so much already."

"That's because I'm a softy when I see someone in over his head."

"Exactly. And I'm so far over my head, I may never get out. I definitely won't without your help."

She studied him, then studied her dark nails. He watched the smile on her face fade into a blur of discomfort when she looked at him again. "I'm not the one who should help you."

"You're the one I need."

"No, you don't get it. I'm angry inside. Jealous of you. Because…" She shook her head, and her voice dissolved into a whisper so faint he couldn't catch her words.

"Why?" He took a step closer. Reached for her hand.

"The bar. The Dusty Saddle. I had hoped to buy it someday. When I had the money." He could see the glimmer of tears. "I didn't know Chris was going to retire so soon."

All the missing pieces clicked into place. Her frustration with him wasn't only from his drunken visit that first night. Or his father's treatment of hers. "I had no idea. I saw a note Chris had posted on the Chamber of Commerce website. And I jumped at the chance."

"You couldn't have known. And it's stupid to be mad at you, but I still feel it. This envy that you can make it into what you want. I need to get over it. But I'm not very good at getting over stuff."

He let go of her hand and shoved his in his pockets. They felt useless against the disappointment in her tone. "I'm sorry. I didn't mean to steal your dream."

Her full lips twitched into a rueful smile. "It might be a little strong to call it my dream. But it was my hope. I need to stay in Benson, and I need more than a nine-to-five, clock-in, clock-out kind of thing."

"Then take me up on my offer. Stay here. Work with me. Help me renovate the bar."

"Did you hear anything I just said?"

"I heard it all. And I promise I'll make it worth your while. I'll make you the manager. I'll give you a raise. And if you stay until we open, I'll give you a bonus."

"Why?" She eyed him suspiciously.

"I have so much I want to do. But I don't know much about running a bar yet and we've already established that I can't read and write very well. I want your input. I want you to help me make some of the big decisions."

"And if I stay until it's finished, you'll give me a bonus?"

"Yes. Enough to make a difference." He cast around in his mind for a number that would help her out of the trouble his dad had caused. Something that would open doors for her. "A hundred thousand dollars. That's enough to help with your dad, right?"

She stared at him. *"A hundred thousand dollars?"*

"If you think it would be fair."

She looked away, shoulders rising slightly. "I don't need charity. That's what this is, right? You feel guilty about what your dad did? About buying the bar when I wanted it? I don't want your pity."

"Jeez, Kit. Look at me."

"No bar is worth paying me all that money." Beneath her dark makeup, her eyes were guarded.

He searched for the reason that would make her say yes. He finally settled on the truth. "I need this. I need a success."

She shook her head. "I don't get it. You *are* a success. You're a rodeo champion. The ladies flock into the bar every night just to bat their eyelashes at you."

"That's different." How could he explain when he could barely articulate it to himself? "My bull-riding success was a miracle. I'm grateful for it. But it's the only success I ever had. I failed out of school. Then I went into the army but my reading and writing problems got in my way again. I want to succeed at something besides rodeo. Something right here in Benson."

"Wait, you bought a bar to impress your dad?" Her smile was incredulous. "I don't see him as the partying kind."

He grinned. "Yeah, well, he's made it clear he'd have preferred another type of venture. But I've spent a lot of time in bars on the road. I went to this bar in Texas that had an amateur rodeo attached, a beer garden, a barbecue…and it felt right. Like all the best stuff in life was wound up in one place."

Kit laughed. "Add strippers and big-screen TVs and you'd have guy heaven here on earth."

He liked her twisted humor. "I think we'll skip the strippers, but the TVs will be a nice touch."

"You really want to pay me all this money just to get this place open?"

He nodded.

"And if I decide to leave after it's all finished, you won't mind?"

His heart sank a little at the thought but he tried to ignore it. "Of course I won't."

She shook her head slowly. "I can't believe I'm saying this but…"

"You'll do it?"

"I'll do it."

"Yes!" He fist-pumped. It was a relief to confess his troubles, to have her help, to know this would work out.

She watched him like he'd gone crazy. "You know you're nuts, right? To pay me so much money?"

He sobered. "You have no idea how many skills you have, do you? How much you know about running a business? Trust me, you are worth way more than I'm paying you." He wanted to hug her, his relief was so deep. He put a hand to his heart instead. "Thank you. Seriously. Thank you."

She nodded. "It's getting late. You'd better get that booze we need. I'll text you a list. And this week, we'll fill out the schedule and the order forms together. Maybe we can come up with a method that's less confusing, too."

"That would be great." He was shaky but he kept his voice steady. "And we'll get a contract drawn up, so you can be sure you'll get everything we talked about."

She opened the door of her Jeep. "Okay, well, until tomorrow then."

"See you soon." He liked saying it. He liked knowing it was true.

He crossed the parking lot and paused at the door to the bar. He felt lighter. With Kit on his side he could make the Dusty Saddle a success. He'd just have to remember not to fall for her, because he was pretty sure he was already partway there.

CHAPTER SIX

TYLER TURNED INTO the rutted dirt driveway on the eastern edge of Benson. A rusty mailbox had Hayes scrawled across it in what looked like permanent marker. A barbed-wire fence delineated the boundaries of the property. Someone, he suspected Kit, had nailed a cattle skull to the post closest to the driveway.

Garth's house was on a slight hill, looking over the plain. He'd chosen a lonely place to live, with sagebrush rolling out in all directions. No wonder Kit had rented a place in town. She was too social to isolate herself out here.

Her Jeep was a bright spot in the driveway. She must be spending her Sunday helping out her dad. He'd picked up from their conversations that she visited her father a lot. Still, Tyler hadn't expected to see her. And if the prospect made his day feel a little brighter, well, they were old friends. And it was always good to see an old friend.

Ever since his disastrous conversation with his dad a couple days ago, Tyler had been thinking about how he could help Garth. He figured

Garth must be feeling lost without his work. The worry in Kit's eyes whenever she talked about her dad confirmed his suspicions. Kit's bonus would help with their financial woes, but Garth needed more than that. He needed a job. And talking with Aaron about repairs to his barn the other day, Tyler had realized that he'd have enough work, eventually, to keep Garth plenty busy.

Kit and her dad were standing on the porch when Tyler parked behind Kit's Jeep. Kit waved, and they came over to meet him. She had a big fan of paint strips in her hand and a strained expression on her face. Her dad wore sweatpants, a bathrobe and slippers, even though it was past midday. They came down the steps to meet him.

"What's going on?" Kit asked. "I didn't expect to see you out here."

"I came to pay your dad a visit." Tyler stuck out his hand to Garth, pleased when his old friend seized his, then pulled him closer to clap him on the back.

"Kit told me you were in town." A wide smile gouged deep creases into Garth's weather-beaten face. "And a bar owner now. Good for you, son."

"Thanks, Garth. I couldn't do any of it without Kit helping me."

"Well, she's real good at that," Garth said absentmindedly. And then went straight to the topic he loved. "It's an honor to have you home, Tyler.

Rodeo world champion. I just about fell out of my seat when I watched that last ride of yours on the TV. You stuck on there like you had glue on your seat. They gave you a mean bull for it, too. Hades is a legend."

"He was tricky, all right. But hey, I was taught by the best. You gave me a great start. Without your help, I probably never would have become a bull rider."

"Well, I thought you wouldn't when you joined the army." Garth's face was grave. "Thought we might lose you in some Mideast war."

"Lucky for me, I guess, that the army wasn't too thrilled with my abilities. And bull riding turned out to be a hell of a lot more fun than boot camp."

Tyler glanced at Kit. Where she'd looked worried before, now she looked upset. He wished he knew why. "Hey, you two look like you're doing some painting. I don't want to interrupt."

"Well, I've been trying to get Dad to choose a color for a few days." Tyler could hear the frustration in her voice.

Garth waved a hand in the general direction of Kit and her paint strips. "We can do that later. Right now we have company. Tyler, want to come up on the porch and sit a while? I could make us some coffee."

Tyler noticed Kit's white knuckles, clutching

her paint colors. "Hey, how about this? Why don't you show me your ideas for your painting project? Believe it or not, I like this kind of thing." He shot Kit a quick wink, gratified to see some of the strain leave her face.

"Okay," Garth nodded. "Let me go inside and get changed. And I'll put that coffee on." Garth climbed the steps with the agility of a younger man and disappeared into the house. Kit stared after him, her jaw set, as if she were clenching her teeth.

"Kit," Tyler said quietly. "I went to see my dad earlier this week. I couldn't get him to listen to me. So I'm here to ask your dad if he'll work for me, managing my barn, once it's up and running. I can't think of anyone I'd rather have."

"That's great," she said, turning to face him. He heard the quaver in her voice, saw the tremble in her lip. "That's really nice of you."

"Hey," he said, reaching with his thumb to brush at a tear that spilled down her cheek. "What's the matter?"

She stepped away and ran her knuckles roughly under her eyes. "It's just, I've been coming out here, day after day, ever since your dad fired him. Trying to get him out of his *damn* pajamas. Trying to get him to take an interest in this house, do his dishes, eat right. Nothing's worked."

She waved her hand toward the porch. "I even

helped him build those porch steps. *Me*. Just because I was so desperate to get him to do *something*."

He looked at the unpainted wooden steps with new admiration. "They're very nice."

"The point is nothing has worked. He *won't* clean his house. He *won't* get dressed. He's quit all of his activities in town, and no matter what I say or do, *nothing* changes. But then *you* show up and he's all excited and happy and running off to get dressed and make coffee."

"That's a good thing, right?" Tyler studied her closely. What was he missing here? "Maybe he just needed a visit from an old friend?"

"Maybe," she said wanly. "Or maybe he's always just preferred you over me."

"What? No… Kit…you're his daughter." He couldn't stand the tears that were starting to slide down her cheeks.

"*You're* his rodeo protégé. That wins out." She used her sleeve to catch the tears and glanced toward the door apprehensively. "I'm being stupid. I should be happy that he's finally interested in something. I just wish, sometimes, that it could be me."

She turned away, but he caught her gently by the arm. "You're *very* interesting. You're smart and capable and funny as hell, and if your dad can't see that, it's a hundred percent his problem.

Don't take his rodeo obsession personally. He was a great rider in his day, and some guys have a hard time leaving it behind."

"And you? Are you having trouble?"

The question took him by surprise. "Not right now," he blurted out. "Not when I'm with you."

Her eyes went wide, as if she saw the feeling behind his words. A feeling so intense it surprised him, too. "Oh."

He wanted to kiss the pallor from her face. Replace the sadness in her eyes with something far warmer. But he wouldn't overstep. He touched her hair, sliding the silky black mass of it behind her shoulder. "You're special, Kit. Don't doubt it."

He heard a sound from inside the house and stepped back, hoping he'd eased some of her angst.

Her dad came through the screen door, dressed in jeans, boots and a flannel shirt. "I've got coffee," he called. "Did you pick a color?"

"We've got a few ideas," he called. Kit eyed him and he gave her a smile he hoped would reassure. "Can I try out your steps?" he asked. "I've never climbed a Kit Hayes signature staircase before."

She gave a small giggle. "By all means," she said, with a flourish of her hand.

On the porch, Tyler had Kit show him her favorite color, a pale blue, and voted for it over

Garth's sage green preference. Then they let Garth have the green color anyway, because, after all, it was his house. And then Tyler offered Garth a position as barn manager, once he had a working barn. And they all toasted Garth's hearty agreement with their coffee.

As he waved goodbye, Tyler felt like he'd done something good today. For Garth, certainly, but hopefully for Kit, too. It had broken something inside him to realize that she felt so disregarded by her father, and that he might play a part in that. Maybe, with a job to look forward to and a sense of purpose, Garth would come out of his gloom. And give Kit one less thing to worry about.

"LILA, CAN I ask you something totally personal?" Kit looked up at Lila, who was perched on a ladder using clothespins to attach white fabric to a wire. It was Monday morning, and they were hanging a backdrop in Lila's photography studio. Which was really the garage of the cottage Lila and Ethan shared.

"Of course." Lila glanced to where Kit held the fabric off the floor. "Anything."

It was hard to ask a question that would reveal such a flaw in her own nature. But she was desperate. "How did you move on from your past? From what happened to you?"

Lila turned and sat on the top step to face Kit.

"You mean with Dale?" Lila had moved to Benson to hide from her abusive ex-boyfriend. Last fall he'd found her and almost killed her. He was in jail now, thank goodness, and Lila seemed completely happy, like she'd moved on from the trauma with ease.

"I'm sorry, maybe I shouldn't bring it up," Kit said. "I wouldn't, if I didn't need your help so much."

"Is this about Arch?" Lila asked.

"It's more about me. And all these bad feelings I can't get rid of. I was so jealous of Mandy when Arch fell for her. And I was so jealous when Tyler bought the bar. But I was starting to accept it, you know? I was starting to be okay with it all."

"So that's great. It's progress."

"I thought so, too. But this weekend, Tyler offered Dad a job at his barn, once it's running. They were close when we were young, and the moment Tyler showed up, it was like Dad was suddenly cured of his depression. And of course I'm relieved about that, but it bugged me that Tyler could help him and I can't. I went right back to that jealous place. And I hate it there. I don't want to feel like that."

Lila nodded sympathetically. "But it makes sense to me. Ever since your mom left, you've devoted a lot of your time and energy to trying to make your dad feel better. And you've been there for him almost every day since he lost his job."

Tears threatened, but Kit blinked them back, needing to say what was haunting her. "I realized yesterday that even though I'm his daughter, I'm not the person who brings him joy. Tyler *is*. They have this bond over bull riding and rodeo. They've had it since we were kids. And it's way stronger than any father-daughter thing."

"You're a great daughter, Kit. And it's not your fault if your dad doesn't find joy in that."

"But I want to stop caring about it, you know? And instead I feel like I've got one foot in this quicksand of resentment and I can't get out."

"You will. But it's a process. It's not simple to get over stuff."

Frustration clenched Kit's hands into fists around the cloth. "Do you know what I hate the most? Is that I sound like I'm whining. *Poor me, Arch didn't love me anymore. And I couldn't buy the bar, and my dad likes someone else better.* I can't stand myself when I feel like this! That's why I need to know how you moved on."

"I hate to break it to you," Lila said gently, "but I don't think it's possible to completely move on from some of the big stuff that happens in our lives. I think you learn to live with the feelings and not let them take over everything. I'm still afraid. I know they'll let Dale out of prison at some point. But I can't let that fear ruin my life, so I try to keep it in one part of my mind while I focus on the good stuff."

"Ugh. I was hoping you had some magic words. Or magic beans. Or anything."

Lila giggled. "Nope. No beans. Sorry. Just stay in the present moment. Appreciate what you have. Try to be grateful that your dad has Tyler in his life. Because Tyler understands him in a way you can't. Unless—" she grinned "—you've developed a secret love of bull riding."

"Not likely." But Kit felt her cheeks flush because, while she wasn't fond of the sport, when a certain bull rider had tried to give her comfort the other day, there had been an unexpected sweetness that she couldn't forget.

Lila climbed down the ladder. "Do you still want to do this photo shoot?"

"I'll do it, but like I warned you, I'm terrible at posing for photos."

"Not true," Lila said. "I've taken a zillion great snaps of you on my phone."

"But this is different." Kit eyed the white backdrop, the tall lamps and Lila's camera, perched on a tripod. "This is serious stuff."

"I take good photos and you're gorgeous. How bad can it be? Now, will you sit down?" Lila pointed to a bench she'd draped with a black cloth.

Kit shuffled over. She felt silly now that she

was here. When Lila had first asked her to pose it had sounded fun. Something different to try that might help her friend. But she had no idea what to do. It didn't help that Lila had the big lamp on and was studying Kit's face under the light with a concerned expression.

"Tell me about your makeup."

It wasn't at all the question Kit had been expecting. "What do you mean?"

"Well…it's hiding your eyes. Would you consider taking it off for the photos?"

"I can't take pictures with no makeup," Kit protested. "I'll look terrible."

"You're pretty with no makeup," Lila insisted. "You don't wear much when you go running and you always look awesome."

"That's running. What if you put these photos in your exhibit? And there I am, no makeup?"

Lila laughed. "You can have final approval. I promise."

Kit knew it was silly. "I'm sure I sound like the most shallow person ever. It's just that my makeup…" She searched for the right word. "It's…"

"…a layer between you and the world," Lila finished for her.

Kit wasn't sure. "I never thought of it that way." Was it a mask? She'd always really liked wearing tons of makeup. She hadn't analyzed it.

Lila came to sit beside her, taking Kit's hand. "Hey, please don't get me wrong. I think you look amazing. Always. But I wonder...this is the look you adopted when you started dating Arch, right? Kind of tough, Goth rocker chick. And it's a good look for you, but I'd like to photograph you the way *I* see you. The person I see isn't Arch's ex-girlfriend, or the town tough girl. I see Kit. My sweet, funny, smart, beautiful, kind friend."

Kit didn't quite know what to say. On one hand her pride was bruised, because no matter how gently she said it, Lila was suggesting Kit's look was outdated. On the other hand, Lila was right. Kit hadn't dressed like this until she started going out with Arch. All the black eyeliner and thick mascara seemed to fit who she'd become when she fell in love with him.

This whole past year she'd wanted, so badly, to move on from that. But change was scary. If she changed, was that admitting her old ways were a mistake? "I guess the makeup shows the side of myself that I want people to see."

"What's wrong with them seeing *you*? Aren't you enough? Just as you are?"

The question sat between them, heavy with meaning. Lila had nailed exactly what ached deep in the raw center of Kit's heart. She hadn't been enough, for her dad, for her mom, for Arch.

Her throat was almost too tight for speech. "I'm not sure."

"What if we try it?" Lila asked gently. "Let me give you a makeover. Or, I guess, a make-under."

Lila was right. It was time for something different. "Okay," she agreed. "Go for it."

Ninety minutes later, Kit looked at a softer version of herself in Lila's bathroom mirror. Lila had cut a few layers into Kit's hair and convinced Kit not to straighten it, so it had dried in gentle waves. Kit's makeup was a delicate palette of browns and pinks that made her eyes look huge, but way more accessible without all the black ringing them.

"What do you think?" Lila asked.

"I'm not sure, honestly." Kit tilted her head. "I'm not sure I look like me."

"Or maybe you look more like you. Or an alternative version of you."

Kit made a few faces. And realized she liked who she saw in the mirror. Lila was right. The black eye makeup, the red lipstick, *was* something to hide behind. Because if she hid who she was, then when she wasn't enough, when people chose a new life, or a new love instead of her, it didn't hurt quite so much.

But right now, she was all about discovering who she was. Not hiding it. "Thank you," she said. "I actually feel really pretty."

"You look beautiful." Lila grinned. "Ready to be pretty for the camera?"

Kit didn't feel as nervous now. This might even be fun. And maybe today could be a start. The day she finally trusted that she was good enough, no matter what choices her mom or her dad or Arch or anyone else made. "Yeah. I'm ready."

MONDAY AFTERNOON WAS shifting toward evening when Tyler climbed the worn granite steps of Benson Elementary. He opened the wood and glass doors and inhaled the paste and chalk-dust smell. With time-warp speed he was that little boy again, squinting at the page, words tangling on his tongue every time a teacher uttered the dreaded "Could you read that out loud, please?"

But he wasn't that little boy now. He was a grown man, looking to improve himself, and that was an honorable thing. He wished it didn't feel so damn embarrassing.

The hallways were empty. His work boots clomped on the tiles.

The office door was on the right and the time-warp feeling continued as he stepped inside. There was the same row of chairs where he'd waited countless times for a lecture from the principal and the dreaded phone call home to his dad.

In those same chairs, he'd waited when his dad had come to get him, white-faced and instantly aged. To take him to the hospital to say goodbye to his mom, in those last moments before cancer stole her from them forever.

He swallowed hard, pushing that memory back. An older woman wearing a bright blue pantsuit bustled in carrying a stack of file folders. "Can I help you, sir?"

Unnerved at being called *sir* in a place where he felt all of ten years old, he cleared his throat. "Yes, I'm looking for a tutor." When her eyebrows went up in surprise he added a lie. "It's for my nephew. I was wondering if maybe the school had a list of people who offered tutoring."

She set her folders down and looked at him thoughtfully. "Benson is a small town. We don't have any tutoring centers. And we don't keep a list, though I suppose we should." She scribbled a note on a piece of paper, as if to remind herself of that idea.

Disappointment and relief were a strange mix. He wanted help. But he didn't want to share the extent of his inabilities, so it was a relief of sorts that she couldn't help him.

"Well, thank you for your time." He turned to go, wondering if it might be better to get help online. Anonymously.

"Hang on," she called, and he turned to see that she'd followed him into the hallway. "Why don't you see Mrs. Lopez in room eight? She teaches second grade, and she helps kids after school. Maybe she could find some time for your nephew."

Coming here was a bad idea. "Okay, I'll look her up another day. Thanks."

"She hasn't gone home yet. I'll walk you to her room." The woman beckoned, a gesture so full of command Tyler's feet obeyed before he'd even decided to follow. She led him down the hall and around a corner. "I'm Mary Kennedy, the principal here. Who is your nephew?"

Tyler cast around frantically for a name. "He actually doesn't go here. He's homeschooled."

She glanced at him, clearly puzzled, and stopped at a classroom with the number eight painted on the door. Anxiety twisted his stomach. He'd spent third grade in this room. The year all the other kids had started to read chapter books. And he'd been still trying to keep track of the alphabet.

"You should probably contact the district homeschooling outreach teacher if his parents are having trouble guiding him in his studies."

"Will do, Mrs. Kennedy," he said. "And thanks for your help. I'll take it from here."

"You look so familiar. Do I know you?"

She probably did, if she ever read the local paper, but he needed anonymity right now. "I don't think we've met. But good to meet you now."

"Yes, nice to meet you, too. Good luck with the tutoring."

He watched her walk back down the hallway, waiting for her to turn the corner before he knocked on the classroom door. A woman with dark hair and brown eyes opened it. "Can I help you?"

"Mrs. Lopez? My name is Tyler. I was hoping to speak with you about tutoring."

She smiled with a gentle kindness that he didn't remember from school. "Come in."

The classroom was decorated with bright colors. She offered him an impossibly tiny chair. He lowered himself carefully and she sat, with much more ease, in another. "I'm so sorry I don't remember you. What grade is your child in?"

Here it was. The moment he dreaded. He thought of Kit's face when she'd realized he'd messed up the ordering. The huge bill he'd paid to purchase supplies from the local liquor store afterward. The frustration on his employees' faces when he'd scheduled them wrong. Kit wouldn't be around to save his butt forever. He had to do this. "I need a tutor for myself."

Her eyes widened. "Oh."

"I went to this school years ago. But I didn't really learn to read or write that well. Or do math. They said I had dyslexia and dyscalculia. Eventually I just quit school."

"What have you been doing?"

"I joined the army at first. Then I became a professional bull rider."

Mrs. Lopez leaned forward and clasped her hands together. "I've heard of you."

"I'm Tyler Ellis."

"Well." She studied him a moment, as if trying to absorb the news. "Nice to meet you, Tyler Ellis." And that was it. No judgment that he'd quit school. No questions about his rodeo career.

"Mrs. Kennedy, the principal, she said you tutor kids. Do you think you'd have time to tutor me as well? I'd pay you, of course. And I'd work around your schedule. We could meet wherever and whenever is convenient for you."

She bit her lip, glanced around the room. As if trying to figure out where she'd fit one more student into her obviously full workload. "I'm not an expert in dyslexia."

"I'd bet you know more about it than anyone else in this town."

"What kinds of problems are you having?"

He described the scheduling problems. Spelling names wrong. Lines that seemed to wiggle and blur when he stared at them too long. Words that never felt familiar, no matter how many times he practiced. "When I was riding bulls, I didn't notice it as much—there just wasn't that much reading. I had an agent I trusted with my contracts and an accountant I trusted with my money. But the day-to-day running of a bar, well, I had no idea there was so much paperwork."

"I can see how that would be very difficult." She took a deep breath and blew it out. "I'd need to give you some assessments, so I can figure out what you know and where the gaps are. Do you have time to take a few tests now?"

Relief, that he'd found her, that she wasn't laughing at him, that she would help him, had him nodding instead of speaking.

She went to a file cabinet and rummaged, while he looked at the alphabet above the whiteboard and the kids' work in rainbow colors on the walls. She set papers and a sharpened pencil on the table in front of him. "Start with those, okay?"

So he pulled his tiny chair up to the tiny table and started writing. The time-warp feeling came back as he carefully read the words on the page, touching each one with his finger to keep on track. Just as he had twenty-five years ago in this very room.

Only he had a different teacher now. And she was humming as she sorted through some papers on the other side of the classroom. And he had a feeling that if anyone could teach him to read, it was Mrs. Lopez of room eight, Benson Elementary School.

CHAPTER SEVEN

"HEY KIT, WILL you take a look at this?" Tyler came through the office door and set the paper on the table in front of her.

"What is it?" Kit put her book down. She'd arrived for her Friday evening shift a little early, and since the bar was empty and Mario was still working, she'd curled up in the big office chair with the next book in her stack of self-help reads.

"It's our contract. I had my lawyer write it up." He paused. "Hang on...you look different. Did you get a haircut?"

It had taken all week to find the courage to try Lila's make-under for herself. But she'd ditched the heavy makeup today and let her hair keep the waves it was born with. "Yeah, kind of," she muttered. Suddenly self-conscious, Kit skimmed the document, getting stuck on the legal language. "It's very official."

It was all there. Her raise and the huge bonus she'd earn if she stayed until the bar was completely renovated and operating. Tyler handed her a pen and she signed at the bottom. "Now you're stuck with me."

He grinned. "I can think of worse things. I'll make copies and give you one." He glanced at the title of her book. *The Satisfied Single Woman.* He shook his head. "Are you sure you need that? It seems like you're doing pretty good on your own."

"Can I add a clause to our contract? That you don't get to comment on my choice of reading material? You should be happy that your employee is trying to better herself."

"I think you're pretty good the way you are. I don't see why you need all these so-called experts telling you how to live."

"Sometimes experts have good ideas. Like the idea I got when I did a little online research the other night." She stood and reached between the desk and the wall, where she'd stored her creation. She'd stayed up until two in the morning cutting it all out, determined to show Tyler that he could find ways around his dyslexia.

He gaped when she pulled out the wood-framed magnetic board.

"It's for scheduling." She'd used permanent marker to create columns for the days of the week, and rows for the regular bar shifts. "I even left extra spaces at the bottom for special events, when you need extra people working."

He tipped the board up so it rested against the wall. "You made this for me?"

She rummaged in her purse and found the plastic bag of labeled blue magnets. "Each staff member has a bunch of magnets with their name on it. When you decide who gets a shift, you just put their magnet on the board. No writing. No spelling. And since the magnets are a different color from the white board, it will be easy to see if two names end up in one space, or if you've left a shift blank." Her heart pounded a little. She wasn't sure if he'd appreciate the help. Maybe he'd feel embarrassed by her interfering.

Tyler reached into the bag and pulled out a magnet with Lila's name on it. He put his finger on the board under the word *Friday*. Ran it down until he came to the section marked *5:30*. He put the magnet in the space. "Lila's working tonight." His voice was low and rough. He cleared his throat, and when he glanced at her, she saw a flush highlighting his cheekbones. Great. She'd embarrassed him.

"This is perfect," he said. "The lines are so wide, the colors help..." He swallowed hard. "Thank you for doing this for me. I can't believe you did. Looks like it was a lot of work."

She wanted to keep it light for him. "I had no idea I was good at making stuff. But after building that staircase, I figured I could do this. And it was fun."

"It's great. I'll get a hammer and nails so we can hang it."

Then he was out the door. But not before Kit caught a glint of something bright in his eyes.

She stared at the scheduling board, trying to take in this new side of Tyler. He showed the world his bull-riding swagger, his upbeat, charming persona. But he'd shared his difficulties reading and writing with her. And now he was emotional over a scheduling tool.

Funny, how she thought she knew him. When she'd first seen him again, she'd pegged him as a rodeo cowboy who cashed in on his good looks. She hadn't expected his depth. The way he'd been so patient with her rudeness. So humble in his apologies. So kind to her the other day at her dad's house. And so genuine, just now, in his gratitude.

Turned out she really didn't know Tyler Ellis at all.

Lila popped her head in. "Your co-bartender is here. Ready for some Friday night craziness." She caught sight of the scheduling board, hard to miss in the tiny office. "What's that?"

"Just something I made to help us stay a little more organized."

Lila's eyebrows arched suggestively. "Helping

out the new boss, are you? And I notice you tried your new look today. I'm sure he noticed."

Kit's cheeks went hot as she stood. "It's not like that. He's asked me to get this place more organized. To manage things with him." Somehow she couldn't bring herself to tell Lila how much money Tyler had offered her. It would take way too much explaining.

"Well, I'm glad." Lila set her bag down and Kit followed her out of the office to start their shift. "We need you back in charge around here."

"Not in charge. Just helping."

"Helping a lot." That from Tyler, who was standing by the bar. Apparently he hadn't made it to the shed. "Lila, I just met your fiancé."

Ethan raised his pint. "Hey, Kit. You look great. And I like your new boss."

"He's okay." Kit gave Tyler a wink.

"She doesn't really think that." The usual Tyler was back, the cocky smile cutting a dimple into his cheek. "I do most things wrong and it makes her crazy."

He was baiting her and she bit, glad to return to their familiar sparring after the undercurrent of emotion in the office. "You're a slow learner, but your pretty face is bringing us a whole new crowd. And even if they are scantily clad and barely of age, they sure do like to buy expensive drinks. How can I complain?"

Lila fanned herself with her hand. "It's getting hot in here." She turned to Ethan. "See? I told you they had chemistry."

"Lila, you're embarrassing them." Ethan pulled her close and kissed her red hair. "Please excuse my fiancée here. She's so crazy about me she's started seeing things."

"Hallucinating, for sure." Kit glared at Lila, who raised her eyebrows in mock innocence.

"I'm gonna get that hammer now."

They watched Tyler walk out. Kit turned on Lila. "*Please* don't say stuff like that."

"I'm sorry," Lila said, not looking very apologetic. "It just came out. The sparks between you two got me all confused."

"There are no sparks. It's familiarity. We were always around each other growing up."

"There were sparks," Lila insisted. "And you know what else? You were smiling more, just then, than I've seen you smile ever since that whole Arch thing went down. So I'm glad there are sparks."

"Ethan, rein her in, please."

He shrugged. "Hate to admit it, but I saw them, too."

"I'm going to stock the bar. Lila, when you are done seeing things that aren't there, maybe you can join me."

"Maybe," Lila said, taking a sip from Ethan's

water glass, "I'm not the one with vision problems." She kissed Ethan on the cheek and followed Kit behind the bar. "Maybe you, my best friend, need glasses."

Kit grabbed a metal bucket from the sink. "Maybe you, my best friend, need to go in the back and get us some more ice."

Lila giggled. "Maybe you, my best friend, are getting a little bossy." She flounced off in mock-indignation and Kit glanced up to see that Tyler was back, chatting with Ethan. His auburn hair caught the light, and when he spied her watching him, a slow smile started. Like he was happy to see her. Happy that she was there.

Kit grabbed the cutting board and the basket of lemons and started slicing. Why was she staring at him like that? All Lila's and Ethan's misguided ideas were getting in her head. Tyler liked cute blondes in cutoff shorts who leaned over the bar to show him their cleavage. She liked guys in black leather jackets and three-day stubble. Clean-cut, jeans-modeling cowboy Tyler Ellis was not her type, and she definitely wasn't his.

TYLER SET THE last box of empty bottles outside the storeroom door, ready for recycling. He glanced at his watch. It was 2:00 a.m. Officially Saturday morning.

"Tyler?" Kit called from the bar. "Everyone is gone. I think I'll head home."

He was still buzzing from the bustle of the Friday-night crowd. And truth was he didn't feel ready to say goodbye to Kit. Working with her was fun. He'd gotten used to catching her eye when it got insanely busy. Teasing each other as they passed. Maybe it was their old friendship rekindling, but she was quickly becoming his favorite person to work with. He hurried into the bar. "Want to stay for a drink? To celebrate signing our contract?"

She'd changed her look. Her hair was more tousled now, hanging in loose black waves around her face. The kind of waves a guy wanted to run his fingers through. And her eyes. She'd ditched the heavy black liner and somehow it seemed like he could see her more. All night he'd been aware of their deep brown color and her thick dark lashes, and the humor and the kindness that shone through far more clearly without the distraction of her intense makeup. Now there were slight shadows under them, like she was tired after their busy night. But she said, "Sure, a drink would be good," and set her purse on the bar.

"What'll you have?" he asked.

"A cosmopolitan," she teased, climbing onto a stool.

"And would that be extra pink? Or extra fruity?"

"Extra vodka. And hold the pink and the fruity." She grinned. "Oh, and can you add some tonic? You get it from that little gun thing over there."

"I figured that out a while ago. With help from a certain someone." He slid the vodka and tonic across the bar and she caught it. He poured a shot of bourbon over ice and went to sit beside her. He raised his glass toward her. "To my bartending guru." It was a joke, but he truly was grateful for the way she'd trained him.

She lifted her glass in response. "You'd be fine without me," she assured him. "Now that half your customers are young women, it doesn't matter how your drinks taste. They just want to flirt."

"It matters to me," he said. "I want to be known as the best bar in town. The best cocktails, with quality ingredients. The best beer, the most interesting selection. Think we can do it?"

Kit looked thoughtful. Then amused. "I think most of your staff doesn't know too much about making cocktails."

"How do you know how to make them?"

"I used to have a lot of parties. Just for my close friends. They let me try out recipes on them."

Inspiration struck. "Would you want to come up with a cocktail menu for this place? We could offer a few specials each month. You could teach the staff how to make them. They'd become better bartenders, and I bet some of the customers would get a kick out of it."

"That's a really good idea, actually."

He couldn't help tease her a little. "See? Change can be fun, right?"

"Some of it, I guess." Her smile was more delicate without the bold lipstick she usually wore.

"We make a good team." He thought of the scheduling board she'd made him, and how much she'd taught him already. "Though I think right now I'm the one benefiting most from our teamwork."

"Nah. I am, too." She rubbed her thumb against her first two fingers. "Money." Then she burst out laughing, as if unable to keep up the mercenary facade. "Seriously, it's fun to work with you. It kind of reminds me of old times. Cleaning stalls together, weeding the garden." She paused, regarding him. "Come to think of it, you got me to do a lot of your chores with you. You Tom Sawyered me, didn't you?"

"What?" He knew she was being funny, but he didn't totally get the reference.

"You know, that book by Mark Twain? Tom Sawyer is a kid who has to paint a fence, but he makes it seem so fun that all the other kids want to do it, too. And they end up painting it for him."

He laughed. "I never got through any of the books in high school. But it's true, I did get you to do a bunch of my chores with me. It made them a whole lot more fun. It's still kind of like that."

"It kind of is." She smiled slightly and took a sip of her drink. "You know what I keep thinking about? The night we went out after the Benson Spring Fling."

He laughed outright at the memory. "The great golf cart crash?"

She giggled. "Yes. I got you to jump over the fence of that fancy community near Mammoth."

"And we stole that golf cart and your driving was so bad, we crashed into a hedge. I thought I was a goner, but I couldn't stop laughing, either."

She wagged an admonishing finger. "Then you decided we should use their hot tub."

His skin heated at the memory. "Hey, I was a sixteen-year-old boy. The idea of you in all that warm water was my adolescent dream come true."

"And it just about worked out for you, until that security guard showed up. And called the sheriff." Kit sobered and she looked like she suddenly saw him in a different light. "Even though the whole thing was my idea, you took the blame. You told the sheriff you talked me into it. That I didn't really want to do it. You got them to drop me off at home before they took you to the sheriff's office."

He swirled the bourbon around the ice in his glass, remembering.

"You stood up for me," she said softly. "No one's ever stood up for me like that. Why did you?"

He looked at her. "You were my girl."

"What?" She squinted at him, as if trying to decide whether he was messing with her. "We were friends."

He laughed. "No, *you* were friends with *me*. By then, I was head over heels for you. You were my girl, you just didn't know it." His heart thudded against his ribs, but there was a certain freedom putting that out on the table. Because it was a long time ago, and she didn't know how close he was to feeling that way again.

Kit stared. "You never said."

"I kissed you in that sheriff's car. That must have told you something."

"Yes, you did." Her pink lips curved into a slow smile. "And it was a great kiss."

"It was." He remembered it perfectly. Sweet, totally sexy and filled with all his years of yearning for her.

"Well, it was nice of you to protect me like that." She gave a wry smile. "I got to know the sheriff pretty well later on, but it was nice not to have to chat with him about my wrongdoings at quite such a young age."

He let that reference slide, though he guessed she was referring to when she'd dated Arch, the local criminal. "It made sense for me to take the blame. My dad had already pretty much written me off as an idiot since I didn't do well in school. Your dad was my rodeo hero. My coach. No way was I going to let his daughter end the night in the sheriff's office. He was furious at me after, even though you were never cited. I did extra chores for months just to get back on his good side."

"Well, I appreciate it. Especially looking back at it now. It was generous."

His laugh was tinged with old bitterness. "Yeah, well, my sacrifice was for nothing. I never got a repeat of that kiss. I was no match for Arch."

"He was one of a kind, that's for sure." Kit stood. "Want me to refresh your drink?"

He slid his bourbon her way. But he wouldn't let her change the subject. Because Arch had changed everything. And the fight they'd had about him still hung like a ghost between them. "Were you guys together a long time after I left town?"

"Four years." She topped up their drinks, confessing in the quiet of the dim, empty bar. "I loved him. Too much. He was in a lot of trouble. He was dealing drugs. The police came after them, and Arch, his dad, his brother, they all just disappeared. He never said goodbye, or called, or left a note. One day he was here and the next he wasn't. And I tried to move on, but deep down in my heart, I think I was waiting. Hoping that he'd come back."

She slid his glass across the bar and Tyler took it, gently swirling the liquid. Surprised that the answer to his next question mattered so much. "Are you still waiting?"

"No," she said sharply as she sat next to him. "He showed up in town last year. Totally out of the blue. He'd been in prison all that time."

Anger reared up on her behalf. "Last I heard they have phones in jail. The bastard could have let you know."

She glanced at him, brows arched. "You still hate him. You were so angry at me when I started dating him."

"Well, I wanted you for myself. My heart was a little messed up. Then you changed. How you looked, how you talked, how you dressed. I hated him for changing you like that."

"I hated that we fought," she said. "That it ended our friendship."

The plaintive note in her voice had him swallowing his tension. "I hated that I was such a jerk. I should have tried to understand, or at least be polite. It's probably fifteen years too late, but I am sorry, Kit."

"Thanks," she said softly, looking at him over the rim of her glass. "Me, too."

He was back where he'd been fifteen years ago. Wanting to kick Arch's ass, wanting her to want him with the same fierce longing she'd had for Arch.

"So what happened?" he asked, pushing those feelings into the past where they belonged. "When you saw him again."

"Trust me, you don't want to know."

"That bad, huh?" He loved that there was laughter in her eyes even as her cheeks went red.

"Let's see. First, I yelled at him in front of the Downtown Market. I slapped him, too."

He tried not to laugh at that image. "I can see how that might not be such a great memory. But honestly, he deserved it."

"Well, it gets better. Or worse, really. Because then for some reason, I invited him to my Halloween party. And made a pass at him. Which he rejected." She buried her face in her hands for a moment. Then she looked up and he saw tears in her eyes, from embarrassment, or maybe sorrow. So many emotions were on her face he had no idea which was which. "And for my grand finale? I threw a bunch of food at him in the diner when I realized he was in love with someone else."

"Holy hell, Kit Hayes, I wish I'd have been there. I'd have joined in and chucked a few burgers of my own."

"You would?" She looked like she really was about to cry now. "Because it was so awful. His girlfriend, who also got hit with a bunch of the food, is one of the sweetest girls this town has ever seen. Everyone loves her. So afterward, it felt like everyone hated me. Or just thought I was this crazy, out-of-control person."

He couldn't help laugh a little. "Well, you always have had a streak of the crazy in you. Remember when you dared me to jump out of my dad's hayloft? You went first and did just fine. I followed and busted my wrist in two places."

She bit her lip, then started laughing. "I'd forgotten that."

"Yeah, and remember when we went skiing and you wanted to go through the trees because you'd seen it on TV or something? You went through just fine and I landed upside down in a snowbank, wrapped around a ponderosa."

She laughed outright now, which was what he wanted for her.

"Screw Arch Hoffman," he added. "He deserved a hell of a lot worse than food thrown at him."

"You're making me feel better about the whole thing. But I shouldn't have acted the way I did."

"Arch always did have a strong hold on you." A lock of hair had stuck to her cheek. He swept it off her face. "But you deserve so much better than him. You always did."

Her eyes met his, and he swore he could study her brown depths all night. Arch must have lost his mind in prison to walk away from her when he got out. But Tyler was grateful he had.

Kit took another swallow of her vodka. "You know what bothers me so much lately? That I've spent over a third of my life on Arch. Being with him, missing him, trying to get over him."

It bugged him, too. The guy didn't deserve a minute of her time, let alone so many years. "I guess that's what happens when you love someone so much." It was ironic how she'd never forgotten Arch, and Tyler had never forgotten her.

"Yes, but now I've been wondering if what I felt for him was really love. I mean, you know how my life was, growing up. My dad worked all the time and my mom was sort of out of it—heading off to yoga retreats or healing workshops. When I wasn't with you, I was a lonely kid. And when we got older, and you were spending so much of your time practicing on the bulls, I was lonely a lot."

She must have seen guilt on his face because she immediately protested. "No, it's not your fault. You were doing what you loved. But Arch came along, and he had this intense personality. An energy that drew people in. When he turned that energy on me, I felt like I was finally seen. Like I was in this big spotlight and everything looked different under there—and I was different, too."

It hurt Tyler's heart to think how badly she must have needed to feel that way. He'd been her friend.

He'd thought he was in love with her. But bull riding had been his first priority. He'd never put her first. No one ever had, he supposed.

"When someone is so hard on everyone, so tough and unreachable, and then they want you..." She seemed to search for the words. "I felt chosen, you know? Like he pushed the whole world away except me. He chose me."

And Tyler had chosen rodeo. "I should've been there for you. I should've showed you how you mattered to me. And your dad...well...maybe I'm responsible for that, too. All those hours he spent with me after work training me to ride bulls. He should have been spending time with you. Maybe if we'd both stepped up, you wouldn't have needed Arch."

She shrugged and took a gulp of her drink, obviously uncomfortable with his regret. "But it's like you said the other day. My dad loves rodeo. And the only kid he ended up with is me. Definitely not rodeo material."

"But definitely special," Tyler said. "I wish I'd let you know how I really felt."

"Hey." She took his hand, and he instinctively wrapped his fingers around hers, so small and soft and warm. "We were kids. And you can't blame yourself for my choices."

She slid her hand out of his and Tyler drained

his bourbon, suddenly needing the fire of it inside him. Guilt and regret were cold things.

"It's late," she said softly. "And if we drink any more we won't be able to get ourselves home."

He nodded and slid off the bar stool, full of so many things he wanted to tell her, about how amazing she was. About how he'd never forgotten her, or loved another, all those years on the road. Instead, he cleared his throat. "I hope you know how much you mean to me. How much you have to give. I wasn't kidding when I said I couldn't get this bar going without you."

Her smile tilted down at the corners, so he wasn't quite sure if it was a happy thing. "Thanks for saying it. And thanks for the talk. Good night, Tyler."

"Good night." He watched her walk away, so small and strong stepping out alone into the dark night. And he wanted, more than anything, to go with her.

CHAPTER EIGHT

KIT SQUINTED AT the building plans in front of her, trying to make sense of the tangled blue lines. She looked at Tyler, smiling proudly next to her, excited that his blueprints for the bar were ready.

It was midday and the weather was warm for June. They were at the picnic table behind the bar, because Kit had been taking her break there when Tyler came to find her. She felt steamy and sticky under her blouse, which could have been from the heat, or could have been because if she was reading these plans right, Tyler was about to build a very ugly building.

She pointed at a giant rectangle that took up most of the page. "So that's the outline? It's going to be huge." It was at least five times as big as the original.

"Well, yeah." Tyler nodded. "Because there has to be room for the restaurant and the dance floor and stage. And I want a big sports bar and space for more pool tables. What do you think?"

"It's…um…" She scrambled for a better way

to say *a giant, charmless box*. If Tyler followed these plans, his bar would look like a supermarket.

"I know change is hard. But I really think this is going to be great."

She gave up trying to find polite words. They weren't showing up and this was an emergency. "I'm not opposed to change, necessarily. But I am when it is going to look like you plopped a giant box down on the edge of town."

He fixed her with a long look, as if trying to figure out whether she was being difficult. He finally gave a curt nod. "Okay, tell me what you'd do."

"Really?" She studied his expression, but he didn't look angry. "You seriously want to know?"

"Sure. You don't like this? Come up with something better."

She tried to gather her thoughts. They were really different from his, but hopefully he wouldn't take it personally. "I don't think you should build one giant rectangle. What about building the whole thing in a horseshoe shape? That way this area—" she gestured around their picnic table "—can be the barbecue and outdoor eating area and it will be inside the horseshoe. The building will protect it from the winds, which can get strong out here."

Tyler glanced around, then back at her. "It sounds like a good idea."

Kit found the outline of the existing bar on the

plans. "Look. You could extend the existing building and add your sports bar there. It could be connected to the current bar by some nice glass doors so people can go back and forth."

"Okay, that makes sense." Tyler nodded. "But what about my restaurant?"

"Attach it as a wing off the original bar," Kit said, starting to feel excited. She might be making this up on the fly, but it was actually a good idea. "It could be one side of the horseshoe shape. That way people can have a drink in the bar while they wait for their reservation."

She glanced at him, noticing the way he bit his lip when he was concentrating. He was cute when he was serious. But she couldn't be distracted by that right now. "And off the sports bar end, you'd build the other side of the horseshoe. You can put all of your noisier activities there. Your dance floor. Your mechanical bull, if you're really going to get that tacky."

"You know I am," he said. He traced the shape she had described on the plans. "This could work." He looked up and raised his hand in a solemn high five. She met his palm with hers, hope warming her heart. "I should give you a bigger bonus," he said. "Because you're a freaking genius."

"And the good part of this design is that we can keep the original bar pretty much the way it is, right?"

He grinned. "You mean keep the sticky floor and ripped vinyl on all the chairs?"

"No." She had to smile at his description. The Dusty Saddle *was* pretty shabby. "I mean fix it all up but keep a similar ambiance to what we have now. So the people who love our bar don't feel like they've lost their home."

Tyler rolled up the papers. "You pretend to be tough, but underneath your black leather jackets and tattoos, you're a softy. I know that now."

"Maybe so." She was smiling so much her cheeks ached. Tension she didn't even know she'd been carrying seeped away, leaving a loose feeling behind. "They matter, you know? Our regulars? I've been here so long, they feel like family."

"I get it," he said. "Sometimes family is who you find along the way."

There was a sadness there. He'd lost his mom to cancer when he was still just a boy. She remembered it. How angry he'd been. How quiet. How he hadn't wanted to play with her for a long time. She hadn't known what to say, so they'd never talked much about it.

"I'll get these plans redrawn," Tyler said. "I like your idea a lot."

"I'm glad. Have you figured out what you'll name your new enormous bar?"

He shook his head. "I hate to admit it, but the Last Rodeo does have a good ring to it, though I know you were just giving me a hard time about that. But I've had other ideas since then. The other night, after pouring Guinness, I was thinking the Perfect Pint. But it probably sounds too Irish. And after this conversation, I'm also considering the Kit Hayes Refuge for Elderly Mountain Men."

"Stop! You're the worst."

His laugh rang across the afternoon quiet. "I may enjoy giving you a hard time, but you're a great person, Kit Hayes. And an excellent bar planner."

She didn't know what to say. She was still reeling at how he'd listened to her. He was changing his entire plan for the bar based on her advice. He trusted her ideas enough to follow them, even when they conflicted with his.

She couldn't remember anyone listening to her like this. Ever.

Luckily he didn't say anything else about the plans. If he did, she might get choked up and embarrass them both. Instead, he eyed the book on the picnic table. "All done with *Single and Satisfied*?" he asked.

She flushed. "It was a quick read."

"Finding Healthy Love." When he looked up, the teasing grin she'd expected was absent. Instead, his expression was serious. "Are you really looking for love?"

Something beat between them. A pulse full of

the meaning that hid behind his question. "I might be doing a little window-shopping from behind the bar. That's about all I have time for."

He laughed and the moment, if there'd been one, was gone. "Good answer." His usual cocky attitude was back. "I find myself doing a little window-shopping on occasion." He grabbed the plans and gave a vague salute with them. "See you around."

"See you." She picked up her book, then set it down. Because watching Tyler Ellis walk away in his low-slung Wranglers and cowboy attitude was far more entertaining than *Finding Healthy Love*.

EVER SINCE TYLER had taken her advice on renovating his bar, Kit had felt lighter. Like she was making a difference at work. She laughed more, and strangely, she hadn't felt the need to read a self-help book in days.

Maybe it was her newfound sense of hope, or maybe it was the fun she was having with her new look, thanks to Lila's make-under. Whatever the reason, she was enjoying this Saturday night behind the bar even more than usual.

Lila poured shots next to her, so Kit gave her friend a playful bump with her hip in time with the music. "How's it going?"

"Busy." Lila set the bottle down and started piling lime wedges on a tray. She added a shaker of salt. "The guys at the end of the bar are going to have wicked hangovers. This is their third round."

"Ouch," Kit sympathized with them in advance. "I hope it's worth it. Where's Ethan tonight?"

"He's doing some kind of night hike with the guys in his veterans group. They're going to howl at the moon or something."

Kit laughed. "He's a good guy. He makes a difference for those men."

"Speaking of men, our boss is looking pretty good."

Kit looked to where Tyler was shaking up cocktails for a group of girls. They'd refused to order from her and Lila, saying they wanted their drinks served by a cowboy. With his tight black T-shirt and his worn jeans, Tyler certainly looked the part. He must have felt Kit staring because he glanced over, shot her a wink, then poured his concoction into the waiting martini glasses with a flourish. "I had my doubts, but he's turning into a good bartender."

"We all have you to thank. You took him under your wing."

Kit felt guilty. She'd never mentioned to Lila that she wasn't mentoring Tyler out of the goodness of her heart. "He's paying me extra to do it. A lot extra."

"Good. He should be." Lila picked up her tray

of tequila shots, shouting, "Okay, gentlemen. Number-one rule. No one gets sick in the bar."

And that was that. No jealousy. No worry that Kit was making more money than she was. That was Lila. Secure in who she was. Happy in what life had brought her. Even before Ethan, she'd been that openhearted.

Kit took an order for six beers and told the customer she'd deliver them to his table. She filled the pints, set them on a round tray and ventured into the crowd. When she spotted her customer she wove carefully through the throng. She set down the pints, accepted the offered tip and turned to go back to the bar. And bumped right into someone's tall, broad chest. The man wore a black T-shirt beneath a black leather jacket, and his strong hands caught her on the shoulders, steadying her. She looked up and gasped at the sight of dark curly hair and a wide, feral smile. *Arch.* Only it wasn't Arch. Of course it wasn't. But this guy resembled him. Kit covered her confusion with an abrupt "Sorry about that."

The stranger held her shoulders a second longer than he needed to. "I'd tell you to watch where you were going, but I enjoyed our collision."

Her heart banged against her ribs, adrenaline still bubbling from the Arch/not-Arch moment. "Glad to make your night. Now, please excuse me, I should get back."

"Of course." He stepped aside so she could pass. She ducked behind the bar. When she turned, the man was right there, leaning forward with a twenty-dollar bill crooked between his fingers. He watched her intently and when their eyes met for a moment, heat sped up Kit's spine. He was ridiculously handsome and obviously interested.

She deliberately helped the woman next to him, who'd been waiting longer. Then the guy behind her, and then every other person who might possibly have been there before this curly-haired stranger. Because he was good-looking, confident and with silver hoops threaded through his ears, he looked a little like a pirate. A dangerous man. Her drug. Her downfall.

Lila was at the other end of the bar and Tyler was swamped with groupies, so Kit had no more excuses not to serve him. "Can I help you?" she asked.

"Are you sure you don't want to ask any of these other fine people if they'd care to go before me?" He'd called her bluff, but she could call his right back.

"Okay." Suppressing a smile, she turned to the mild-mannered-looking guy who approached the bar. "What can I get you?"

Her downfall watched her with a slow smile growing on his face, long dimples shadowed under the stubbled growth of his beard. When she'd handed the nice guy his scotch and soda, she turned to the gorgeous man again. "Ready now?" she asked innocently.

This was fun. She was flirting. Window-shopping, just like she and Tyler had joked about. But this guy was funny, and he was wickedly handsome, so maybe she was ready to do a little more than window-shop.

"Always ready," he said, with a tilt to his eyebrows. "I'll take a shot of Jack Daniel's. And a pint of that ale you have on tap. The one from June Lake."

"Jack Daniel's and a microbrew," she commented, reaching for a shot glass and the bottle. "Interesting combination."

"I'm a guy with many interests," he countered. And when she slid the shot toward him, he set his money on the bar and held out his hand. "Ian."

She shook, thrilling a little at his warmth and his firm grip. "Kit."

"Very nice to meet you, Kit. If I'd known that the most gorgeous woman on the east side of the Sierras worked here, I'd have stopped in a long time ago."

She rolled her eyes. "I've only known you about thirty seconds, but I still expected a better line than that one."

He put his palm to his forehead in mock dismay. "That was really bad, wasn't it?"

"Terrible, actually." She shut off the tap and handed over the pint.

"Here," he said. "You're clearly a very busy woman. Keep the change, and go help some other people. Check back with me in a few minutes. I promise I'll come up with something better by then."

She laughed, charmed by the humor in his dark eyes, the confident humility. "Sure, Ian. Good luck with that."

A few of Tyler's groupies had gotten fed up waiting for him and waved their money at her over the bar. She took their orders and glanced at Ian as she poured vodka into one of the large cocktail shakers. He gave her a nod and lifted his Jack Daniel's in a brief toast.

He was hot. And funny. And witty. And he liked her. And maybe she liked him a little, too.

She glanced at Tyler as he accepted a kiss on the cheek from some girl on the other side of the bar. Yes, she was attracted to him. Just like every woman was. But she wasn't his type and he wasn't hers. Plus, it seemed he was doing a little more than window-shopping tonight, too. So she'd get to know Ian a little. Maybe she was ready to get back out there. Ready to try dating again. Maybe Ian was the guy to try it with.

TYLER RESISTED THE urge to wipe the young woman's lipstick off his cheek in front of her. She'd said she had something to tell him. When he leaned in, listening for a drink order or maybe an autograph request, he'd gotten that kiss instead.

He handed her the drinks and accepted the tip with thanks. Then grabbed a napkin, stepped into the shadows by the storeroom door and used it to wipe his cheek. Not that he was opposed to kisses, but lately, he'd felt like they should come from the right person. Maybe staying in one place for the first time in years was making him want to settle down.

Or maybe that was Kit. Because if she leaned in to give him a kiss, he'd be a very happy guy. Not that she would. Because she didn't see him that way at all.

"Hey, Tyler." Relieved that a masculine voice called him, he tossed the pink-stained napkin in the trash and turned to the crowd. His brothers were there, and he high-fived Parker across the bar.

"Glad you're here." He cuffed Miles on the shoulder.

"We found you a couple horses," Miles said. "So we're here for the free beer."

Tyler filled two pint glasses and set them on the bar. Parker took a satisfied sip. "That's good. Haven't been in here for a long time."

"And who knew you had such gorgeous bartenders." Miles nodded his head toward Lila, who was shaking a cocktail and laughing at some joke Crater was telling at the far end of the bar.

"She's taken," Tyler informed his brother. "Very, very taken."

He shrugged. "Just my luck."

"Miles has a thing for redheads." Parker nudged his brother. "Down, boy." He nodded his head toward Kit. "Is that who I think it is?"

Tyler wanted to shoot back, "She's taken, too," but he couldn't. Kit was free to do whatever she pleased and right now, it was clear that what pleased her was the dark-haired man in black leather, with a white-toothed smile and the ability to make her laugh whenever she walked near him. Not Tyler's business. Not a reason for him to go plant his fist between the dude's eyes, as much as he wanted to. "That's Kit Hayes."

"You two used to be inseparable," Miles said. "It's nice that you're working together." His brother eyed him shrewdly. "Is that why you spend all your time working?"

"I spend all my time working because I'm expanding this business," Tyler shot back.

"Yeah, right."

"Does she know that guy?" Parker tipped his head in the direction of Kit's admirer.

"I dunno." Tyler shrugged with a lot more nonchalance than he felt. "She knows a lot of the people who come in here, but I don't recognize him."

"I think he's bad news," Parker said, downing another gulp. "We met him in the parking lot. He asked us if we wanted to buy weed. When we said no, he asked us what we liked. Said he could get anything."

Stress coiled in Tyler's gut. Kit was pouring the guy another shot of JD. He laughed at something she said, but his eyes were on her chest, not her face. The drug-dealing scum wasn't good enough to even look at her. Or speak to her. Tyler's hands went to fists at his side.

"Easy there, bro," Miles cautioned. "Don't you have bouncers for this kind of stuff?"

"Yeah, but I hate to make a scene if I don't have to. Just give me a minute to deal with him." He slid past Lila and made his way to Kit's end of the bar. He tapped Kit gently on the arm. "Can I speak with you?"

Kit glanced at him, obviously surprised. "It's crazy tonight. Can we talk later?"

Her dark eyes had a new sparkle in them. It made him sick to think that a low-life drug dealer put that there. "The guy in the black leather? You need to cut him off. Don't serve him any more."

"What?" She looked shocked, then handed the beers she'd poured to a brunette in a white cowboy hat. She turned so her back was to the drug dealer. "He's not drinking that much."

"Trust me, just cut him off. We need to get him out of here." He'd leaned close to speak, so the guy wouldn't hear, but it was a mistake. She smelled like vanilla and spices. He took a step back.

Lila brushed by with a tray of empties. "What are you two arguing about?"

"Tyler's trying to kick that guy out of here. He hasn't done anything," Kit hissed.

Lila glanced at the dealer. "Good," she said simply.

Kit flashed an outraged glare at her friend. "What do you have against him?"

The smile Lila flashed her was sweet, but Tyler saw steel underneath. "Because the last thing you need is Arch Hoffman Part Two. And that's exactly who that guy is." Lila marched off to the sink in the back. Kit stared after her.

Tyler hated to pile on the bad news, but she deserved an explanation. "He tried to sell my brothers drugs out in the parking lot. I'm sorry, Kit, but I can't let him stay."

Her pale skin went paler and Tyler grabbed her elbow. "Are you okay?"

"I need some air." Her voice was choked, and she yanked off her apron and shoved it into his hands.

She stepped into the crowd and her black-haired

friend rose as if to follow her. Kit, in high-heeled cowboy boots, only came up to the guy's chest. But her hand, raised palm-up toward his face, sent a clear message. "*Don't* follow me," she said to the drug dealer, and pushed her way through the crowd and out the front door.

The guy looked at Tyler, hands raised in a help-less gesture. "What did I do?"

"You dealt drugs in my parking lot," Tyler an-swered, stepping around the bar so they were face-to-face. "So I'm asking you to leave my prop-erty and not come back."

The guy looked a lot less handsome when anger and pride twisted his features. "It's a crappy lit-tle bar anyway, man." He shoved out through the crowd.

Tyler followed, quickly letting Ernie and Loo-mis know what the deal was. "Loomis, did I hear a rumor that you fill in behind the bar sometimes?"

"Not if I can help it," Loomis answered. "You need me to?"

"I gotta check on Kit," Tyler said. "Can you go back there for a few minutes?"

"Sure, boss." Loomis paused. "Did that guy do anything to Kit? Because I can go after him." He didn't need to explain more. "I'll crush him" was loud and clear in the bouncer's posture.

"He hurt her pride a little. Nothing more," Tyler

assured him. He clapped the big man on the shoulder. "Thanks."

Tyler stepped out into the parking lot to see a big black pickup peel away. Probably the indignant drug dealer. Good riddance.

There was no sign of Kit, so he walked around the side of the building, picking his way through the darkness. She was there, a darker shadow sitting on the shadowed picnic table. "Hey," he called. "It's Tyler."

She watched as he approached. He stopped, wary, a few feet away. "I wanted to make sure you're okay."

"I'm fine. I just needed a breath of air."

"I'm sorry that guy came in tonight."

She sighed. "It's not your fault. It's just part of bartending."

"I guess so. Want to take the rest of the night off?"

She looked at him as if he was crazy. "No. I'm not some delicate flower who's going to fall apart because some bad man came into the bar. I just needed to get some air."

"I don't like you sitting out there alone in the dark. What if he comes back?"

"Then I'll happily kick his ass. Just like I did yours that first night."

He couldn't argue with that. "Okay then. I'll just go on in. Unless you want to talk."

"I don't."

He got up to go.

"Wait." Her voice was quiet in the dark. "Can I ask you something?"

"Sure, of course."

"When you look at me, what do you see?"

He was instantly wary. "Is this one of those trick questions? Like when someone asks if they look fat?"

"It's just a question. What do you see? Because obviously, screwed-up guys like Arch, or this guy tonight, Ian, they see something in me that they really like. I'm trying to figure out what it is."

He wasn't sure how much to tell her. Because some of what he saw when he looked at her wasn't G-rated. Definitely not what a boss should see. But that wasn't what she needed to hear. "Well, first of all, you're tough and independent and capable of taking care of yourself. And since guys like Ian must realize, on some level, that they're totally messed up, maybe they feel drawn to someone like you, who solves problems and gets stuff done."

She watched him warily, as if trying to figure out whether he was telling the truth. "You're beautiful, of course. You must realize that. But the way you dress, the tattoos, it's all a little edgy. And it seems logical that edgy guys like edgy-looking women."

He watched the doubt cross her features. Remembered how the guy she'd loved forever had chosen someone else. "You're totally beautiful, Kit. Please trust me on that."

Her laugh was a little forlorn and he was surprised to hear a hint of tears in it. It loosed something in him. He hated her feeling this bad. So he kept talking. "You have no idea how much energy you bring when you walk into a room. Haven't you noticed how every head turns? And not just because you're so pretty, but because you're funny and you take charge. And because you take care of everyone."

She shook her head. "You're being nice."

"No, I'm being honest."

"So if I'm as great as you say I am, why am I drawn to guys like this?"

A crescent moon was hanging in the sky, just above the ridgeline. He studied it a moment, thinking. "Maybe it's like we talked about the other night. Because they're dangerous and risky. Maybe you can sense that and you're attracted to it."

She sighed. "Great. I have a sixth sense for drug dealers."

"Or maybe you see dating as a way to have adventures. To do something a little wild. It's your eight seconds on the bull."

She looked at him wide-eyed. "What do you mean?"

"Maybe dating guys like Arch or that guy is the way you get your adrenaline rush. Like bull riding is for me."

"So you're saying my life is boring, and I look for guys to make it exciting."

The idea obviously upset her, so he sat next to her on the bench, putting an arm around her to offer comfort. "Look, there's nothing wrong with looking for that kind of rush. I just think that if you crave some kind of excitement in your life, you have to be careful where you get it from. I've seen guys quit the rodeo, then start drinking or doing drugs, because they're trying to re-create the way they felt during that eight second ride in the arena."

She leaned her head on his shoulder and he allowed himself a moment to breathe in her perfume. He could live on it, it smelled that good. "You're gonna be okay, Kit. Don't be hard on yourself because you flirted with the wrong guy."

She put her arm around his back and tucked herself closer under his arm. Maybe she was cold. Maybe she didn't even realize she was doing it. But Tyler wasn't complaining. It felt amazing to sit with her like this. Like this was how they should always be. He pressed a gentle kiss to her hair, unable to resist the silken feel of it against his mouth.

"I've been reading all those self-help books. Trying to understand so much. But I feel like I'll never get it. That I wouldn't recognize the right kind of guy if he was standing in front of me holding a big sign with Mr. Right written on it."

And it hit him, right there, that *he* was that guy with the sign. He'd known it on some level for weeks. Next to her, every woman he'd ever met paled in comparison. He'd never wanted a committed relationship before. He'd traveled too much. Been too focused on his career to give love a whole lot of thought. But Kit was different for him. Kit was *it* for him.

He let out the breath he'd been holding, wondering what to do next. Now that he knew his feelings, every cell wanted to blurt them out. It would be so easy to tip her chin up, to kiss her lush mouth the way he'd been wanting to ever since he saw her again. To see if she'd let him touch her in all the ways he'd dreamed of.

But there was too much at stake for him to get this wrong. He needed Kit's help to make this renovation happen. He needed her expertise, her great ideas, her way of seeing them through.

And she and Garth needed the money they'd get from this partnership she and Tyler had formed.

If he told her how he felt, and she didn't feel the same way, he could ruin everything, for all of them.

So yeah, he was the guy holding the sign, but he couldn't show it to her. Not yet. But he *could* spend more time with her. And try to help her feel better, if she'd let him. "What about trying something different that doesn't involve guys in leather jackets hitting on you in the bar?"

"What did you have in mind?" That breathy, teasing note was back in her voice, and when she tilted her head to look at him, it took a good chunk of his self-control not to drop his lips to hers.

"Ethan offered to take me rock climbing tomorrow morning. You want to come?"

"You think I should climb up a cliff?"

"Why not? It's exciting and it's better than dating losers. You might even like it."

She gave him that solemn, studying look he was getting used to. He tried again. "Meet us here at seven tomorrow morning. Wear shorts or leggings or something. And shoes you can hike in. Lila's going, too, so I'm sure you can borrow her climbing shoes."

"What if I fall?"

"There are ropes to catch you."

"What if I get hurt?"

"I'll bring bandages." He pulled her a little

closer in a bracing hug. "Plus, you're tough. You'll heal. Or you'll find a self-help book to read, and then you'll heal."

She giggled. "*Healing Your Broken Ankle*. It sounds like a fascinating read."

She'd gotten him smiling again, just like she always did, and it was balm for this new angst in his heart. "I'm sure it's a bestseller. Right up there with *Romance on the Rocks*."

Her laugh crackled through the quiet night. "Or how about *Hitting the Wall*?" She pulled her arm away from his waist and stood. "We've got to get back in there."

She was right and he stood, reluctantly. "Loomis is covering the bar. But yeah, we should go in."

They followed the path around the building. "Thanks for the pep talk, Tyler," she said when they got to the front door.

"I hope it helped," he said, not wanting to go in. "Tomorrow morning? Bright and early?"

"I'll think about it." She smiled. "It's a little hard to picture myself voluntarily climbing a cliff."

He let her go inside first, while he hesitated, looking up at the sky above the Dusty Saddle. He wasn't much of a spiritual guy, but he sent a little prayer up to the star-strewn universe. That she'd find her way. That she'd see all that she was worth. Because he could see it. Way too clearly for his own damn good.

CHAPTER NINE

KIT CLUTCHED HER coffee cup and huddled in Ethan's SUV, listening to Lila explain climbing holds and foot positions. How could her friend be so chatty? They'd both worked last night. Why was Lila bursting with energy while Kit was still trying to figure out how to be awake?

Oh, yeah, Lila was in love. Kit was pretty sure Lila had never set foot on a boulder before she'd met Ethan. Now she climbed with him every chance she got.

And now Kit had been talked into it. Also by a guy. That thought rankled. She wished she'd agreed to go one of the many times that Lila invited her along, rather than waiting until Tyler talked her into it.

She'd lived way too much of her life conforming to what guys wanted. Waiting for them to suggest something fun. Still, it was nice of Tyler to ask. To try to help her. And he'd had a good point with the whole adrenaline rush idea. If Arch had provided her that rush so often when she was young, maybe she'd never learned how to get it for herself.

She yawned and glanced at Tyler, but he had his head tipped back on the seat, cowboy hat covering his face. He was wearing long cargo shorts and hiking boots, and she took the opportunity to get used to him looking like any other outdoorsy guy. No Wranglers, no cowboy boots. Just Tyler.

Pushing up his hat he said, "What, you don't like my shorts?"

She tried to play it cool. "Just wondering how you can be awake without coffee."

"Don't like the stuff. Though I hear it makes you smarter. I could use that." He winked at her and she laughed, startled that he could make light of his reading troubles. Just one more thing she liked about him.

Ethan bumped them a few miles down a dirt road that snaked through a steep valley. He pulled over at the foot of a granite cliff and got out. "This is it. You guys ready?"

Kit looked at the rocks rising so far they blocked out the sky. "We're climbing that?"

"Not the whole thing. There's a ledge not too far up. You guys will climb up to that and rappel down." Ethan pulled open the tailgate and Tyler joined him to haul out duffel bags stuffed with ropes, harnesses and bits of metal.

Kit looked at Lila. "You *like* this?"

Lila grinned. "Trust me. You'll love it. And Ethan's a great teacher."

Kit sat on a rock, watching as Ethan got the ropes set up, paying close attention when Lila pulled on her harness and slid her feet into climbing shoes. She'd be doing this herself in an hour or so, and she wanted to learn everything she could beforehand.

Lila scaled the rock face in almost no time and sat easily on the top of the ledge. She waved, making Kit's heart thud at how far away from the ground Lila looked. Tyler had been standing with Ethan, but now he walked over to Kit. "Are we crazy to do this?" he asked, keeping his voice quiet.

"You rode bulls. This should be a piece of cake."

Tyler peered at Lila, still perched on the ledge, still waving happily at them. "Bulls aren't so high off the ground."

"You can do it," Kit told him, having no doubt that he would. The guy was all muscle. "And because you're my boss, I'll let you go first."

He smiled that slow, wide smile that had sold so many Wranglers. "Mighty generous of you, Kit. Mighty generous."

When he went to stand by Ethan she followed, wanting to listen to the instructions one more time. Hoping that if she heard them enough times on solid ground, she'd be better able to follow them on the rock. Lila arrived, jubilant after her climb, and pointed out various invisible-to-Kit handholds that she'd been able to use at the bottom of the cliff.

Then Tyler was roped in, ready to start.

"On belay," he said, using the words Ethan had taught them.

"Belay on," came Ethan's deep voice in response as he tightened the rope so there was no slack.

"Climbing," Tyler said, groping for a handhold on the granite.

"Climb on," Ethan said.

"As if it's that easy," Tyler muttered.

"Your shoes will stick to really small footholds if you put your weight on them. Trust your feet."

"Famous last words," Tyler said, but he put his foot on a small outcropping and slipped his fingers into the crack Lila pointed out and there he was, standing on the cliff face. After that, he seemed to get the hang of it pretty quickly, inching up a lot more slowly than Lila had, but steadily, with no slips or missteps. Then he was on the ledge, a huge grin on his face, a fist pumping the air in triumph.

By the time he'd rappelled down, Kit's heart hammered in her ears. Tyler was a professional athlete. Lila was really athletic and had climbing experience. Ethan was ex-army. They were naturally good at this.

She, on the other hand, was a bartender. A sporadic 5K jogger. A dabbler in martial arts and senior-citizen pole dancing. She was about to make a fool of herself.

She tried to focus on everything Lila said as she helped buckle Kit into her harness. Kit slid on the stiff climbing shoes. She went through the checklist with Ethan that finished with the words "climb on."

Then it was just her and the rock, which had grown several stories in the past thirty seconds, the ledge looking impossibly high, with no hand- or footholds in sight.

Tyler stood beside her. "You've got this," he told her quietly.

"Trust your feet, Kit," Ethan intoned.

"Oh my gosh, if he says that one more time..." Kit whispered, and Tyler grinned. Kit slid her fingers into the granite crack, surprised to realize that she *could* grip it, and it felt solid. "Bye-bye manicure."

Tyler shook his head as if in disbelief. "That's what you're worried about?"

"Well, that and breaking my neck." She put her foot onto the outcropping and stood.

And slipped, landing with a jarring thud on the ground, staggering to keep her balance, grateful that Tyler gripped her arm before she went over, her heart careering in her chest, her breath coming in gasps, her pride hanging in tatters.

"It's okay, Kit." Ethan had the perfect climbing instructor voice, more solid than granite. "Just put your entire focus on the rock."

"And don't forget," Tyler said, in his best Ethan imitation. "Trust your feet."

"Thanks for those words of wisdom."

"You can do it," he said. "I'll give you some space."

He walked away and it felt a little lonely without him. Because now it was just her versus this very large rock.

"Right." Kit wiped sweaty palms on her black leggings. She could do this. She wanted adventure, she wanted to push herself to try new things. To feel alive.

Well, she felt alive all right. The nerve-charged, hyperalert type of alive that people probably felt right before they took the risk that finally killed them.

Lila wandered up and took her gently by the elbow. "You're on belay. You won't fall any farther than you just did."

"My mind wants to do this. But my feet won't get moving."

"You are forgetting that you are my kick-ass

friend. Who was the star of the seniors' center pole-dancing class?"

Kit giggled. "Not me."

"Yes, you," Lila said firmly. "And who has read every self-help book in the Benson library?"

"That would be me," Kit said, laughing.

"Who is the most gorgeous, popular bartender at the Dusty Saddle?"

"Well, that would be Tyler, nowadays."

"True," Lila agreed. "He has perhaps stolen that title from you. But what I'm trying to say is that you can do this. No problem. Just ignore the rest of us and focus on kicking this cliff's butt."

"Kick cliff butt." Kit pulled her friend in for a hug. "Best pep talk ever. Okay. I'm doing this." She walked to the base of the cliff and called to Ethan, "Climbing."

"Climb on," Ethan said. "Now, put the ball of your foot on that bump in the rock and stand right on it. Don't hesitate. Trust your feet."

There *was* a life lesson there. She was sure of it. Putting her foot on the outcrop, her fingers in that manicure-annihilating crack, was one of the harder things Kit had ever done. She stared at the rock and tried to block out Tyler and Lila and the fact that they'd both done well and she'd fallen on her first step. She shouldn't compare herself. All that mattered was this rock. And Ethan, since he'd be the one to catch her fall.

She wriggled her foot in to make sure the ball of her foot was right over the bump. Then she tightened the grip with her fingers and stood. And stayed, with her heart thudding in her ears.

"Now look for your next hold," Ethan said quietly.

She scanned the rock and saw a small bump, about knee-height above her free leg. A foothold. Glancing up, she saw a tiny ledge. She inched her right hand up the rock and grabbed on.

"When you're ready," Ethan coached, "just go for it."

She'd assumed rock climbing would be difficult. But she wasn't expecting this. The shaking in her standing leg as her muscles grew weary. The distance between her and the ground, only a few feet but looking so much more vast. The mind-whirling knowledge that she was supposed to scale this cliff, gripping onto tiny bumps and cracks. She was terrified.

"Keep breathing. One step at a time," Ethan reminded her.

She wanted to tell him she was done. That this wasn't her thing—too much could go wrong.

"This is your eight seconds, Kit."

Tyler. Who knew a little about what she was running from, and what she was moving toward. About how much she wanted to learn to live. He was right. This was her eight seconds. Except it was taking her a whole lot longer than eight seconds to climb this rock.

She brought her focus to the hold in front of her, narrowing her mind and body to this next step. A step only she could take, for herself. She went for it, putting all her weight on that new foothold, grasping the ledge in her damp fingers. Then she was climbing. Really climbing. Scanning the rock for cracks and bumps she could use to lever herself up the cliff, her whole world made up of those hand- and footholds, and the harshness of her breathing as she pushed herself harder and higher than she'd ever imagined going.

Kit was surprised when the ledge she reached for was *the* ledge that marked the end of the climb. She pushed up on it, flopped down on her stomach and raised a fist in exhausted triumph. Closed her eyes to absorb the whoops and cheers from her friends below.

Then she was rappelling down, which was so much easier than going up. When her feet hit the ground Lila enveloped her in a warm hug and Ethan high-fived her, and then Tyler held out his arms. Kit ran to him, fueled by gratitude and triumph, and when she jumped, he caught her. She wrapped her arms around his neck and her legs around his waist, laughing while he spun her around once in triumph. He slowed, then stopped, and the spinning world narrowed to the deep green intensity of his eyes, the feel of him under her, the way he'd made her feel with every conversation, every shared confidence, every silly joke.

He made her feel too much. She slid off him slowly.

"You were awesome up there," he said quietly, letting her step away.

"Thanks for your help." She stared at him, stunned by how much she wanted to kiss him. "I'll go help Lila clean up."

"Yeah me, too." He seemed as dazed as she was. "I'll help Ethan."

As Kit wrapped ropes under Lila's watchful eye, she glanced at the cliff again. Climbing that rock had been a risk, but a manageable one, with ropes to catch her. Acting on these unexpected feelings for Tyler would be far riskier. No matter how drawn to him she was, she had to remember all that could go wrong. And keep in mind that breaking old patterns meant resisting the kind of risk he offered. The kind that could blow your whole world apart if something went wrong.

TYLER SURVEYED HIS STAFF, clustered around him at the old picnic table behind the bar. They'd shown up on a Monday for early-morning champagne and a chance to cheer on the excavator as it started digging the foundation for the new additions.

He'd come a long way from that first staff meeting where they'd looked bored and barely met his gaze. He knew them now. He'd worked hard among them and he sensed he'd earned at least some of their respect. In fact they'd asked *him* if they could all kick off the construction together.

And another thing was different. Kit. At that first meeting she'd been furious. Now she was his closest ally, and maybe something a whole lot more. He didn't know what to call it.

Aaron waved from the seat of the excavator. "Hey, Tyler. If you want this place ready by the fall, we have to get busy."

Tyler nodded. He shook the champagne bottle a couple times, popped the cork and let the bubbles burst out. "To all of you. You've been a part of the Dusty Saddle for a long time. It's a great business. Thank you for staying on board as we take it to the next level."

"What are you going to call it?" Loomis asked.

Tyler looked at Kit and caught the smile blooming on her face. "Got any new ideas?" he asked her.

She glanced at the blueprints laminated in plastic and nailed to the back wall of the bar. "Tyler's Money Pit?" she suggested.

Everyone burst out laughing. "A pretty accurate description," he admitted. He poured the champagne into the waiting glasses and Kit opened a second bottle so even the crew members could have a taste. They passed the glasses around. "To the Dusty Saddle," Tyler said. "Also known as my money pit."

Glasses clinked and voices rose in excited conversation. Aaron fired up the excavator and scooped up a huge pile of dirt and everyone cheered. Then they headed for the table of food Kit had set out, chatting and laughing as they helped themselves to muffins and fruit.

Kit stepped away from the crowd to glance at the blueprints, and Tyler followed. "We'd never have gotten this far without you."

She glanced at him from under her thick black lashes. "You'd be okay."

"Nah. Not even close." He clinked his glass softly to hers. "To my partner in all of this. I'm so glad to have you by my side."

She shot him her teasing smile. "To my partner, who's really my boss. But he has this strange need to pretend we're in an equal relationship."

"I may have the bucks, but you have the brains."

Their gazes met for a moment and held. He could stay there, looking into the deep brown darkness of her irises, for a long, long time. He wanted to hold her like he had when they climbed yesterday, but that moment had passed. So when she took a sip, he did the same. She elbowed him and her eyes narrowed and her mouth widened in a sassy smile, the way it always did right before she gave him a hard time. "I really think you should call it the Money Pit. Seriously."

"Hopefully, with you by my side, we can find a way to avoid earning that name. Can I show you my budget for the first phase of construction? And you can tell me if it makes any sense?"

He couldn't wait to show her. He'd worked on it all last week, with some help from Sheila, which is what he now called his tutor, Mrs. Lopez. She made time for him twice a week and assigned him homework in between. She'd taught him some eye exercises. They made him look ridiculous when he did them in the mirror, but they seemed to be keeping lines on the page from turning into writhing snakes.

Kit nodded and followed him inside. They sat in the office to go over the spreadsheet, and they were so close he wondered if he was wise to expand this room after all. Because once he did, they wouldn't need to sit like this. Knee to knee, shoulder to shoulder, with her heat warming his edges and her scent wafting like ether in his brain.

THE BUDGET LOOKED good to Kit, though the figures were so enormous it made her head swim. "It balances," she assured Tyler, setting down the calculator. "The foundation, the framing, the pipes, the walls and the roof. It all balances."

"It's a pretty simple budget right now." He

reached for the papers and slipped them into their folder. "I still have to make one for the interior construction, the finishes, the fixtures. It's a little overwhelming to think about."

"You'll figure it out. It seems like you did really well with this one." She wondered how he'd done it when he had so much trouble with numbers. But he hadn't mentioned his problems for a while and it didn't seem right to make him talk about it. So she switched to teasing him.

"How did you get so rich, anyway? Rodeo prize money isn't that great."

"That's what the underwear commercials were for. The more skin I showed, the more zeroes my agent negotiated onto my contract."

She burst out laughing—totally disarmed by his honesty. "So you're spending underwear money on this place." Delight at this juicy piece of information had her mind going. "This gives me ideas for new names. How about Tyler's Skivvies? Or Tighty-Whitie's?"

He rolled his eyes. "Don't you have to be somewhere this morning?"

Kit glanced at the clock. "Actually, yes, I've got to get on the road."

"Where are you headed today?"

She hadn't been planning to tell him yet. Not when the plan was so new. Just barely born in the dark last night when she'd thought about their after-rock-climbing almost-kiss. And how incredibly tempting it had been to turn it into a real kiss. But wouldn't that be just like the old Kit? Throw away a chance to do what she'd always wanted so she could kiss a guy?

She needed to keep her focus on her own dreams. And her dream had always been to travel. "I'm going down to Mammoth, to talk with a travel agent."

"You're taking a trip?"

She took a deep breath for courage. "A long one. I'm thinking of leaving. After we're done building this place."

He seemed to still. Just a faint tightening of muscles in his jaw and his fingers on the folder. "Leave? As in, for good?"

"I don't know yet. I'm just starting to make plans. Between the money you're paying me and the job you offered my dad, I can finally do what I've always dreamed of—see the world, travel."

"Travel." His voice sounded wooden. As if he was having trouble understanding.

"To stay in other countries. To live somewhere else besides here."

"I didn't realize you were that unhappy in Benson."

"I'm not unhappy." She tried to explain what had seemed so clear in her own mind last night. "But I'm also not satisfied. You went off to see the world. You had this incredible career and so much success. And all that time you were gone, I was here, doing this." She gestured around the office. "Can't you see how I'd want to try something else? To have a more interesting life than I have now?"

"Yes." He nodded slowly. "I do understand."

"Great." He seemed upset, but she knew in her heart that she was doing the right thing. She couldn't stay just because they had chemistry. "So I'll see you later then."

"See you later," he said. "Thanks for helping with the celebration this morning."

"Of course." She gave an awkward wave, leaving him alone with his budget. She walked quickly to her Jeep, her excitement dampened by the disappointment she'd seen in his eyes.

THE GOOD THING about discovering Kit's travel plans was it had Tyler working hard for the next couple weeks. He stayed in the barn mainly, not taking many shifts behind the bar, to put some space between them. Because she was leaving in the fall. And she *should* leave if that's what she wanted. But that meant he needed to get over these feelings he had for her.

Easier said than done. It was the little things that haunted. How her breath felt, so soft on his ear, whenever she leaned close on a busy night to give him instructions. Or how, on a weekend night, with music blasting from the jukebox, she and Lila would break into a dance behind the bar, and Kit would pull him over to dance with them.

Watching Kit behind the bar was a revelation. She never stopped for a moment, taking drink orders while she made others, and somehow tossing crisp comebacks at the guys trying to get her to pay attention to more than their drinks. He knew just how they felt. He wanted her attention, too. But that wasn't going to happen. So he worked.

He'd been up early this morning, soon after sunrise. Now he walked through the barn, relishing the cool before the day heated up. Hard to believe it was already July.

They'd made it through July Fourth last weekend, hosting their first barbecue. It had been a chance to try out the most promising chef they'd found, and the guy had done a great job.

They'd had to have the barbecue in the front parking lot though, instead of in the barbecue area. *That* was a full-blown construction site. In fact, running a bar while you were adding entire sections onto the building had proved more challenging than he'd imagined. Their daytime customers had all but disappeared, since most people didn't enjoy construction noise with their drink. Though a few folks liked it and would take their beer in a bottle and stand around watching the crew at work. Any change was exciting in a small town.

Still, he'd have to close the entire bar at the end of August to do the finish work inside and to update the original Dusty Saddle. He'd been worried about how to keep his staff on board, but Kit had suggested he average each staff member's pay for the last six months. He'd pay them that amount while the bar was closed, to make sure they didn't find work elsewhere. It was a good idea, like so many she had.

And here he was, thinking about her again. Wishing she was present to appreciate the renovations he'd made here in the barn.

The tack room had been expanded, and there was an office, a classroom, changing rooms and bathrooms down one side. There was even a small medical room, because his students weren't getting out of bull-riding school without a few cuts and bruises.

The stalls looked great, too, but he wouldn't use them much. He wanted his animals out in pastures where they'd be happiest.

That's all he wanted. Just a few happy horses and bulls. Nothing big. He wasn't a rancher, wasn't planning to be one.

For now he wanted to take a minute to be grateful for what he had. He'd bought this property just a couple months ago. And already he had this great barn.

He stopped at the wide front doors. It was a perfect summer morning. The sun sent rays up from the east, and soon it would chase away the chill of the mountains. The air was a soothing mix of pine and sagebrush and that dry, rocky smell of high desert. He'd missed that scent all his years of traveling. Just like he'd missed these mountains, this town. It was all mixed up with who he was and what he wanted for his future.

Tyler heard wheels crunching on gravel and squinted down the lane. Garth was bumping along in his battered blue pickup. He parked and leaped spryly to the ground. Slamming the door behind him, he caught sight of Tyler, tipped the brim of his hat and crossed the gravel between them with a crisp step. "Morning, boss." His smile said it all. The smile of a man with a purpose. A man who was happy to be back on the job.

Tyler grinned and pulled Garth in for a clap on the back. "First day on the job. I'm glad you're here." He wished Kit were here, too. She'd be happy with the way her father wandered through the barn, opening cabinets and examining the stalls. It would put a smile on her face to see it. No matter how much he tried to tell himself that he didn't care for her, the truth was, he did. And even though she might be counting the days until she hit the road, if he could make her smile up until the time she went, he would.

CHAPTER TEN

KIT MADE HER way around the plywood walls of the restaurant. Construction was speeding along. Tyler had crews working seven days a week. Aaron stormed around the construction site like a manic general, ordering his troops to dig this and frame that. Trenches for plumbing were everywhere, bright orange cones and caution tape creating a colorful obstacle course she had to navigate to get to the path that led to the barn.

The barn was officially finished and her dad started work today. She'd planned to walk down to see it, and him, later on her lunch break. But Tyler had burst into the office a few moments ago to announce that the horses were coming and she *had* to be there to see them arrive.

It was nice that he'd come to find her. He'd been avoiding her ever since she'd told him she planned to leave. Maybe he felt betrayed because they were building this bar together and she wouldn't be around to run it with him. But that had never been their agreement. The contract was clear. She had to stay until the bar was open. That was it.

She'd missed him, though. Funny how she could work here for nine years, quite happily in his absence. But now when she took a shift and Tyler wasn't with her, she didn't enjoy her job nearly as much. She'd come to depend on his silly jokes, his laughing good looks, the warm feeling she got when he was nearby.

The trail approached the barn from the rear, where wood fencing delineated corrals and the edge of a huge pasture. A man stepped out from the barn to shake out some kind of floor mat. "Dad?" she called.

He waved vigorously. Enthusiastically. She hadn't seen her dad do anything with any kind of energy since he'd lost his position with Tyler's father.

"Congratulations on your first day." She grabbed the other end of the mat and helped him shake.

Pride was evident in his eyes. "You're looking at the official barn manager for the Tyler Ellis Rodeo School."

"Dad, that's incredible!" She'd known Tyler was going to give her dad a job. But to give him a title like this, a position of authority…tears threatened, but they'd only embarrass both of them. She shook the mat again, a little more vigorously, then set her end down so her dad could carry it inside.

She followed him silently, not trusting herself

to say any more, because the way he walked, straight-backed, square-shouldered, *this* was the dad she knew. He was back, after all these lost months. And she could never thank Tyler enough—though she would try.

He was leaning on the opposite entrance to the barn, his back to her, looking out to the parking lot. A dark cowboy silhouette against an amazing view of winding road and pines and mountains rising up beyond.

Kit walked the length of the barn, enjoying the cool shadows on this hot morning, the perfectly appointed stalls, the rooms he'd added. The changing room had been her idea, complete with the rustic wooden sign that could be flipped to say men or women, depending on who was using it at the time. Because even though bull riding was typically a men's sport, Kit had argued that maybe women would like to try it, too.

Are you volunteering? Tyler had asked at the time, teasing her. But he'd implemented her idea, and it was a great feeling to see it here, finished.

He turned and an excited smile broke across his face. "You got here just in time."

A truck and horse trailer were making the turn off the distant road and into the drive.

"You look like a kid at Christmas," Kit said, catching his excitement.

"Christmas in July. I've wanted horses of my

own for years." He took her hand, gave it a brief
squeeze. And as always, when he let go, she
wished he wouldn't.

They watched the truck and trailer rattle toward
them, dust rising and settling on the sagebrush
and scrub that lined the lane.

"Thank you again," she said. "For hiring my
dad. For giving him such an official-sounding
position."

"My pleasure. He's gonna do great here." The
truck and trailer were parking now, and Tyler
beckoned. "Come on." He started down the ramp
that led out of the barn. "Come meet my horses."

"I'm not going to be any help."

"You're always a help," Tyler said, and led the
way forward.

Kit's dad caught up with them, his eager steps
so at odds with the shuffling gait he'd adopted
throughout the past few months. "Tyler's got himself some of these broke mustangs from Marker
Ranch."

Kit froze. Marker Ranch. That was Arch Hoffman's family ranch. His sister was using part of
the land for a wild mustang sanctuary. "Tyler's
getting mustangs?"

Her father grinned. "He sure is. Great choice.
They're smart. Great trail horses. Sweet as anything as long as you train 'em right. Todd Wil-
liams is at Marker and he's a great trainer."

"He's a great guy, too." Todd had been a friend of Kit's. But when he met and married Nora Hoffman, Kit had started avoiding him. She liked Arch's sister, but it had felt too awkward to be around anyone related to Arch.

The truck was parked and the doors opened. Todd hopped out of the driver's side; Nora hopped out of the other. She didn't greet them, just turned to open the second door in the king cab. But Todd spotted Kit. He strode over, nodded to Tyler, but went straight for her, pulling her into a giant bear hug. "Great to see you, Kit. It's been way too long. You're working for this guy now?" He released her and shook Tyler's hand. "Good to see you, Tyler. We're so glad you're taking Rachel and Carson."

Kit laughed, glad that some things never changed. "You're still naming horses after famous environmentalists?"

Todd grinned. "Yes, but I'm running out of names. Nora wants to move on to scientists."

"Plant biologists, to be exact." Arch's sister came around the truck with an adorable baby boy in her arms.

Kit stared at his gummy baby smile. "You guys had a baby? I didn't even know—" She'd done such a thorough job of avoiding anything to do with Arch that she hadn't known Nora was pregnant. "He's so sweet," she said. What else had she missed out on by avoiding anything that might hurt?

"This is Owen," Nora said proudly. She picked up Owen's tiny hand and waved it. "Say hi, Owen." Owen stared at Kit solemnly.

"Great-looking kid," Tyler said. "Can I hold him?"

"Sure." Nora passed the baby over.

Tyler held Owen to his chest, looking at the little guy with a delighted face. "Hello, cowboy," he said. Owen's flailing hand pushed up the brim of Tyler's hat. Tyler made a funny face and the baby giggled.

"And a bromance was born," Nora said. She turned to Kit. "Great to see you again. I've been thinking of you a lot this past year or so. I kept hoping I'd see you around. But with the baby, I haven't managed to get into the bar."

"It's fine. I totally understand," Kit said. "And I could have tried to see you." She wanted to fix this. Wanted to wrap up any loose ends related to Arch. "I had a hard time when your brother came back. I'm sure you heard."

Nora smiled faintly. "I heard a few things."

"Like flying food, I bet."

"Well, the diner incident *has* become a Benson legend," Nora teased, but Kit could see in her eyes that it was kindly meant. In fact, she was surprised to see so much warmth in Nora's big gray eyes. And a hint of tears, too. "You did a lot for me, you know," Nora said. "Remember when we talked in the grocery store and you told me to be more accepting of Todd? You helped me trust what my heart was telling me."

"I remember that day," Kit said. "Glad I could help."

"I just wish—" Nora flushed pink. "I'm just sorry things didn't work out the way you wanted. With my brother. I wish I'd come to see you and said that a long time ago."

"It's okay." And Kit realized that it *was* okay. That talking to Nora was not nearly as uncomfortable as she'd imagined. That Arch's not loving her had been really hard, but it had also led her here. To this project with Tyler. To seeing her dad happy and fulfilled. To finding herself a couple months away from a brand-new chapter of her life.

"Let's do this," Todd said. "Tyler, are you ready to meet your horses?"

"Sure am."

Tyler handed Owen to Nora and smiled at Kit. "Are *you* ready? Because I have this feeling that Rachel might make a pretty good horse for you."

For her? Tyler had bought a horse with her in mind? She hadn't ridden since they were kids. She studied him, trying to figure out if he was teasing.

"Good luck with that, cowboy," she finally tossed back, and went to stand a safe distance away.

Nora came to stand with her while Tyler, Todd and Kit's father slid the ramp from the trailer and conferred on a plan to unload the horses.

"A horse for you, huh?" Nora smiled, bouncing Owen gently in her arms. "Tyler seems like a great guy."

"We're old friends," Kit said quickly. "And colleagues."

A smile played around the corners of Nora's mouth. "Hmm…if you say so. Though I'd say your friend and colleague has a big crush on you. Which is totally understandable because you are beautiful and warmhearted. I hope you know that whatever choice my brother made, it doesn't change that one bit."

"It means he met someone *more* beautiful and *more* warmhearted. I've met Mandy Allen. She's lovely."

"Arch needed a change," Nora said. "He was desperate to move on from who he'd been. Mandy makes him feel like he can be that new guy. But I'm so sorry that you got hurt."

"Thank you. But it's okay. He's happy?" she asked. "With Mandy? In San Francisco?"

"He's very happy."

"That's good," Kit said, and she truly meant it. "That's really good."

"And I predict," Nora said when Tyler glanced at them and gave Kit an excited thumbs-up, "that you're going to be really happy, too, if you let that guy into your heart."

Kit shook her head. "Things between us are a little complicated."

"Good things aren't always simple." Nora grinned. "You know, someone really wise once told me we don't choose who we love. We just love."

Kit recognized her own words. "But she said that a long time ago about a very different guy," she corrected gently. "And I'm a different person, too. I'm leaving Benson soon."

"Where are you going?" Nora asked.

"Mexico." She'd printed her plane ticket and it was sitting on her nightstand. "I'm going to attend a language school there, then I'm planning to head to Central America. Maybe South America after that."

Nora's eyes were wide. "Wow. That's an incredible adventure."

Kit didn't let herself look at Tyler. Because every time she did, the excitement over her plans faded a little. "I can't wait," she told Nora.

There was a *clank* as the trailer doors opened, and Todd walked a beautiful slate-gray mare down the ramp. She had a mottled coat, a long mane with white threaded through the gray, a dished face and pretty dark eyes. "Oh my gosh." Kit stared. "She's gorgeous."

"Meet Rachel," Nora said. "She's pretty special, isn't she?"

Kit nodded and felt something settle into her heart. "She's perfect." And knew that now there was one more thing that she'd miss when she finally left town.

AFTER THE HORSES ARRIVED, Tyler had left them in Garth's care and spent most of the day at the construction site with Aaron, going over decisions. He'd even jumped into the work when one of the framers had called in sick. It had been a long day and it wasn't over yet. He was taking a shift behind the bar tonight. But first, he wanted to check on the horses one more time.

He'd found Garth leaning on the fence, watching Rachel and Carson eat. "Great first day on the job," Tyler said as he joined him.

"Seems like the horses are settling in just fine." The old man nodded his approval. "You picked a couple good ones. Rachel is mighty pretty and strong, too. And Carson, well, that is one tough horse. You could ride him all over these mountains and he wouldn't tire."

"I'm going to count on you to give them both

regular exercise. I doubt I can take them out often enough." His hunch that Garth missed riding was confirmed by the smile the other man couldn't contain.

"I'll make sure they both have everything they need."

"I'd like to get at least two more horses. Maybe in a few weeks, once we get into a routine here, you can come with me to pick them out." Garth would never let Tyler buy him a horse. But if there was one at Todd's ranch that his friend liked, Tyler would make sure to get it and turn it over to Garth full time.

"It's a good thing Todd's doing," Garth said. "Training these mustangs."

"Better than letting them suffer under the government's neglect. And you can't beat Todd's prices." Todd charged an adoption fee to cover his expenses and that was it. "Anyway, I'd better get up to the bar before it gets too busy. I'll see you tomorrow, Garth."

"Night, Tyler."

He watched Garth walk to his truck, happy to see the pride back in the man's posture. Glad he'd been able to help Kit and right his own father's wrongs.

He walked through the barn to make sure it was all locked up. He was looking forward to being behind the bar with Kit. The problem with avoiding her so much was that he'd missed her. Seeing her at the barn today had confirmed what he'd suspected. Staying away from Kit didn't diminish how he felt. Not one bit. So he might as well take any chance he could to be around her while she was still here.

Emerging from the barn, he was surprised to see Kit leaning on the fence, watching the horses devour their hay. "Didn't expect to find you here," he said quietly from a few feet away, so as not to startle her or the animals.

"I know I need to get up to the bar…" She looked a little flustered.

"It's okay. You have time." He stopped next to her. Rachel's head lifted and she eyed him cautiously, then blew out a heavy breath and went back to eating. "I didn't know you still liked horses."

"I don't usually." She bit her lower lip, as if she was worried. "I think they're beautiful, but I never really felt like I wanted to be around them much. But Rachel… I don't know. She's just so pretty."

"You used to be a great rider."

She flashed him her familiar sardonic grin. "I think the last time I was on a horse was with you. So basically a lifetime ago."

"Well, I need to start getting to know her and Carson before I ride them. Maybe you can help with that."

"How does that work? Getting to know a horse. Do you talk about your childhoods? Play trust games?"

He laughed and Carson glanced his way. "You do this. Spend time near them. Put a halter on them and take them for walks around the pasture. Brush them. Feed them. Even though Todd has trained these two completely, they were wild not long ago. So it's better to make sure they trust you before you start riding them."

"I'd like to try it," she said. "But I might not be much good at it."

"You'll be fine." He pointed at Rachel, who had moved closer to the fence and stood a couple feet away from Kit. "She likes you. She wouldn't come that close if she didn't."

Kit reached slowly through the fence rails, holding her knuckles out. Rachel instantly looked up from her food, brought her nose to Kit's hand and snuffled.

Tyler wished he had a camera, to catch the delighted smile that lit Kit's face. "What did I tell you? She trusts you already."

"What time do I have to get here tomorrow to practice my horse whispering?" Kit said quietly.

"They'll have their breakfast at seven. So how about nine?"

"Okay," she said. "I'm up for it."

"Kit." He wasn't sure how to say what he

wanted to say. She faced him, waiting. "I'm sorry I got weird, about you leaving," he finally said. "I understand why you want to go. I guess I'm worried that I'll miss you when you're gone. But that's no reason not to spend time together before you go. Let's do stuff together. We could go riding, hiking, whatever you want. But I don't want things to be awkward between us anymore."

"Neither do I," she said, and took a step toward him. He opened his arms and she wrapped hers around his torso in a quick hug. "I've missed you, too," she murmured as he reluctantly let her go again. "I'm sorry if my travel plans upset you."

"Nah, I'm good," he lied. "As long as you teach me all your bartending tricks before you go."

"What kind of tricks?" she asked, turning to take the path toward the bar.

"I dunno." He fell into step beside her. "What do you have left up your sleeve? How about some good shaker tricks? Like in that Tom Cruise movie."

Her peals of laughter rang like bells in the quiet evening. "You want to be like the character in *Cocktail*?"

"Well, maybe not that whole dance routine thing, but I wouldn't mind flipping a few glasses around."

Her smile was everything he needed in this moment. "I'll see what I can do, cowboy." They'd reached the bar and she tugged open the door, holding it for him. "Go wash some of that horse dust off before you get behind the bar tonight."

There was a streak of dirt on her cheek, and he brought his thumb up to wipe it off. "Same to you, actually. Who knows? I might make a cowgirl out of you yet."

"Good luck with that," she said, turning toward the women's room.

He watched her go, thinking that there were so many sides to her. The sweet girl he'd caught looking longingly at his horse tonight. The businesswoman who was keeping this renovation project on track. Tonight he'd get to see sassy, sexy Kit behind the bar. If he was lucky, he'd get his friend back as well. He tried to ignore the voice in his head, cautioning him that he liked all these sides of her way too much for his own good.

KIT SLID THE halter tentatively over Rachel's soft nose. The mare huffed out a breath visible in the cool morning air, but let her slide the strap over her head and buckle it.

"Good," Tyler said quietly. "Now you know what to do from here, right?"

Kit took hold of the lead rope, its rough coils familiar in her hand. "I think so."

"I'll start walking Carson. Rachel will want to follow him, but make sure you hold her still until you're ready. You're making friends, but you're also the boss here."

Tyler and Carson started off and Kit waited until there were a couple horse-lengths between them. "Let's go," Kit said, and Rachel moved forward instantly, clearly concerned that Carson was leaving without her. "Steady," Kit assured her. "We'll keep up." The mare settled, walking briskly by Kit's side, but not pulling anymore. And Kit tried to get used to the huge animal being so close.

At first, Rachel's big presence made Kit jumpy. But after a while, it was as if the horse's hoofbeats beat a rhythm that drove tension away, leaving a quiet satisfaction behind. The mare's movements kept Kit present, right here in this moment. And as they walked through sage-dotted meadows with majestic mountains rising nearby, she realized that this moment, walking with Tyler and the horses, was a very good place to be.

LATER THAT WEEK, on Friday morning, Kit tried to remember that peaceful feeling as she and Tyler sat at a table in the bar and tried to figure out the new decor for the Dusty Saddle or the Last Rodeo or whatever Tyler was going to call it. He'd gone quiet about the name, which had Kit nervous. Because it probably meant he'd come up with something he knew she'd hate. Which wasn't really her problem. It was his bar, and he could name it whatever he wanted, but still, she couldn't help wondering.

"Tell me what you like about this." She pointed to the red-and-white-checked fabric sample Tyler had pulled out.

"It's cheerful," he answered. "And it's kind of rustic, right?"

"Well, yes, it's cheerful," she admitted, searching for the right words. "If you like the tablecloths they put in Italian restaurants."

"Oh," he said, looking bemused. "I didn't know."

She'd been too blunt, and she tried to fix it. "Let's go over the design again."

"I was thinking of this color for the walls." Tyler indicated a burnt-orange paint strip.

"It's going to look all Southwestern."

"Well, Southwestern is Western, right?"

"We sound like an old married couple," Kit groaned, putting her head down on the table. "One of those bickering couples who never agree on anything."

Tyler grinned, stretching lazily in his chair, arms over his head. Kit tried not to notice the way his T-shirt pulled tight over his abs. "Well, we've known each other long enough to earn bickering rights."

"I didn't realize there was such a thing." Kit

giggled. "But now that I know that I have them, I'm going to bicker hard in support of this cream color for the walls. And then all the trim could be this warm brown stain," she added, pointing to the sample. "And then we could pick a matching color for the booths." She opened the sample book and showed him a strip of rich burgundy fabric. "See? Warm, simple, welcoming."

"But won't one solid color be boring?"

"Maybe we could do a subtle pattern. But we'll also have a bunch of stuff on the walls. The new sconces are going in, plus we'll have all the old signs and saddles. *And* the new glass case of your rodeo memorabilia. I think boring is the least of our worries."

"All right, then," Tyler said. "You've convinced me. Go ahead and call in the order. No more bickering."

"Oh, good," Kit said, rubbing her eyes. She'd come in early to walk Rachel every day this week, because it made her feel happy to be around the sweet, beautiful horse. But she was going home to crawl into bed after this and try to get some sleep. "What's next?" she asked, stifling a yawn.

"Nothing," Tyler said.

"What do you mean, nothing?"

"What I mean is that we just made the last decision about decor. After this order, we just wait for construction to finish up, then it all gets delivered and installed, and we'll be ready to open."

No more ordering. It was amazing to contemplate. A relief to realize. They'd spent hours this past week making decisions like this. Debating patterns and chair shapes and table sizes. "I can't believe it," Kit said, feeling a strange twinge of loss. It had been a huge challenge to figure it all out, but it had been kind of fun turning Tyler's dream into a reality, one design choice at a time. "How many weeks until we have to close?"

"A couple. Aaron says the last week of August. Then we can reopen at the end of September, if we push."

"Gosh," she said, trying to take it in. "It's really happening, isn't it?"

"I think we're on schedule."

"So does that mean you'll have time to teach me how to ride again?"

He threw back his head and laughed, and the rich sound filled the empty bar. "Words I never thought I'd hear. But yes. I'll have time to teach you to ride. And I'd be happy to do it. You want to start now?"

"Right now?" Her desire for sleep fell away at the thought of riding Rachel.

"Yup." Tyler's dimples slashed down his lean cheeks. "When I said I'd make a cowgirl out of you, I wasn't kidding." He stood and held out his hand, and she let him pull her out of her seat. And they walked down to the barn together.

"She's so pretty." Kit ran the brush over Rachel's coat, a mottled dark gray, as if storm clouds were rolling over her. Her mane fell down her neck in gray and white waves. Kit held out her hand and the mare's black nose found her palm and nuzzled softly, whiskers tickling.

"You've done a great job with her so far," Tyler said.

"Thanks for letting me spend so much time with her." Kit stepped back as the mare raised her head and snuffled at her hair. "Now come on, that's not hay."

"Nope, it's silk," Tyler said, reaching for Rachel's halter to pull the mare a few steps back. He didn't seem to realize he'd given her a romantic compliment. "I remember our last ride. It came to me on the way here."

"You do?"

"It was our junior year. We went riding in the hills behind my family's ranch. You were on that palomino you liked so much."

"Sunrise—such a sweet horse."

"When we got back, your dad was all excited because he'd gotten me into this bull-riding clinic a friend of his was organizing. He pulled me away to talk about it, and when we were finished, we turned around and you were gone. There was Sunrise, unsaddled, brushed down, but no Kit."

The memory was so old, it shouldn't still carry a sting. "I remember that."

"What happened after that ride?" Tyler asked. "Why'd you leave? I feel like that day is the last fun memory I have of us."

"You and my dad were talking rodeo. I guess I realized that you two had this connection that I could never share. And I didn't want to be the third wheel anymore."

"I'm sorry about that." Tyler's voice was quiet; his hand stroked Rachel's nose in long sweeps. "I can see it now. How it must have felt, him paying all that attention to me. I didn't think about it—I was so hungry to learn everything he knew."

Kit shrugged. "You were a kid. It wasn't your job to know."

He smiled. "I do remember that you joined cheerleading pretty soon after that." Mischief cast a gleam in his eyes. "I remember *you*, in that uniform."

Her face went a little hot and her heart went a little proud because she'd worked out really hard and worn that uniform well. "It was fun. Something of my own, you know? That had nothing to do with my dad or you."

But it had. Because her dad hadn't even realized Kit was on the cheerleading squad. Hadn't been home to see all the time she'd spent at practice or drilling with her pom-poms in the backyard.

That had been the start, Kit thought, of her personal rebellion. Of eventually quitting the squad and layering on the makeup. Of skipping class to meet Arch and let his older-guy, bad-boy attention become the balm that soothed her orphaned soul.

"So are you ready to ride?"

It was a simple question, but it felt complicated. Because he was inviting her back to those days before she donned her tough-girl shell. Back when she was just a girl galloping these rugged hills with her best friend.

And like any armored animal, the thought of life without that shell seemed uncomfortable. Maybe even impossible.

"You promise you won't laugh at me? Because you've spent all these years as rodeo king, and I've been behind the bar."

"I'll never laugh."

"Even if Rachel dumps me in the dust?"

"I remember how you rode. You never hit the dust. Just left me in it." His eyebrows rose in a slow challenge. "I'm getting you a saddle."

A part of her wanted to say no. To shy away from the good memories he'd excavated. Without them, it would be so much easier to walk away from this town. From the bar. From Tyler.

But it was too late. She ached to be on a horse again. To be that girl who'd known horses better than she'd known herself. "Fine. Get the saddle." She stroked Rachel's sleek shoulder as she watched Tyler disappear into the shadows of the barn, wondering what else he'd dug up besides memories just now. Because along with the old hurts about her dad and her old love of horses, there was a warmth deep in her heart as she watched him go. A soul-deep knowledge that she'd carried with her growing up. That he was her friend. That he had her back. That somehow, in some way, he was the boy for her.

SEEING KIT ON a horse again was a little disorienting. On one hand, Tyler recognized his childhood friend immediately. She swung a leg easily over Rachel's back, tucked her red cowboy boots into the stirrups and backed the mare neatly away from the fence. She took charge like she'd been in the saddle yesterday, rather than over a decade ago. Her whole posture on horseback was familiar to him, her squared shoulders, her legs strong in the stirrups, her seat so solid in the saddle.

But this wasn't the young girl he'd chased over the hills. This was Kit, with hair that fell to her waist in black waves, with beauty that stole his reason and a mind that ran circles around his.

The smile she gave him was shy, so un-Kit-like, it woke him up. He realized in an instant what kind of limb she was going out on to take up riding again.

"You look great up there. Like no time has passed."

"But it has."

"Not today." He encompassed the Dusty Saddle with a general wave in its direction. "None of this has happened. It's just you and me riding again. Give me a minute and I'll get Carson saddled."

It only took moments to catch Carson, who was eager to rejoin his friend. The big gelding stood calmly while Tyler ran a brush over him, checked his hooves and threw his saddle and bridle on. He swung onto Carson's back, then glanced at Kit. "You ready?"

"Ready for a sedate walk," she reminded him. "Don't you dare take off on me. We're not sixteen, you know."

But he felt sixteen. Sixteen and crazy about her and wanting, more than anything, to see her smile wide, like she did back then. Before her dad and mom ignored her one too many times. Before Arch took her in, taught her to be like him and then tossed her aside. "Just a walk." Tyler led them south of the barn, where they threaded their way through sparse pines and out into open fields. Here, the entire Sierra range unfolded in jigsaw spires along the skyline.

He glanced her way, wanting her to appreciate

it the way he did. "Doesn't get much better than this, right?"

He saw the glory of it reflected in her wide eyes. "It still takes my breath away," she said quietly.

"Want to trot?"

"Pushy much?" But he saw how she deepened her seat and eased the mare into a slow jog, so they passed him by on the wide path and Kit's laugh slid through the space between them like drops of rain.

This was working. This was making her happy. And if this could bring her joy, who knew? Maybe he could, too.

He didn't need to urge Carson on because the gelding was happy to catch up. Easier said than done, because Kit was rising in her stirrups now, asking Rachel for a speedier trot. Tyler asked for the same, but just when he was catching up to her, she eased her mare into a lope, sitting back in the saddle again, riding the rocking horse gait easily, like all these years since their last ride together hadn't affected her a bit.

So he sat back, too, using his calves and thighs to ask for a gallop. When he'd caught up, Tyler reached for his hat and handed it to her across the jerky distance between them. And she leaned in and grabbed it, laughing, and held it to her head, letting out a cowgirl whoop as she asked the mare for a little more speed, leaving him eating her dust, just like she always had.

CHAPTER ELEVEN

Kɪᴛ ᴡᴀs ᴛᴇᴀᴄʜɪɴɢ the bar staff how to make cocktails. Well, *trying* to teach them. She kept losing track of what they were working on. Which was making her crazy because this wasn't rocket science. There was no reason to be so distracted.

But it was extremely hard to focus with Tyler there. Even after working together constantly, rock climbing with Ethan and Lila, taking countless horseback rides and hikes this summer, she couldn't seem to settle into an easy friendship with him.

Her desire for him still rose at unexpected and inconvenient times. Like when he walked into the bar, or when they toured the construction area and he helped Aaron lift a beam and she was mesmerized by the way the muscles in his arms moved. She loved their friendship and their work partnership, and she didn't want to ruin them with anything romantic.

Plus, every day that she was on her own, trying new things and pushing her travel plans forward, she was proving to herself that she'd changed.

That she could be strong and interesting and adventuresome on her own. That romance and relationships weren't the only place she could find excitement in life. Still, she couldn't shake this attraction to Tyler. She hated to admit it, even to herself, but her feelings had evolved into a full-blown crush.

He, on the other hand, didn't seem the least bit interested in her. Which showed how ridiculous it was to lust after him. She'd thought there was something between them at the stable when the horses had first arrived, and on the day she'd first ridden. But lately it seemed as though to him, she was just the trusty employee he relied on. The old friend he enjoyed having adventures with.

It was better that way. But it stung a little. She had to try so hard not to stare at him, while he never looked her way. Like right now. He was completely absorbed, hanging out at a table with Tim, laughing as they tried to upstage each other with their stylish ways of wielding a cocktail shaker. Tyler had been serious about wanting to imitate Tom Cruise. Lately there'd been bottles flipped behind the bar before he poured, glasses tossed to her when she needed them. It was silly, but she had to admit, it was a lot of fun, too. And the customers loved it.

Focus. She was covering three drinks today: the cosmopolitan, a Manhattan and martinis of all kinds. She glanced at the clock. Tyler was paying them for only another thirty minutes. She had to hustle if she wanted to teach both dry and sweet Manhattans.

"Guys, finish up the circus tricks," she called to Tyler and Tim. "Everyone, you're all officially martini experts. Go clean up." There was a scraping of chairs as people headed for the sink to rinse their shakers.

Tyler walked her way and she braced herself against whatever weird and bumbling thing she might do in his presence, now that she had all these feelings for him. Like fall over a chair or mention his pecs by accident. It seemed better to say nothing.

"This is a good class," he said, stopping across the table from her. "I appreciate you teaching us. It will be great to have everyone on the same page."

"It's not a problem," Kit said, crossing her arms across her chest. Then uncrossing them. Because nothing felt quite comfortable around him anymore.

"I have to take off now. Can you lock up when you're finished here?"

"You're not staying for my Manhattan lesson?"

He looked around, clearly uncomfortable by her question. Oh, no, did she sound all needy?

"I know I should. I was hoping you could teach me later. There's somewhere I really need to be."

"Sure." She noted the way his hands clenched. He was nervous, too. But she had no way of knowing if his tension was due to her, or because of wherever he was rushing to.

"Thanks, Kit. See you later." And he jogged out. Jogged. As if he couldn't wait to get to where he was going. She watched him through the glass door. He jumped into his truck and zoomed away, leaving a cloud of dust in the parking lot.

"I heard he's got a girlfriend." Bella came to stand beside her. She was one of their newer bartenders. A pretty blonde in her early twenties. Funny and smart. "My aunt lives across from the place he rented. She says he has a woman visiting him a few times a week now. Some pretty lady with dark hair." She sighed. "I can't blame her. He's so cute. A nice guy, too. I'd be happy to visit him anytime."

There was no reason for this weird flare of jealousy. Of course Bella thought he was cute. And of course Tyler had found someone to be with. He was Tyler Ellis. He'd probably been propositioned by every woman who walked into this bar.

"Okay." She swallowed the strange tightness in her throat. "Did you get your shaker cleaned out? Ready for the next drink?"

"I sure am," Bella said, flashing her a grateful smile. "This job is so fun. I'm really glad you hired me."

"I'm glad you wanted to work for us." Kit turned to the group, clapping her hands. "Okay, everyone, it's Manhattan time."

"The boss is away," Tim called. "Can we use real booze?"

Kit looked around at them, all tired from their Friday and Saturday night shifts. Until they hired more staff, it was all-hands-on-deck on the weekends—especially with the Dusty Saddle being the suddenly cool place to be. "Okay, I'll buy you a Manhattan." A cheer went up, but she shushed them. "Only *if* you make a perfect one. You make a bad one, and you have to pay."

That got their attention. She'd have to keep this teaching strategy in mind.

"All right," she said. "Take a moment to read over the recipe on your table."

She couldn't help it. In the silence that followed, her gaze strayed to the parking lot, where the dust from Tyler's departing truck had long since settled. And she wondered again where Tyler had gone. And, if Bella was right, *whom* he'd gone to.

KIT POURED OUT a few glasses of champagne and looked around the crowded Mammoth Gallery. It was a beautiful evening and even more people were coming through the door to see Lila's photos.

Lila had worried that she might not get a big crowd on a Wednesday night. But Kit wasn't surprised so many people were here. Lila's photography was gorgeous. She'd framed each print in simple, weathered wood, perfect for the desert scenes.

Kit had offered to support her friend in the best way she knew how—to set up a small, elegant table in the back of the room and serve drinks.

She was so proud of Lila tonight. Her friend had been a well-known photographer in Los Angeles before she fled to Benson to hide from her ex-boyfriend. With Dale in prison now, Lila was free to let her work shine again. Some of the guests tonight had come all the way from LA to celebrate with her and welcome her back.

Apparently the *Los Angeles Times* was going to be here, too. They were writing a feature piece on Lila's experience—her life in hiding and her life now, reclaiming her art.

Kit spotted Ethan leaning on a post in the back of the gallery, his face pale and drawn. She beckoned him over. "Are you doing okay?"

He shook his head slightly. "I know there's no reason to worry. But I still feel so protective, you know? After tonight and this article in the *Times*, the whole world will know where to find her. What if Dale has some creepy friend he sends for her?"

"Then you'll take him out with one swipe of your fist. And Lila will help with her awesome martial arts moves. And I'll break bottles over his head."

It worked. A smile crept along Ethan's tense face until he was laughing a little. "Good to know we have a plan."

"I am nothing if not organized," Kit said. "Now, take these glasses of champagne. Drink one to take the edge off your vigilance. You're huge and tattooed, and when you get worried, you start scaring people. Take the other to your gorgeous fiancée. She's been answering so many questions, she must be parched."

Ethan took the glasses obediently and made his way through the crowd to where Lila, looking stunning in a black cocktail dress and heels, was listening to an earnest-looking woman pointing at an ethereal print of a Joshua tree.

"There you go, taking care of everyone again."

She turned toward the voice, surprised to see Tyler. He looked amazing, as always, in black jeans and a button-down shirt. "Hey, you startled me. I didn't see you there."

"You were too busy fixing everything for Ethan to notice me."

"It's Lila's special night. I want it to go perfectly."

Tyler whistled low. "Ethan told me what happened last year. How that guy almost got hold of her. He sounds scary."

"He was." Kit shuddered at the memory of the one time she'd seen Dale. "He came into the bar to get information about Lila from me. I didn't know who he was—she had never said anything about him. But his eyes were so cold, I knew something was wrong, so I lied. Told him she'd quit her job a long time ago."

Kit didn't want to think about it. If she'd been more busy, or less alert, she'd have told the truth— Lila was working later that evening. And Dale would have been waiting for her. "Let's talk about something else."

Ethan wound through the crowd toward them. "Want me to pour the wine for a bit?" he asked. "You guys can check out the photos."

"You just want an excuse not to be out there mingling," Kit teased gently. "Which is great, because I'd love a break."

She filled a glass with champagne and offered it to Tyler, then poured one for herself before letting Ethan take over.

"There are some amazing photos she took of the Dusty Saddle. I'm sure you'll want to buy them." Kit led him that way.

Tyler grinned. "If you ever leave bartending you could have a career in sales."

She gave him a mock glare, then let him admire the photos. The old Dusty Saddle sign against a brooding sky. The building covered in snow with winter-frosted Sierra peaks rising behind. The barn, before Tyler had fixed it up. While most of Lila's photos were black and white, this one had been taken last spring, when a wet winter had caused wildflowers to bloom thick and lush around the weathered walls.

"You're right," Tyler said, staring from one to another. "I do want to buy them. Who knew I had such a talented bartender?"

"I knew." Kit elbowed him. "Just one more reason why you should listen to me."

"Oh, I'll listen to you. I just might not do what you say." He elbowed back with that wide grin that sent heat down Kit's spine. *Ugh. No heat.* He thought of her as a buddy. They were friends. Why did these other feelings have to get in the way?

But she knew why. Chemistry. She wanted Tyler. She was incredibly attracted to him. And she had to find a way to live with that.

Tyler stopped their wandering path through the gallery with a hand on her arm. "Are those photos of you?"

Kit followed his gaze and felt her cheeks heat. "Oh. Those."

He walked to the exhibit hanging near the office door. Kit followed, sipping her champagne and wondering if maybe she should disappear. These photos were the results of the day she'd modeled for Lila. As promised, Lila had allowed Kit to approve the prints before including them in her show. But it was one thing to look at them in Lila's kitchen. Here, the intimacy that Lila had captured with her camera felt like a little too much to show Tyler.

Especially now, when all of her feelings for him made everything seem more complicated.

Tyler stood stock-still, staring at her photos. Maybe he liked them. Maybe he didn't, and couldn't think of what to say. Kit did them both a favor and slipped away into the crowd, putting as much distance between them as possible.

IT WAS DIFFICULT to know which photo to look at first. Tyler's gaze landed on one to absorb the beauty there, only to be instantly drawn to another. Lila had done something brilliant here. Each black-and-white photo, soft and shadowed, showed one alluring part of Kit. In the first shot, she faced away from the camera with no top on, revealing the hourglass shape of her torso. Her hair was pulled to one side and the light caught the contrast between her intricate tattoos and her pale skin. It was artistic, completely innocent and totally sexy at the same time.

In another photo, Lila had caught Kit's rattle-snaked arm with the alluring shadow of her full breast behind it. The next focused on the stubborn line of her jaw and the sweet curve of her neck. The last in the series was the only one that showed her face. Kit looked over her shoulder at the camera, her eyes huge and vulnerable without her dark makeup. There was a startled expression in her eyes, yet her full mouth was set in a defiant line, as if she was ready to fight back against whatever troubled her.

Lila had captured the dilemma that was Kit.

He turned to tell Kit how much he loved them. But she was gone. Instead a man he didn't know stood behind him, studying the photos, too. He caught Tyler's eye. "Pretty incredible, aren't they? I'm thinking of getting them. Perfect for the bedroom wall."

Tyler's hands coiled to fists before he had one coherent thought. But when his mind caught up, he knew there was no way that this guy would have these photos on his bedroom wall, or on any other wall for that matter. These were too personal, too private, too perfect to be in some stranger's hands. A stranger would have no idea what Kit had risked here, how hard it must have been for her—normally so guarded—to show herself to the camera.

He nodded to the other man, not trusting himself to say anything, and went to find the gallery owner, who was only too happy to sell all the photos of Kit to him. And he bought the photos of the Dusty Saddle and his barn as well.

He had no idea what he'd do with Kit's photo series. It would be way too creepy to hang them. But the need to protect these images of her ran too strong to resist. He'd done his best to become her friend this past month. To put his feelings aside and help her have the adventures she needed. To support her as she tried to get herself onto a healthier path with men, with life, with herself.

And it was working. Kit was stronger and more vibrant and happier than when he'd first walked into the Dusty Saddle. Her self-help books had been replaced by travel books and Spanish textbooks. She was so excited for her travels and whatever life had to offer her next, now that she felt free to leave town.

The problem was, all that excitement and strength and vitality made her more beautiful to him. He was aware of her every movement behind the bar, her every smile. He'd fallen in love with her. Completely. And it was all he could do not to take her in his arms and show her how he felt.

Maybe he was making a mistake, being so understanding, giving her so much space. He was letting her go without a fight. He'd fought for everything else he had with a single-minded drive. His rodeo career. This bar. Learning to read and write. Maybe he needed to step up and fight for her, too. To try to show her how much she belonged here. How much they belonged together. Then maybe she wouldn't need to get on that plane and go.

For now, he signed the forms to have the gallery ship her photos to his house.

He was disappointed when he didn't see her in the crowd. He wanted to view the rest of the photos with her. Because everything was much more fun with Kit making dry comments that only he could hear.

He spotted someone he knew near the door and set aside his thoughts of Kit. He'd invited his friend Gray to meet him here tonight.

Gray had been a great bull rider, a hard partier, always ready for a good time. And that's how Tyler still pictured him. So it always took a moment to adjust to the sight of his friend in a wheelchair. Gray had lost the use of his legs when a bull trampled him. Now he was an accountant living near Palm Springs.

Gray swiveled his wheelchair as he approached. "Hey, Tyler! Good to see you."

They shook hands. "Thank you for meeting me here," Tyler said.

"It worked out since I've got a race here in Mammoth this weekend."

"Yeah, what's up with that? You're doing some kind of trail race?"

"You bet." Gray's face lit up. "You've got to see my off-road wheelchair. It's awesome. The thing *flies* down the hills."

"You're an adrenaline junkie, man."

"Aren't we all? Not being able to walk doesn't change who I am."

Tyler laughed. "I'm glad nothing will change your kind of crazy. So you're doing okay?"

"I am, actually. Getting used to it, at least. I'll be all right. Now let's get that dinner you promised me. And tell me about this business of yours that you want help with."

Tyler figured it was best to be honest. "*Need* help, is more like it. I'm kind of desperate to have someone deal with all the finances, at least for a while." He was making progress under Sheila's tutelage. His reading had come further than he'd ever thought possible. But numbers were still tricky, and Kit checked all of his records for him. That's where he hoped Gray would help out once Kit left.

He and Gray headed out the door toward a restaurant Tyler liked. Over dinner he told Gray about his reading and writing problems and his struggles to run the bar. It felt good to let someone else in on his private issues. And to share with Gray that he had a disability, too. It wasn't nearly as serious as Gray's, certainly not as life-altering, but his friend understood how frustrated he felt.

At the end of the meal, when Gray offered to

take on the work, and said he might even consider moving to Mammoth—but not to that cow town Tyler called home—Tyler knew he had a friend he could trust. Gray would have his back, always. And he'd make sure Tyler didn't mess up everything he and Kit had created together at the Dusty Saddle.

BY SOME MIRACLE, Kit had Friday night off. Despite craving a quiet night with a hot bath and a good book, she decided to invite her father for dinner. She still hadn't told him about her travel plans, and with her departure date a month away, it was time to have the conversation she'd been dreading.

She made spaghetti and meatballs, a dish he liked enough to motivate him to come over to her house. She prepared garlic bread and salad, and put a candle in the middle of her little kitchen table. The house she rented was small, but she liked to think she'd made it cozy and comfortable.

She waited until they were finished eating before she brought up the subject. "Dad, I have a deal with Tyler that I want to tell you about."

Her father brightened, as he always did, at the mention of Tyler's name. "He's turned into a fine man, hasn't he?"

"He certainly has." Kit steeled herself. "I've been helping him with the renovations to the bar, so he's giving me a bonus. A lot of money…and I want to use part of it to help you out."

He shot her a suspicious glance. "What do you mean, help me out?"

"I want to pay off that loan you took against your pension."

He leaned back in his chair. "You use that money for yourself. I'm not your responsibility. Don't worry about me."

"Of course I worry about you. You're my dad."

"Nope." He shook his head emphatically. "I got myself into this pension mess and I'll get myself out."

Frustration at his misplaced pride rose. "You *aren't* getting out of it. You're stuck under it. And I already *do* help you. I've been covering your mortgage. I pay your utility bills."

He stared at his plate. This wasn't going well at all. "I don't mind helping out." Kit gentled her voice, needing him to hear her. "Please let me. Once it's paid off, your pension from the ranch and your paychecks from Tyler will be plenty for you to cover all of your own bills again. Doesn't that seem like a good solution?"

He was silent for a long time. "All right. If it will make you happy."

"It will. Thanks, Dad. And there's one more thing." She took a deep breath and blurted out the news on the exhale. "I want to take a big trip."

Garth looked relieved to be talking about something other than his financial troubles. "It's about time you had a vacation." This from the man who'd never gone farther than a camping trip in the Sierras, which were in his backyard.

"I want to do more than take a vacation. I want to travel. For months. Maybe longer."

His gaze darted to hers, then flickered away. "You want to live somewhere else?"

"Maybe. I need a change. I really do."

When he finally spoke, his voice was more gruff than usual. "Where are you heading?"

"I'm thinking about Mexico. Then Central America. I'm not sure which countries yet, exactly. I want to learn to speak Spanish. And see the rain forest and the ruins. I want to sit on tropical beaches."

"You're that unhappy here? In Benson?"

The concern in his voice had her placating him. "Not totally. I just want to see something different."

"You can see different things right here in the United States. They speak English and it's a hell of a lot safer."

"I want to go farther than that."

He sat up straighter. "This is about Arch, isn't it? I've seen how unhappy you've been ever since he showed up last year."

She stared at him in surprise. She'd never told

him about Arch coming home. Or about him leaving again. "It's not, really. It's about me."

"You think I haven't noticed how unhappy you were? And how much happier you've been since Tyler came back?"

She thought she'd hid it all from him.

"I can understand you wanting to see the world. I just hope you're not making this choice because of Arch. He's controlled too much of your life already. Don't let him influence this next chapter, too."

His words stunned her. "I'm not," she said with a lot more certainty than she felt. "This is what I want."

His lips pressed together. "Just as long as you're not running from your memories. Because the problem with you and Arch is down in your heart. Until you solve it, you'll just take it with you wherever you go."

The truth of that settled on her shoulders. "When did you get so wise?"

His smile, so unused lately, creaked into place. "I had some extra time on my hands recently. I got to sit around and think."

They both laughed, relieved that his sitting-around-and-thinking days were over, thanks to his new job. She didn't want him to worry about her travels anymore, so she brought up the one topic she could count on to make him happy. "Tell me more about your and Tyler's plans for the rodeo school."

As she listened to his ideas and saw how his eyes lit up as he spoke, she realized that the very thing she'd resented all these years was what was saving them both now. His love of Tyler, his pride in his protégé's rodeo success, had lifted him from the depression of the past few months.

And Kit would never be okay leaving Benson if her father was unhappy. She'd never be able to leave if he didn't have this new job he loved so much.

It was ironic, really, that her father's love of Tyler, and of the rodeo—a love she'd resented so much, for so long—was the very thing that was setting her free.

CHAPTER TWELVE

IT HAD BEEN a long, hot Saturday, followed by a long, hot night. Word must have gotten out that this was their final night before they closed to finish the renovations. People had packed the bar, even spilling outside to sit at the tables Kit had set up.

They were closed now. Everyone had gone home, the bar blissfully empty. Kit looked around for Tyler to say goodbye. He'd been such a flirt tonight. Ever since Lila's show in Mammoth, he'd seemed a little different. Maybe she was imagining it, but it seemed like he was looking for reasons to be around her. To stand a little closer to her behind the bar. Which was torture, since she was already so aware of him; of his spiced scent; of the way his voice, low and full of laughter, would murmur some joke close to her ear, just for her.

She wished she didn't like it so much.

He came out of the office. He must have been putting tonight's earnings in the safe. "Hey, has everyone else left?"

"Yeah." His T-shirt was tight, black and it clung

to him in the heat. Suddenly she wasn't ready to go home.

"You want some ice water?"

He slid onto a stool and took the glass she offered. "That was a fun night."

"Fun and crazy," she agreed. "And a little sad for me. Our last night as the Dusty Saddle I've known and loved. When we open again, it will be different."

"Better, though. I promise." He grinned at her. "You're not going to miss all the beer stains on the floor, right? Or the way the sink behind the bar always clogs?"

"No. I won't miss those things." She paused, remembering something she'd seen earlier. "What were you laughing about with Crater and Stan? You were doubled over."

"Those guys are a kick. Did you know how Crater got his name?"

Kit smiled at the memory. "You mean when he accidentally set off those explosives at that big mine in Nevada? Yes, I've heard that story many times."

Tyler shook his head as if he still couldn't believe it. "Stan said the crater is still there. That it's legendary."

"It's how Crater became a prospector. No one will hire him. Though he doesn't seem to mind that much. I'd get lonely, working out in the desert all by myself."

"It seems to suit Crater okay. I think when you really love what you do, maybe you don't mind the loneliness so much."

Kit studied him, sensing he was speaking from experience. "Were you lonely when you were on the rodeo circuit?"

He studied the ice in his glass. "Sometimes, sure. But bull riders are a community. You see the same guys at all the competitions and get to know one another pretty well. You're not really competing against one another, you know? It's you against that bull, and no one wants to see anyone get hurt—even though the odds are high. You stick together."

"Sounds like you had some good friends." She wanted to ask about the other way of keeping loneliness away. About women. There must have been hundreds wanting to ease his solitary lifestyle. But it wasn't her business. Just like this mystery woman he was supposedly dating wasn't her business. Still, she was dying to ask.

"I did have friends. I lost a few, too. Lost my best friend about six years ago. A bull cut him clean through."

"Jeez." Kit almost choked on her drink. "That's horrible."

"It was hard. And then my friend Gray got paralyzed. That's what made me think about quitting. I promised myself I'd finish the season, go for the world title one more time, then get out. So that's how I ended up here."

The thought of Tyler in a wheelchair brought a lump to Kit's throat. He was so vibrant and alive. The kind of guy who was meant to be behind the bar, bringing people together. "Your friend, how's he doing now?"

"Actually, I've been meaning to tell you about him. He was at Lila's show—I wanted to introduce you, but you disappeared on me."

She flushed, remembering how shy she'd felt when he was looking at her photos. She'd actually gone to hide in the restroom. "Yeah…sorry about that."

"Well, his name's Grayson—Gray for short. He went back to school. Became an accountant of all things. He's thinking of moving to Mammoth, which would be great. I'll hire him to keep the books, do payroll and all the accounts. He could also help with the rodeo school if he wants to. I think he's going to say yes."

"That's great." It was a relief to know that Tyler would have assistance with the books. He seemed to be doing better with his reading and writing, but she liked knowing he'd have someone to double-check everything once she was gone. Then she thought about what he'd just said.

"Not to be rude, but won't he make the rodeo students lose their nerve?"

His grin was classic Tyler. Unapologetic. Infectious. "If they lose their nerve, then they never had it in the first place. If you are getting into bull riding, you've got to get in it with your eyes wide open. Gray would be a great example to the students. If bull riding teaches you anything, it's that life is short. And we're all here by the grace of God and that grace can leave at any time. So you've got to grab on to every minute and make the most of it."

His words went straight into her soul and she took a gulp of water to dull the impact. She was thirty-two years old and she'd only recently learned this lesson—mostly thanks to Tyler and his attempts to get her out on adventures. Because of him, these past few months had been the fullest and happiest she could remember. It scared her how many years she'd let slip on by, unappreciated, unlived, barely noticed.

Suddenly the need to live, to feel alive, was overwhelming. "Hey, you want to do something crazy?"

His eyes went wide. He set his glass down carefully. "Right now? What did you have in mind?"

"I don't know. Swimming? We could head over to one of the lakes."

"Are you sure? The water's pure snowmelt."

"That makes it even more exciting." Cold water waking her up, bringing her alive again, was exactly what she needed after this hot day…after all these hot, uncomfortable feelings sparked by being near Tyler.

His smile was one she remembered from their youth. A smile that said he was ready for anything. He grabbed his keys off the bar. "Okay then, let's go swimming."

RIDING IN TYLER'S TRUCK, the night sky whirling by her window, Kit felt like she was sixteen again. The town was asleep, and they were zipping down dark roads, hell-bent on mischief.

The road wound up toward the rise of the Sierras, the twists and turns illuminated only by Tyler's headlights. "Turn here," Kit ordered, spying the sign for the lake.

"It's closed for the night."

"It's a county park. It's not like they can afford a night watchman or anything."

"Your powers of persuasion haven't changed a bit." He parked in the gravel parking lot and glanced at the dashboard. "It's cooler up here. Sixty degrees outside. You still sure you want to do this?"

"Absolutely." Kit shoved open her door. "You don't have to, though. If it's too cold for you."

Tyler grabbed his door handle. "You bait me

and I fall for it, every time. I'll race you." He was out of the truck, slamming the door shut behind him, running through the headlights' glare to the shoreline beyond.

Kit shut her door and bolted after him, letting the chilled air rush over her tired skin, shedding her shirt as she ran. She pulled up next to Tyler and kicked off her boots as he did the same. In a fluid motion he had his shirt off. They stood, panting from their efforts, looking out at the black and icy water. "Jeans?" he challenged, and reached for his belt buckle.

Suddenly she was aware of what they were doing. Two adults in their thirties shedding their clothes for each other. But that wasn't what this was about. This was about embracing life the way Tyler described, knowing that tomorrow was never guaranteed.

"Jeans." She yanked hers down, kicking them off. Her bare feet sank into the sandy shore; the night chill raced over her skin, enlivening and awakening each nerve.

She lunged toward the lake, knowing if she stopped for an instant she'd never have the nerve. The frigid water forced a screech from her lungs and numbed her toes, but she threw herself forward and went under anyway, letting the icy silence close over her head and steal a few moments of her breath. She pushed off the bottom with a whoop, sailing up into the night air in time to see Tyler, clad only in briefs, muscles carved in the headlights' glow, dive into the water and disappear under.

She stumbled toward shore, gasping for air, all the heat and sweat of the day obliterated. She turned as Tyler shot up out of the water like a jack-in-the-box shouting, "Holy hell, that is so damn *cold*!" He jogged in her direction, and she couldn't pull her gaze away from his muscular frame.

He grabbed her hand and held it tight as they navigated their way to the beach again. On shore, he pushed her sodden hair behind her ear. "That was invigorating," he said with a slow smile.

"It was." He was stealing her breath the way the cold water had. Standing so close, water beading off his body, no clothing to hide the power of his frame. She couldn't stop her hand from going to his shoulder, her fingers from tracing his biceps. She saw the desire she'd been feeling for weeks, the want she'd been trying to ignore, reflected in his eyes.

"Kit." His fingertips traced her jaw, stopped at her chin and gently tilted her face up to his. "You're so damn beautiful." And he brought his lips to hers, the warmth of his mouth a haven from the cold night. He was strong and so soft and she'd been trying not to kiss him for so long but she had no willpower left. Her hands slid behind his neck and she pulled him down to deepen the kiss. His arms circled her back to support her, to crush her to his bare chest. His wet skin against hers drew a moan from her throat that he caught with his next kiss.

It was perfect. Beyond anything she'd imagined, and she'd thought about kissing him way too much.

The chirp of a siren sliced through the quiet night, and they jumped apart. The blue-and-red lights of a sheriff's car joined Tyler's headlights to brighten the scene.

"You've got to be kidding me." She looked at Tyler, soaking wet and almost naked. He glanced back and burst out laughing.

"And history repeats itself," Kit said, shivering and laughing at the same time.

A deputy stepped out of the car. "Folks, you know the county park is closed, right?"

Tyler took a step forward, but Kit put a hand on his arm to stop him.

"Let me handle this. It's my turn." She took a couple steps toward the deputy, trying not to think about the fact that she was only wearing her wet bra and underwear. "It was my fault. I really wanted to go for a swim and I talked this man into going with me."

"There's a fine for being in the county park off hours, you know."

"I figured." Kit kept her voice as sweet as she could make it while her teeth chattered. "Would you mind if we got dressed while you write us the ticket?"

"We'd really appreciate it." Tyler was beside her, evidently not content to let her deal with this alone.

The deputy squinted at Tyler and in the light Kit saw that he was a rookie, probably not much above legal drinking age. "Are you... Hey, you're Tyler Ellis! I heard you were back in town." He came toward them with eager steps, holding out his hand to shake Tyler's enthusiastically. "I'm a huge fan, Mr. Ellis. It's a pleasure to meet you. Welcome back to Benson. The whole town is real proud of you."

"Why, thank you, deputy. I appreciate the warm welcome." Tyler's voice was as charming as ever, despite the situation. "Would you mind giving my friend and me a chance to get dressed? Then I'll come to your car to take care of that ticket."

"Tyler—"

"Hey, this was my idea," he lied, just like he had so many years ago. "Let me deal with it."

"Sounds good, Mr. Ellis," said the deputy.

"Call me Tyler, please."

"Okay, Tyler. You all get dressed now. I'll wait by my car."

They gathered their clothes from the beach and

ran to Tyler's truck. "Oh my gosh, put the heat on, please?" Kit begged as her skin made contact with the cool leather of the seats.

"Will do." Tyler turned the engine on and hit a few buttons. "Did I tell you how glad I am that I paid extra for the seat warmers?"

"I'm glad, too."

"Hang on." Tyler reached behind the seat and pulled out an old towel. "Use this." Kit grabbed it and dried off, while Tyler used his T-shirt to do the same. Warmth started to seep from the seats, slowing her chattering teeth.

Reaching for his jeans, Tyler glanced at her. "I've got to say, a night out with you, Kit Hayes, is never boring."

"I'm going to take that as a compliment."

His glance skimmed her body for a split second. "It is. It most definitely is."

She tried to ignore how much she liked it, when he looked at her that way. And how his muscles bunched in his arms and thighs as he pulled his jeans up. The sculpted contours of his shoulders, his back, his abs were all beautiful. She'd been wrong to think of him as pretty. *Pretty* implied feminine, and there was nothing girlish about his raw strength—great enough to take on a furious bull.

Somehow she focused on getting her clothes on.

"I'm going to talk to that deputy," he said.

"You should let me handle it. I owe you one from way back when."

"You can pay me back in more bartending lessons. I've got this." He reached across her lap to the glove compartment and pulled out a pen and a few bumper stickers with a bucking bull and the letters *PBR* across them. "These might come in handy." He tugged his jacket on over his shirtless chest, then was out the door.

Kit yanked her shirt over her head, then tugged on her socks and boots. Flipping down the visor, she glanced at her makeup, relieved that the promise of waterproof liner and mascara was genuine. She met her own eyes, almost black in the dim light. And smiled.

She'd done it. She'd jumped in a frozen lake at three in the morning, just because. Just to be awake. Just to make sure life wasn't passing her by. And she'd kissed Tyler. And it had felt amazing.

The door opened and Tyler was back, sliding into the driver's seat with an easy grace. "All right then, have you had enough excitement for tonight?"

"I think so. Thanks for taking the blame. Again."

"No problem. You're my..." He paused for a tiny second. "...my friend. I'm happy to do it. Plus, I got lucky that he's a fan."

"At least let me pay the ticket."

"There's no ticket." The tilt of his eyebrow, the

confident smile, told her how much he was loving this.

"What do you mean, no ticket?"

"I signed those bumper stickers, and he didn't mention the ticket."

Kit tried to take it in as Tyler pulled out of the parking lot. She kept forgetting who he was. To her, he was Tyler, her old friend. Her new, somewhat bumbling boss at the bar. The guy she couldn't stop thinking about. But to most of this town, and a lot of the world, he was a superstar. "Wow. You really are famous."

"To certain people, yeah." He glanced at her. "I take it you're not a big fan of bull riders."

"Maybe I am now," she teased.

"I kind of like that you don't see me the way the deputy does. You and Lila and everyone at the bar make me feel like a normal guy. I haven't felt that way in a long time. It's kind of a relief."

"So you don't like it when your adoring fangirls show up at the bar every weekend?"

"I'm not sure there's a guy in the world who'd complain about a bunch of pretty girls paying him a visit. I'm retired, not dead."

She couldn't help but laugh, despite the tiny edge of jealousy. Which reminded her of all the other jealousy she'd felt lately. "Can I ask you something?"

"Of course."

"Are you seeing someone?"

He glanced at her. "No. What makes you say that?"

"Bella said some woman was coming to your house. With dark hair?"

"That's Sheila, my reading tutor." He laughed. "Good to know that the Benson gossip machine is alive and well."

"Oh." Her cheeks went hot and she looked out the window, wishing she hadn't asked.

Tyler slowed, then pulled over at a wide gravel turnout alongside the road. "Can I ask you something?"

"Of course," she said, her heart pounding, as he unbuckled his seat belt and reached over to play with a lock of her hair.

"Why do you care if I have a girlfriend?"

It was the question she'd been afraid of. "I don't know," she whispered.

"I do." His hand slid to her shoulder, gently massaging her tight muscles. "Do you want me to tell you?"

"I'm not sure." She was being a coward. This thing she'd dreamed of was right in front of her now, but she couldn't find the courage or the craziness to reach for it.

"It's because you and me, we have this thing between us. This chemistry. It's there when we're working, and when we're at the barn or out riding.

And the more time we spend together, the more it grows. Haven't you noticed?"

"Yes," she breathed, closing her eyes against the intensity in his, so the only thing she felt was his hand, soothing all her sore spots, and his voice, wrapping her in sweet words.

"I've been trying so hard not to act on it, because I know you are focused on healing. And because you're leaving. But it's getting harder and harder not to touch you. Not to pull you close and kiss you."

His words permeated every pore of her skin, driving out the cold, making her feel every second of her breath and of his. Because he was closer now, his hands in her hair. She opened her eyes and freed herself from the seat belt so she could turn toward him.

"I don't want you to not touch me anymore." It was garbled enough to give him pause, but she saw when comprehension clicked. The way his eyes widened for an instant, then narrowed in on her mouth. Then his hands were in her hair and his mouth was on hers in a kiss so scalding she could feel the heat travel down her spine, over her chest. The fire of it had her grabbing on, to his shoulders, to his upper arms, to anything that would ground her. Because kissing him was like trying to hold on to something electric.

His hands slid to her back, pulling her as close

to him as he could in the awkward confines of the cab. His kisses rained heat on her mouth, her neck, her shoulders. He pulled away, brought his hands to her hair and fixed her with an intent gaze. "I want to start seeing you. I want us to be together. Can we do that?"

The reality of what he asked seeped through the heat like glacial melt. "I don't know." She slid away from him. "I don't know what to do. I'm leaving."

He dropped his head for a moment, as if her words had physical impact. "Yes, you are."

She didn't want to say no. Didn't want this incredible night to be her only chance to feel this way with him. "Can we think? About what to do?"

He let go, then moved toward his side of the cab. "We can. Though lately I feel like there's been too much thinking between you and me. Maybe we need to stop thinking and see this thing through. And take whatever consequences come with it."

"Like eight seconds on the bull?"

"Yeah," he said, putting the truck into Drive and pulling out onto the road. "Kind of like that." He reached over in the dark and found her hand, wrapping it in his. "Come on. I'll take you home. And you can do all the thinking you want."

TYLER HAD NO idea he could get so hooked on one person. His experience with women was limited to short-term relationships. And he'd never been too bummed when they ended. But something had changed when he moved to Benson. Maybe it was because he'd come home ready to put down roots. Or maybe it was something about Kit that made him want so much more than she was able to give.

All morning, he'd kept it businesslike between them, while memories of last night haunted him. Images of her body, dripping wet and shivery by the lake, warm and wanting in his truck, were branded on his mind. And the memory of how it had felt to finally kiss her was something he'd hang on to forever. He wished the kisses they'd shared had sated him somehow. Instead they'd made him want so much more.

But she wanted to think. Though how thinking would help them, he had no idea. Unless he could think of a way to make her stay, there was no solution for them. If only he could get her to *stop* thinking, convince her to just feel, she'd see what he saw so clearly. That they were meant to be together. That she should stay here with him.

Meanwhile, they had a bar to pack up. They'd officially closed today for the final stage of the renovation.

Most of the staff was here, boxing up the alcohol behind the bar and loading it in his truck, packing glassware, utensils and memorabilia into the storage unit he'd had delivered.

It seemed like Kit might be avoiding him, and he understood. Because for him, even being in the same building as her today was like walking on recently cooled lava. He knew he seemed calm on the surface. But under the thin, cool crust of his friendly facade were all of his molten feelings. All of his desire. Simmering away, keeping him on edge.

One positive was that the discomfort kept him working hard. The progress was gratifying. He'd single-handedly packed the office and moved all those boxes to the barn. They'd use the office there for the next few weeks.

He'd packed almost the entire storeroom liquor supply himself. It was amazing what you could do with a whole bunch of pent-up frustration. He grabbed a box from the stash in the main room and returned to the storeroom for another load.

He was wrapping bottles of dark rum when the door opened and Kit walked in with a bottle of liquor under each arm and one in each hand. "I found these behind the bar," she said. "Unopened."

Tyler was in front of her in an instant, reaching for the bottles in her hands.

"Not those. The ones under my arms, please."

Her words came out breathy, reminding him of her voice when he'd kissed her last night.

He reached for the bottles, sliding them out and setting them on the nearby shelf. She set her bottles down as well. She faced him, her eyes were huge in the dim light, searching his like she was looking for something, and damn if he knew what the hell he was supposed to give her. Because he'd laid it all out for her. How he wanted her. And all she'd said was that she needed to think.

"I want..." He couldn't find the words for all that he wanted from her.

"I know," she said quietly, her gaze not leaving his. "I know." She stood on tiptoe and kissed him, lightly, a breathy brush of lips to his, as if she were testing out how it might feel.

It felt incredible, but he forced himself to stay still and let her try it again. Maybe this was her method of thinking. Maybe she was curious to see if she still liked kissing him.

She seemed to come to some sort of decision, because her hands went to his neck and she tugged, so he leaned down, his mouth inches from hers. "Kiss me again," she murmured. "Like you did last night. If you want to."

His blood felt chaotic in his veins, there was so much want humming through him, around them, bringing the dead air of the storeroom to life.

"Of course I want to." His hands found her hair, his fingers wove through the silken lengths.

She didn't answer, not in words. Just parted her sweet lips in an invitation he couldn't possibly refuse.

She was so damn tiny and he remembered, in a hot instant, how her body had felt against his at the lake last night. How she'd felt so chilled, yet still fiery beneath his mouth. Then the memory of it blended into now as his lips touched hers again, as his hands held her, as the heat and softness of her registered in his brain. So familiar, so exotic, the taste and scent of her searing away everything except the feel of her under his mouth.

The door slammed into his back. "Where the hell is the—" Lila gasped. "Oh damn—" She dissolved into laughter. "I'm so sorry, you guys." Then she was gone, the door swinging on its abused hinges.

Kit moved away from him, her hand over her mouth.

"Come back." He reached for her, not caring about Lila or anything except feeling Kit in his arms again.

She shook her head, then went to the small mirror on the wall and ran a fingertip over her mouth to fix her lipstick. "This isn't the right time. Or place. We need to get back out there."

"When is the right time? Tonight?"

"I—I don't know."

He caught her hand before she could walk out. "Don't play games with me. Please?"

"I'm not trying to play games. I'm just... I just don't want to hurt you."

Frustration boiled over. "I'm fine. I don't need you to worry about me. It's you who asked for space to think. And I would have kept giving you that space. Except *you* came in here and kissed *me*."

She went pale at his words. "I'm sorry."

"You say you don't want to hurt me, but I think we need to call this what it is. *You* don't want to be hurt again. When you fell for Arch, it turned into this thing that messed with your head for the next decade. So you're scared to fall for me now. But don't let that fear rule you, Kit. If you do, then you're letting Arch ruin this thing between us, on top of all the other damage he already did in your life."

"It's not about Arch," she protested. "I'm over him."

"Yeah, I think you are," said Tyler. "But I *don't* think you're over the way he hurt you. And you can't have love risk-free, Kit. There's no such thing. So you have to decide if you're willing to take a risk with me or if you're going to keep hiding."

He turned away from her, breathing in gulps,

trying to get his frustration under control. He stayed that way, his back to her, until he heard the *whump* of the door swinging shut behind her, when she walked out of the room.

CHAPTER THIRTEEN

IT HAD BEEN a few days since their encounter in the storeroom, and time wasn't on Tyler's side. It was the end of August and Kit was leaving later in September—unless he could convince her otherwise.

And maybe he wouldn't convince her. But his heart felt like it was caught in a vise every time he thought of her flying away from him. Which was why he stood on her porch on this Wednesday morning, with a big bunch of daisies in his hand.

If he'd learned one thing from life, it was that when you fell off the bull, you got back on. You kept trying for your dreams. That belief had won him a world championship. Maybe it would win Kit's heart as well. If not, at least he'd know he'd given it his best shot.

She looked sleepy and surprised when she answered the door. "Tyler, what's up?" Then she spotted the flowers and looked even more confused. "What? For me?"

"Yes. I was hoping you'd go out with me today. On a date."

Her brows drew together. "Us dating makes no sense. I'm leaving soon."

"All the more reason to spend time together while you're here. Come on, Kit. I like you. A lot. I think that's pretty clear. And I think you like me. We're a hell of a lot more than friends already. So go out with me. Spend some time with me."

She laughed softly and covered her face with her hands. "I don't know."

"It's a perfect date. You won't be able to resist. We're going fish-bothering."

She dropped her hands and her smile widened. "Oh my gosh, I'd forgotten about fish-bothering. Are you serious? You have stuff for it?"

"In my truck. With a picnic. Get dressed?"

She glanced down at her faded pink flannel pajamas.

"Or you could go like that. I won't complain."

"Hang on. I'll get dressed."

"Here, take your flowers. Put them in water, maybe."

She took the daisies, breathing them in for a moment. "They're lovely. Thank you."

"Anytime."

"Okay, I'll go get dressed."

She disappeared into her white cottage and Tyler sat on the bench outside her door, trying to look casual when inside he celebrated. He'd taken a chance and it had paid off—he was one step closer to reaching his new dream. A life here in Benson with Kit by his side.

KIT PULLED ON shorts and a T-shirt, then rummaged for socks and a sun hat. She'd planned to stay away from Tyler. He'd been right in the storeroom—she *was* scared. The last time she'd loved someone it had taken her over a decade to recover. And she didn't remember Arch's kisses burning like Tyler's. She didn't remember such scorching longing from just a few whispered words. Tyler felt like something she might not ever find her way back from, and yeah, that was frightening.

But she'd missed him these past few days. So much. Her thoughts filled with those kisses, with an aching desire to kiss him again.

She might have been able to resist him, though. She was discovering that she could be pretty tough, especially when terrified. What she couldn't resist was him at her door with daisies, standing there with his straw cowboy hat shading his smiling green eyes. What she couldn't resist was him offering her a piece of their childhood. A chance to relive something that was special only to them.

Fish-bothering. Something in her stomach fluttered like butterflies. But she never got those. She grabbed a sweater, laced her hiking boots, then found a jar for her daisies. As she stepped out the door, Tyler rose from the bench and offered her his hand. He held it while they walked to his truck.

"You're not joking. This really is a date."

"You're slow," he teased, "but you get there eventually, don't you?"

"Next time you show up on my doorstep early, make sure you bring coffee along with the daisies."

He grabbed a steaming cup from the center console. "Like this, you mean?"

She accepted the cup, shaking her head. "You know me too well."

"Maybe. Though I'm looking forward to knowing you a lot better."

She took a sip, needing to take this one step at a time. The coffee was from her favorite café, hot and rich. "You didn't happen to get—"

"A croissant?" He indicated a brown paper bag. "Yup."

"How did you know?"

"I've seen the crumbs in the office," he said with the teasing grin she loved.

"Right. So you know one of my flaws."

"That you leave a trail of bread crumbs behind? Nah, that's not a flaw. It means I'll be able to find you when I need you."

Kit laughed, then dived into her croissant.

Tyler drove a few miles along the highway before he turned onto a dirt road. It got more rutted as they went on, Tyler steering the truck over bumps and ditches so big that Kit had to hang on to the handle above the window.

"We're off-roading?" She couldn't help laughing at the ridiculous way the truck rocked over the ruts, the two of them bouncing like popcorn kernels in a popper.

"We're heading to my favorite lake. I guess when I mentioned a picnic I forgot to say that it might be a challenge to get there."

"Just a small detail." She braced herself as the truck hit a steep rut.

"Hang on and enjoy the ride. I'm taking us where no deputy will find us."

"If I didn't know you well, I'd worry about that comment."

Tyler laughed, gripping the steering wheel tight as the rear tires skidded on the loose gravel of the wash. He navigated them up the opposite side and she was relieved to see the road ahead was hard-packed dirt, veering sharply toward the base of the mountains.

"It certainly has been an exciting date so far." She eased her vise grip on the handle.

"It's the next adventure, right?" The truck jostled over a few small boulders in the middle of the road.

"Or our next *bad*venture."

"Very funny," he said, pulling off onto a small side road and parking the truck. "We're here. Grab your coffee and I'll grab the rest."

TYLER WATCHED KIT sort through the pile of junk he'd brought and congratulated himself on coming up with the idea for this date. Her eyebrows were drawn together in arcs of concentration as she tied a paper clip and a feathered lure onto a piece of string. Then she tied the other end to the bamboo pole.

"I can't believe you thought of fish-bothering. This is so awesome."

"I thought you'd like it." He tied a length of string to his pole, then tied a few lures and a floater on the other end.

"When did we come up with this?"

"Miles and Parker took us fishing with them. And they caught a whole bunch of trout and you cried."

She flushed under her cute straw sun hat. "That's right. I wanted them to throw the fish back in but they started a campfire right there and cooked them up."

"And you went on a hunger strike." He shook his head at her in mock dismay. "You always were stubborn as hell."

"But you liked to fish, so you came up with this idea that we'd still fish, but we'd make sure we never caught anything so I wouldn't feel sad. You said that if we did catch a fish, it was so dumb that it deserved to be caught." She laughed as she stood and went to the lake's edge, where she executed an elaborate cast.

"And you named it fish-bothering," he finished, going to stand beside her. "Because we weren't going to catch them, just bug them a little."

She flashed him a smile. "I like our date so far. I can't think of anything better than being out in the mountains, by this pretty lake, bothering the fish. Thank you."

"Yes, ma'am." He tipped his hat at her for effect, because it made her laugh when he played up his cowboy image. And he wanted to see her laugh. He wanted to see her do anything, looking like this. It was so rare to see her fresh out of bed with no makeup on. Her skin was clear and pale, her eyes so dark they stood out on their own. The best? She looked at him like he mattered to her. A lot.

Damn, he had it for her bad.

They sat on the rock slabs that gave Granite Lake its name, letting the rising sun warm them.

At first she tried fish-bothering his way, holding the pole in one hand and tossing the line in the water with the other. But after a while she moved to lie on her stomach, on a big rock right at the edge of the lake. Her pole was beside her, her line trailing in the water.

"What are you doing?" he whispered, keeping quiet in case any fish were nearby.

"Fish-bothering the Kit Hayes way. Come try it."

He set his pole down, then lowered himself to the granite next to her.

"Look," she mouthed, pointing subtly.

From this angle he could see what she saw. The dark shadows of trout flickered through the water around her lure. They weren't biting, but they were curious.

He rested his chin on his folded hands and watched the fish. He was remarkably comfortable. Kit's sweet and spicy scent mixed with the clean air and the slightly dank smell of lake edge. The gurgling sound of lake water washing against rock was soothing.

He felt Kit's gaze on him and looked her way, dazzled by her smile, her small teeth so even and white behind lips so rarely this natural pink. Her cheek rested on her folded arms. She watched him, not the fish.

He wanted to kiss her, to show her how much this time together meant to him. But he didn't want to overstep and ruin anything. Having this day together was a precious gift he knew he had to handle with care. So he reached out his hand instead and she met him halfway, holding his big hand with her small one. And they remained that way, watching the shadowy trout, until it was time for lunch.

After lunch, they curled up on their blanket, and Kit let him wrap his arms around her, pulling her close, cradling her like two spoons in a drawer. He fell asleep, inhaling the sweet scent of her hair, feeling like everything he'd ever wanted was in his arms. And she slept, too, waking him when the sun had shifted behind the pines, casting a cool shadow over them.

He drove back to town slowly, and as soon as they were past the bumps, she slid over to sit beside him, her head on his shoulder. And Tyler didn't know when he'd felt more relaxed and happy and at peace with the world, as he did in that moment, driving to Benson with a sleepy Kit Hayes tucked under his arm.

KIT LOOKED AROUND the brand-new barbecue area at the Dusty Saddle, trying to take it all in. Tyler had strung fairy lights over the seating area, illuminating twenty-five new picnic tables scattered about.

He'd asked her to come outside, to admire his handiwork before they went out. It was her birthday, and he was taking her to dinner.

"You like it?"

"It's fabulous." She turned around slowly, absorbing the magical atmosphere he'd created. "On nights like this when it's so warm, customers will love sitting out here."

"Tonight would be a great night for that, too." He raised two fingers to his lips and let out a piercing whistle.

The door from the almost-finished kitchen burst open and people came pouring out of it. "Oh my gosh!" Kit exclaimed, stepping back in alarm.

Tyler caught her with an arm around her back as the crowd yelled, "Surprise!"

Lila was at the head of the group, a sparkly tiara in her hand. She set it on Kit's head. "Happy birthday, sweetie." She handed Kit a basket wrapped in layers of cellophane. "Don't open it here," she whispered when she hugged Kit. "It's adults-only."

"Thanks for the warning," Kit said, putting the basket on the table. "I can't believe you planned all of this."

"I had a little help." Lila shot a glance at Tyler and they high-fived.

Kit was swarmed with well-wishers. The entire staff of the Dusty Saddle was there, as well as high-school friends who'd stayed in the area. Her father was there, and Ethan, of course, and Gray, Tyler's new accountant, who was now living a few miles away in Mammoth. Aaron and his wife enveloped her in big hugs, as did the entire construction crew. Crater, Stan, Marcus and Doug had shown up, looking a little awkward until they got a beer in their hands and took over a picnic table slightly away from the crowd. Nora and Todd rushed in, excited to have a night out without the baby.

The new chef, Billy, fired up the barbecue and soon the aroma of steaks and burgers permeated the night. He'd prepared a huge buffet, and people filled their plates. Bella and their newest bartender, Ryan, inaugurated the outside bar, pouring beer and mixing drinks.

"I can't believe this," Kit said when she bumped into Tyler a while later. "I can't believe you did this for me."

"You can't? What better way to break in the barbecue area?" The smile he gave her was melting. She couldn't get used to it, even after all this time spent in his company. "When are you going to figure out that you matter to everyone here?"

"But still…this party." She watched wide-eyed as a DJ set up to one side. "It's just so much. When did you guys do this?"

He grinned. "Well, don't get me wrong, I loved our date yesterday and all. But Lila and Ethan did a lot of the party organizing while we were out at the lake."

"Sneaky," she said, giving him a light punch on

the arm. She didn't know how to act around him after their sweet date. They weren't a couple, so she was opting for slightly flirtatious colleagues right now.

"I know you've worried that you haven't lived a full life here in Benson," he said, lowering his voice so only she could hear. "But look around. All these people jumped at the chance to celebrate you. It was the easiest party to plan because everyone wanted to pitch in. People love you, Kit. You've made a big difference in this town."

She looked around the crowd, at all these people she knew, gathered in one spot, and her eyes flooded with tears. She'd been looking at her years in Benson as a waste. As time spent stuck. But all *this* had happened. These people, these connections had happened.

And Tyler had given her that knowledge. "Thank you!" She threw her arms around his neck, hugging him tightly. She felt him hesitate for a moment, then his arms encircled her back, so warm and strong that she clung tightly, for longer than colleagues would. He buried his face in her hair before he set her away from him.

"I'm sorry." She felt heat rise and coat her face. "I didn't mean to..."

"Didn't mean to what?" he prompted, and she noticed an intensity in his eyes. "Show everyone how we really feel? I'm ready to do that, Kit, whenever you are."

They'd taken things slow yesterday. Nothing more than a kiss he'd brushed across her cheek when he'd taken her home. A sweet and innocent interlude in the passion that had a grip on them. But she saw that passion in his eyes now and it thrilled her. She was getting used to it. Needing it. Thinking about it last night when she should have been sleeping. He was right. Maybe tonight was a good night to throw off some of their restraint.

Lila put a cosmopolitan in Kit's hand. "It's what all his groupies drink," she teased. "Plus, it's festive."

Glad for the distraction, Kit took a swallow of the sweet and sour cocktail, and swayed to the music the DJ had put on.

"Hey," Tyler said, "Before you go mingle, I have another surprise for you."

"Because all this wasn't enough?"

"It could never be enough," he said. "Not for you. Come on." He took her hand and led her to the bar, grabbed a glass and started tapping on it with a cocktail spoon. Slowly, conversation around them ceased and the music stopped.

"Many of you have wondered about the new name for this new bar of ours. Kit has been wondering most of all, and has come up with some pretty interesting suggestions." He glanced at her with a wink that had her grinning in return. She'd enjoyed coming up with those names.

"Well, tonight, in honor of her birthday, we'll end the suspense. The new sign is up, so if you all will head to the parking lot, you can join us for the unveiling."

A murmur of conversation rose from the crowd as they headed to the front.

"What is it?" She took his hand, tugging it like an impatient kid as they walked.

"You'll see."

"The Bucking Bull," she guessed. He shook his head.

"The Prickly Spurs."

"What?" He shot her an incredulous glance.

"The Last Rodeo." He kept walking, pulling her gently alongside him.

"Tyler's Groupie Gathering Place."

He stopped and took both her hands in his, laughing. "Try to be patient. I know it's hard for you, but no more crazy guesses."

He started walking again.

"Tyler's Taproom has a pretty good ring to it," Kit said, unable to resist making him crazy. Then they were in front of the building and up on the roof, far larger than the original sign, was a tarp. Aaron and a couple of his crew were up there, too. They waved cheerfully when they spotted her.

"Ready?" they called.

Tyler looked at her. "Are you ready?"

She nodded, too busy praying the name wasn't something she'd hate to actually answer.

Tyler gave the thumbs-up and the guys tugged on some ropes. The tarp slid down to reveal a sign that read The Dusty Saddle. The letters were framed in sheet metal and lit with big lightbulbs. It had a very cool vintage look to it. A neon saddle, blinking on and off, tilted near the final *e*.

Everyone started clapping. A few people cheered. "So?"

She could hear the worry in Tyler's voice. But she wasn't sure she could speak because there were tears. "You…" She had to stop and clear her throat. "You did that? For me?"

"It's a good name."

"But I thought…all the changes you've made… that you wanted it to be completely different?"

He shrugged. "I did. But that was before you taught me that some things are fine the way they are."

She threw her arms around his neck for the second time that night. And squeezed tight, gratitude filling her heart. "Thank you," she said into his shoulder. "Thank you for listening to me."

"Sometimes," he added when she pulled away, making her laugh.

"Yeah, sometimes. But those times mean a lot." She let herself lean against him and take comfort when he slid an arm around her shoulders. They stood side by side, admiring the new sign, and the new old name. People lost interest and wandered back to the party, and there in the parking lot, under that amazing sign, he lowered his head and kissed her, gently, on the lips.

"Careful," Kit whispered. "Kissing is dangerous for us."

"I remember," he murmured, and wove his hands through her hair, holding her steady while his mouth ravished hers for a very long time.

TYLER WALKED AROUND the barbecue area, picking up beer bottles. It was after midnight and the party was winding down. Small groups of people were scattered around the picnic tables, laughing and talking. The DJ was packing up, but had left a country music mix playing. Billy and the kitchen staff had cleaned up the food a long time ago.

It had been an incredible party. Though he and Kit had missed a full half hour of it making out in the parking lot. Which, come to think of it, was his favorite part of the evening by far.

Suddenly he heard a round of applause from the mechanical bull arena and a bunch of voices whooping and hollering. And a few distinct cries of "Go, Kit!"

He set down his box of bottles, then jogged across the barbecue area, up the steps to the deck, and popped his head into the door of the newly built arena that housed the mechanical bull.

Kit sat astride the bull, wearing someone's straw cowboy hat on her head. Her tight black top accentuated every curve. And her cute red cowboy boots peeped out from the hem of her jeans.

Tyler stumbled a few steps forward, mesmerized. He spotted Lila in the crowd, and Bella, but he couldn't help notice that there were a lot of guys in here. Guys whose eyes were fixed on Kit. Because her straddling that bull was about the sexiest thing imaginable.

He had half a mind to pull her off, but the concentration on her face showed that she was determined to see it through. Ernie was at the controls and Tyler put a hand on his shoulder. "Take it easy, okay?"

Ernie nodded. Kit's arm went up, the signal that she was ready. Her other hand clutched the bull.

Ernie eased the lever forward and the bull started moving. Tyler was pretty sure the silence in the room was the collective breath held by every guy in the place.

The slow-motion bucking was downright erotic. Kit was good. Ernie cranked it up and the bull turned and dived and turned the other way, and she stayed on no problem. Making it look easy. Making it look like a lot more than just bull riding. He was torn between pride and a protective feeling so extreme that he had to shove his fists in his pockets to keep him from unplugging the entire contraption. Instead he elbowed Ernie. "It's been way more than eight seconds."

Ernie emerged from his trance, hit the buzzer and stopped the bull. Kit slid off, hands raised in the air in triumph. And the collective breath slid out in a sigh. Conversation resumed and the music started up again and Tyler felt like something in his DNA had been altered. Or maybe it had happened a long time ago but he was only noticing now. Noticing that there would never be another woman on this planet he wanted more than he wanted Kit Hayes.

It was late, the party was clearing out, and Kit, standing on the deck and swaying to the music in his arms, leaned away and covered her mouth to hide a yawn.

"You're exhausted," Tyler said. There were shadows under her eyes he hadn't noticed before. They lent a vulnerability to her face that he'd almost never seen. "Let me drive you home."

"No, I'm fine." She yawned again. "But I think I need to leave, if you don't mind."

He wasn't letting her travel the dark roads half-asleep, even if she lived close by. "I'll drive you. Then you can give me your car keys and I'll stop by here on my run in the morning and take your car to your house."

"I'm not sure I want your sweaty self in my car," she said with her teasing smile.

"Kit, I'm serious. Let me drive you home."

She yawned a third time. "Okay."

She said goodbye to some friends while Tyler checked in with Lila and Tim, who said they'd oversee cleaning and locking up. Then he took Kit's elbow to guide her to his truck. Halfway there, Lila's voice stopped them, calling, "Kit, wait!"

They turned and Lila jogged up with the present in her hands. "Hey, thought you might need this," she said with a wink, pressing the basket into Tyler's arms.

"Lila!" Kit protested, grabbing the basket from Tyler.

"What? Just looking out for you." Lila planted a kiss on Kit's cheek, then went back to the bar, her laugh trailing.

"Girlfriends," Kit said in explanation and set the basket in the back of his truck.

Inside the cab, she shivered, so he put his jacket around her. The feel of her small shoulders under his hands, the action of wrapping her up, stirred a tenderness in him that he'd been trying to keep below the surface. This is what he wanted to do all the time. To look after her. To be the one to keep her warm when the cold bit in.

She was biting her lip and he remembered how tired she was. The reason she was in his truck right now. He reversed and drove out of the parking lot, heading toward her house in silence. He tried to slow his breath, to calm the intense need to know what she wanted and what, if anything, could happen between them. To cool the heated memories of their kisses earlier tonight, and how she'd looked riding that fake bull. He tried to be satisfied with this. Kit, sleepy and happy after her party, riding in his truck. Watching the dark night flow by with half-open eyes. Trusting him to take care of her and get her home safely.

This might be all they had, and it had to be enough.

CHAPTER FOURTEEN

TYLER TRIED TO focus on the county road that ran around the edge of Benson, keeping an eye out for Kit's street. But he could feel her gaze on him. He glanced her way, wondering if she wanted to talk.

"Could you pull over?" Her voice was a surprise in the silent dark.

Tyler slowed onto the shoulder of the road. "Are you okay?"

"I am." She unhooked her seat belt and slid across the seat to him. "But I want to kiss you."

His breath faltered into tiny wisps of oxygen. Her hands slid gently from his jaw to the nape of his neck, and he obeyed when she pulled him softly toward her, toward that mouth he'd dreamed of kissing over and over, toward the satin skin he'd imagined touching again.

He slid a hand carefully into her pretty hair and knew, with the first whisper of her lush soft lips under his, that he was in trouble again. Because what he felt couldn't be tamed with a kiss. Instead it roared out of the cage he'd been keeping it in all evening. Her mouth was ajar, her dark eyes widening to soulful pools as he pulled away, shaking.

He fumbled for the emergency brake, shoved the gearshift into what he hoped was Park, threw off his seat belt and kissed her again. He lowered his hands to trace the line of her waist. When his hands cupped the curve of her full hips he swore the planet tilted a little on its axis.

Somewhere in all the spinning and the heat of her kisses and the bliss of her tongue as it brushed his, he slid toward her, pulling her onto his lap, deepening the kiss, finding the softness that she hid behind her quick wit and sharp words.

She did something to that part of his brain that reminded him to be cautious with her. She must have felt the same mindless need because she shifted, straddling him. His fingers sought the snap at her waist, unzipping her jeans, needing access to her softest skin there. Then he realized what he'd done and broke away from her blinding kisses, rested her head on his shoulder, grabbing oxygen with each gasping breath.

"Is it too much? Jeez, Kit, this thing between us…"

He could feel the resonance of her low laugh against his shoulder. "It's fine. It's good. Really good."

Gratitude at her reassurance steadied him and her full lips drew him back for more. He kissed her slowly, forcing his hands to stay where they were, losing himself in her breath, in her sweet mouth, in the white-hot heat that seared whenever she shifted her weight over his lap.

A sudden light flooded the cab, causing them to freeze, then a harsh loudspeaker voice blasted the nighttime. "Roll down your windows and remain inside the vehicle."

"You've *got* to be kidding me." Kit's eyes were wide as she slid off him, pulling at her shirt, zipping her jeans, smoothing her hair, tugging his jacket back in place over her shoulders.

Tyler slid to the driver's side, his mind blank with disbelief that this was really happening. Again. He rolled down the window.

Somehow the deputy must have decided that his massive floodlights weren't enough illumination because, as he approached, he used a bright flashlight to wipe out what was left of Tyler's vision. "Everything okay in here?" he asked. "No way!" He lowered the light, and Tyler squinted past the multicolored dots decorating his retinas to see it was the same deputy they'd encountered at the lake.

"Hey," he said weakly.

The deputy peeked into the car. "Nice to see you again, ma'am."

Kit, in typical Kit-style, burst out laughing. "I wish I could say the same."

"Do you folks actually have a home? Because I think you need to spend some more time indoors," the deputy drawled, a slow grin lurking around his boyish mouth.

"At this point, I couldn't agree more," Tyler said.

"Ma'am, I assume you're okay? Do you need anything?"

"Besides privacy?" Kit shook her head. "No, I'm just fine, thanks."

"Look, I'm not going to give you a ticket, but it's late. And it seems like whatever you're doing probably shouldn't be done at the side of a public road. I'll just tell you to head on home now."

"I appreciate that." Tyler put his hand on the gearshift. "We'll get going now."

"Not sure who you're going home to," the deputy added. "But you might want to rub off that lipstick before you get there."

Tyler glanced at himself in the rearview mirror. Kit's lipstick was everywhere. On his mouth, his cheeks, across his nose.

He glanced at her and she dissolved in peals of laughter. She pulled a packet of tissues from her purse. "Sorry about that."

Tyler wiped his face, knowing he probably smeared red everywhere. "How many bumper stickers would it take for you to not tell this story to everyone you know?"

The deputy grinned. "I'm not sure there are enough bumper stickers in the world for that. But I'd take a nice night out at that restaurant you're opening."

"Done." Kit said it the same moment Tyler did.

"Well, I'll see you around, then," the deputy said. "Though hopefully not in the middle of the night."

"I'm not sure we can promise that," Kit said. "We do get off work pretty late."

"I guess I'll look forward to many good meals at the Dusty Saddle, then. Drive safely now."

They listened to his footsteps crunching over the roadside gravel. To the slam of his car door and the blur of his lights as he pulled away. "Unbelievable." Despite his humiliation, Tyler felt a grin spreading across his face. "I think it's a sign."

"I agree." Kit shoved her thoroughly mussed hair from her face. "It's a sign that we cannot be trusted after dark."

"Or maybe it's a sign that we should take this thing between us indoors."

He waited, pulse thudding, for her response. Finally a smile tipped up the corners of her mouth. "You know, I think you might be right. Want to come over?"

"Uh-huh."

"Then what are you waiting for?"

"I have no idea." He buckled his seat belt and

stepped on the gas, and got them to her cottage in no time. Jumping out, he raced to open her door, and she slid into his arms. He kissed her long and slow. Then he pulled away to lock up his truck. "It's always a pleasure getting busted by the sheriff with you," he teased her. "But I'll be glad for some privacy."

She glanced around. "Let's go in. He's a nice guy but he has a bad habit of showing up right when things get interesting."

He followed her toward her front door. "Is that what this is between us? Interesting?"

She shot him a look so full of promise it almost brought him to his knees. "I think it's going to be very interesting," she said.

KIT LED TYLER into her house feeling that nothing was ever going to be the same again. Because even though this thing between them couldn't last, it mattered. And it burned hot enough to alter the very chemistry of her being.

He shut the door behind them. And her small hallway suddenly felt a whole lot smaller.

But she'd invited this. She wanted this. And what the hell, if she was going to risk so much of her heart she might as well burn up in the process. So she reached for his shirt. Pulled it over his head. And pointed down the hall.

He looked dazed. Happy. He nodded and led the way.

She watched the muscles of his back as he walked. The way his jeans clung to him so well. It hit her then. His butt was world famous. Adorning billboards and magazines for jeans and underwear across the globe. The thought brought a smile to her face. It was a really, really nice butt.

"Left," she breathed, when he hesitated in the hall, unfamiliar with her home. That one word was hard to form, she was so mesmerized by him.

In her bedroom he stopped, as if not sure what to do next. So she did it for him. Kicking off her boots, pulling off her top, her jeans, while he watched intently. In bra and panties, she slid into the smooth cotton sheets. Watched as he pulled off his clothes, desire stopping her breath when he stood before her, stark naked and glorious.

She made room for him, and gasped as he lay down beside her, the feel of his skin against hers so foreign but so delicious. She faced him on her side, her fingertips skimming his hair, the faint ridge of his cheekbone. He kissed them as they passed his mouth, a featherlight kiss that sent shivers.

"Are you good?" he asked.

"Very," she assured him. Now that they were here, now that this was happening, she knew it was right. If she was never with him, if she never followed these feelings to this outcome, she'd always regret it.

She ran her fingers over his chest, tracing a scar there. "I didn't notice this before."

That scar said he'd come close to dying a few times. That he could have been like Gray, stuck in a wheelchair forever. She fought the fear for him that made no sense after the fact.

He must have seen her distress because he took her hand and kissed the palm. Then placed it on his heart. She traced the arc of his ribs, the solid wall of his abs. He watched her with narrowed eyes, his breathing hitching as she skimmed the top of his hip. Then he rose on an elbow to slide his lips over her mouth, to push insistently for a deeper kiss. He wove his fingers through her hair and leaned so she rolled onto her back. His hand cupped her breast, his fingers traced the satin of her bra and his lips caught her low moan.

He found the clasp of her bra and released it, catching the strap and sliding it down one arm. She helped, reached for her panties, wanting them gone, unable to stand anything between them any longer.

His hands traveled restless over her skin.

"You're incredible," he whispered in her ear, his warm breath waking every nerve there, tuning all her senses only to him. His voice, his kisses, his hands as they heated her skin and slid across her stomach, her hip, between her legs. She moved into his touch, his circling fingers pure, thought-destroying sensation.

He paused and she opened her eyes, his slight smile coming into focus. His words came out on ragged breath. "Protection."

Oh, that. How could she have invited a man over and not thought of that? She put a hand over her forehead. "I don't have any." Then she remembered. "Lila's basket. It's in the truck."

"I'm on it." He jumped up, naked, and disappeared down the hall. She heard the front door open, and after a pause, slam shut. Then Tyler was back, diving into bed with chilled skin and the basket in hand.

Kit lay back, hand to mouth, giggling. "I can't believe you went out there. Naked. Did anyone see you?"

His grin was unrepentant. "I didn't stop to find out. I had more important business to attend to." He untied the ribbon that held the cellophane shut.

"Lila said it was adults-only." Kit sat up and peered in. She pulled out a box that looked promising. Until she read the label. "Vibrating egg?" She cast it aside.

Tyler picked it up and examined the box with interest. "This could be fun." He gave it a little shake. "My friends never give me presents like this."

Kit laughed. "I think she wanted me to get out more. I guess I've been a little boring lately."

Tyler leaned over and kissed her bare shoulder. "Not a word I'd ever use to describe you. And this thing, by the way, is for staying in. I don't know what our deputy would say if he found us out and about with a vibrating egg."

Kit giggled and dumped the basket, ignoring the tubes of massage cream and a packet of edible panties in favor of the neon pink condom packets. "There."

"Are you sure you don't want to try these?" Tyler held up the panties.

"Another time." She tried to ignore the hollow feeling that they probably didn't have too many other times. She was leaving soon.

Tyler took the condom packets from her and set them on the nightstand. He scooped up the other contents, tossed them in the basket and set it on the floor. "Now, where were we?" he said, and she saw that his smile had gone feral, no more jokes and teasing.

He kissed her down onto the bed, continued down her body, erasing all her thoughts of being anywhere but here, under his hot mouth and his generous hands. He loved her until there was only one feeling—a consuming, aching need for him.

When she asked, in a voice she barely recognized as hers, he ripped open the hot-pink wrapper and sheathed himself. He kissed her, exploring her mouth, taking his time, until she tasted only him, breathed only him, felt only the weight of his hard body over hers, and then, better than anything she'd ever known, the strength of him within her.

Mindlessly, her body followed the rhythm he set, as if she'd always known it, as if she'd always followed it while they'd worked and talked and teased over the past months. His strength had been hers lately and nothing changed now as he murmured "so beautiful" again and again in her ear, as she kissed his neck, his shoulder and finally, clung to him, his kisses catching her cries before they left her lips.

Afterward he held her close, her head on his chest, kissing her hair, caressing her shoulder. She was grateful he said nothing. There was nothing to say in the face of this new knowledge. That there was some spark so fiery, some emotion so intense between them, that Kit had seen tears in his eyes to match her own.

TYLER WOKE TO sunlight streaming across a tumbled bed. He cracked an eye to see Kit, curled next to him. The white sheets and comforter had been kicked partway off to reveal her creamy skin, her black hair spilling all around her. Her lashes made dark crescents; the hollow of her neck was another shadow, and he resisted the urge to kiss it.

He pulled the sheet over her to cover the million temptations she presented, naked, next to him. He needed to let her sleep. She'd let him love her over and over last night. A night that came to him in a series of images, of remembered desire so strong he felt like no matter how many times he kissed her, or how many ways he made love to her, it wouldn't lessen, wouldn't slow.

Rolling onto his back, he pinched his finger and thumb between his tired eyes. The fact was, the more he made love to her, the more he wanted her. That hadn't been the plan. When she'd invited him over, he'd been elated and relieved. Because he'd thought maybe, if they finally acted on all the tension between them, it would lessen. And with less desire, maybe there would be less love. And maybe he'd be able to function when she was gone.

Now he knew the opposite. The more he'd touched her, the more he was connected to her by invisible threads of desire, of understanding, of a deep knowledge of who she was and how he loved her.

He glanced around the room, bright in the morning sun that the filmy white curtains did nothing to dilute. He'd been surprised when he first saw it. Kit, with all her black leather and dark makeup, with the exotic tattoos he'd traced with his tongue last night, had a bedroom that was all innocence. A white wrought iron bed, white sheets…a small bouquet of pink roses on the nightstand.

He was reminded of some kind of shellfish. A mussel with its inky dark shell. The hardened image she showed the world hid a delicate, fragile inner creature. It was humbling that she showed that part of herself to him.

She stirred, sighing in her sleep. Then her thick lashes fluttered, opened, and her dark eyes, unfocused at first, homed in on him. "Oh." They widened. "Hi."

"Hi." Her confusion was adorable and he rolled to face her, to touch the satin of her hair and push the wayward strands behind her ear. But that ear was so sweet, pink and perfectly curved, he kissed it, then her cheek, then her mouth. She gave a whimper as his tongue met hers that launched him on a journey across her incredible body, to find other places that sparked that sound, his hands intent on memorizing her curves, his mouth following his fingers to her breasts, to her belly, to the curve of her hip and down to taste the sweet and salt of her.

She tugged his arm and grabbed the last ridiculous pink condom off the nightstand, and it was the only hint he needed to lose himself inside her, to feel her hands across his back, pulling him closer and deeper until there was nothing but her. Her faint spicy perfume his oxygen, her small gasps his need, her eyes a window into the only world he wanted to live in.

When they lay tangled in damp sheets, when she curled against him like she was made to fit with his body, her voice uncoiled in the silence. "You're better than I thought, you know."

He met her dark gaze and saw how the humor lit her up, tilted her mouth in that sexy, sassy way he'd fallen in love with. "What do you mean? You thought I'd be bad at this?"

Her shoulder rose in a faint shrug. "I didn't know. I mean, you're always talking about those eight seconds…"

He laughed and kissed her teasing mouth, ran his hands over her body, tracing the curve of her waist, the rise of her hips. "I'll show you eight seconds. And then I'll show you eight more and another eight…"

Her mouth found his, demanding his silence with a passion he could feel all the way to his heart. He'd give her the most memorable seconds he could. He'd sear his touch onto her skin, brand himself on her soul, so maybe she'd stay. Or, if she left, she'd remember him. And hopefully, when she was ready, she'd know where her home was and whom she belonged with, and she'd come back to him again.

CHAPTER FIFTEEN

KIT LOOKED AROUND the new and improved Dusty Saddle, trying to take it all in. The rebuilt shelves and brand-new taps were so clean and professional; the refinished bar gleamed in the new overhead barn lights. The brown leather stools she and Tyler had picked out looked fantastic.

Tonight was opening night. Then her job was done. But she was trying not to think about that. Because the past few weeks with Tyler had been incredible, and they made her want to stay.

Fortunately, she had no time to think right now. She was still trying to train the bar staff in tonight's signature cocktail. The Fall Fantastic. Spices and whiskey that, when combined, was like drinking potent pumpkin pie.

Glancing around to make sure she had everyone's attention, Kit cut a strip of orange peel into a perfect spiral then held it up. "Behold, the garnish." Lila and Tim clapped. The three of them had come up with the orange spiral together, outvoting Mario, who wanted some kind of plastic pumpkin in the drinks.

The eight bartenders-in-training each had a paring knife and a cutting board with an orange on it. Kit held up her orange and demonstrated again. "Don't cut the skin too thick or it won't curl."

It had to be perfect because tonight was special. An invitation-only event. Tomorrow they'd open to the general public and Tyler's version of the Dusty Saddle would be officially up and running.

Kit walked around to inspect everyone's handiwork. "Okay, now let's talk about muddling. Slice half an orange and put the pieces in the shaker. Start squishing the fruit with your muddler, twisting your wrist a little."

Tyler walked in at that moment. Ran in, more like it, skidding to a halt beside her. "Did I miss the lesson?"

"You can sit there." She pointed to an empty table with an orange and a knife.

He leaned closer, trying to speak quietly. "Did you check with the kitchen about food for the staff party?"

She could feel his breath heating her neck, heating other things, too. "Yeah, they're doing trays of finger food. And I paid the DJ to stay."

He grinned. "When should we tell them the last two hours of their shift is a party?"

"Let me make sure they all have this cocktail down first. Then you can break the good news."

"I better get on it, then." Tyler picked up the paring knife and the orange. "I don't want to fail the Kit Hayes master bartending exam."

"That would be terrible," she said, laughing. "A blow to your career from which you'd never recover."

He started slicing while Kit surveyed the room and decided the oranges were muddled enough. "Okay, everyone, over to the bar, please. I need each one of you to demonstrate how you make this drink."

Tyler presented her with a perfectly coiled orange peel. "Do you have time for a break after this?"

Kit's blood heated at his suggestive tone. It had been hard to stay professional these past few weeks, when they'd slipped away from work as often as possible to be together. Their relationship had been tucked between long days and nights of hard work, a patchwork of incredible stolen moments…kisses in the storeroom, late nights and early mornings tangled in her bed or his.

Kit glanced at her to-do list. "I do have something about a quickie on here."

Tyler grinned. "I like your thinking. Can we really make time?"

"Are you kidding me?" She elbowed him gently. "It's opening night. Everything has to be perfect."

He glanced at the bar staff, then planted a quick kiss on her cheek. "I'll have to wait, I guess."

"Yes, you will. But if I'm still awake after closing, I'll make it worth your while."

"If you're still awake… Honey, I'll make sure you're wide awake—"

"Kit!" Tim called. "My cocktail looks like vomit."

She stepped away from Tyler's caressing words, wanting everything that he was promising, right now. "I'll be right there," she called to Tim. And reached for Tyler's hand to feel a moment of his skin on hers before she went back to work.

TYLER ALLOWED HIMSELF a few moments to walk through the various rooms of the Dusty Saddle. The whole place looked fantastic. From the colorful lights strung over the dance floor to the dark masculine colors of the sports bar, Kit's magic touch was everywhere. He stopped in the kitchen to make sure Chef Billy had all that he needed. The energy was high, the prep cooks' knives flying as they chopped. Billy cursed—worthy of a pirate—as he urged them to go faster, to be more careful, to be ready.

Tyler glanced at his watch, stunned at how quickly the time had passed this afternoon. He had ten minutes to get dressed for the opening. He jogged to his truck for his clothes and then to the men's room to change and was at the office in time to see Kit walk out and knock him even more breathless.

She was always gorgeous. His definition of beauty. But he'd never seen her in the burgundy dress that wrapped around her curves as if it had been designed for her. He'd never seen her in black high heels, with thin straps around her ankles. Part of her hair was pulled up with a clip; the rest cascaded down her back in waves.

"Too much?" A flush formed on her cheeks. "I wasn't sure."

"Not too much." His voice came out sounding like a rusty gate. "You look great. Just…really great." Although he'd found his voice, he hadn't located many words yet. *Great* didn't cut it, but it was all he had.

She gestured to his black jeans and his black Western shirt with white trim. "The man in black. You look nice, too."

"Thanks." There was an awkward beat of silence between them. Like she wanted to say something else. He did, but he couldn't say any of the thoughts that tangled in his mind. Because they all had something to do with how he didn't want her to leave. He settled for, "I'm so grateful for you."

She flushed pink. "But this is all yours. Your bar. Your big night."

He reached for her hand. Held it tight in his own. "I could never have made it happen without your help. You saw me struggling and you helped. Even before I offered you that bonus, you reached out to me."

"I was difficult."

"You saved me. Kit, this is your night, too."

She blinked and looked away, as if she were fighting tears. When she finally looked at him he could see them glittering in the brown depths of her eyes. "You've changed everything for me, too. And for my dad. Everything is better because of you."

His throat clogged. So he didn't try to talk. Just tucked her hand under his arm. Loving how she stepped close to his side and leaned on him just a little.

"Ready to go greet our guests?" she said.

He nodded. Cleared the emotion out of his throat. "Let's do this thing."

They unlocked the doors together. Opening night had begun. And he was so glad to have Kit right by his side.

Crater, Stan and a few of their miner buddies were the first to arrive. Tonight Crater sported an old plaid blazer over his usual plaid shirt. And Stan had a tie on. An odd orange tie, but Kit gave them both a big hug, touched by their efforts. "Can we get you a drink?" she asked.

Crater looked a little sheepish. "Stan and I, and a few of the others, we're gonna start our night in this new restaurant of yours. Then we'll come to the bar after."

Kit took his arm. "Well, let me walk you over and make sure you get the best seat in the house."

She left them in the hostess's capable hands, then strolled back, stopping to shake hands with various people she knew. Then someone came through the door, so familiar in his shabby suit, and her heart swelled. "Dad." She rushed over to give him a hug. He looked out of place, clutching his dressier cowboy hat. "I just came by for a quick tour. I won't stay."

She took him to Tyler to say hello, then they wandered the rooms together. She pointed out all the changes they made while her dad said, "Well, I'll be..." every time. She tried to persuade him to stay, but he said no and left. But not before giving her a pat on the cheek and saying, "I'm proud of you. You know that, right?" For the second time that evening, she had to blink back tears.

A dark-haired woman caught her arm, saying, "You must be Kit. I'm Sheila. Tyler's tutor. And this is my husband, David."

Kit flushed. The woman she'd been so jealous of was pretty and middle-aged, with a tall, gray-haired man on her arm.

"Oh my goodness, so nice to meet you." She squeezed Sheila's hand. "You've changed Tyler's life."

"From the way he speaks about you, I think I can say the same," Sheila said. "The place looks great. I hear you had a lot to do with the design."

Kit nodded, realizing that this might be her only chance to tell Sheila what she truly felt. "I've known Tyler since we were kids. I saw the problems he had in school. The problems he had when he first started here. I can't thank you enough for helping him."

Sheila flushed. "Now don't make me cry. I'm a teacher. I'm just doing my job." She gave Kit a quick hug. "We'd better get to the restaurant for our dinner reservation. How exciting to have a new place to eat."

"Enjoy," Kit said, liking this woman immensely. "I'll come by in a bit to make sure everything is just how you like it."

Sheila gave her a bright smile and David inclined his head. "Great to meet you, Kit. Good luck tonight."

"Thanks."

Tyler appeared at her side. "It's crowded. I can't believe everyone showed up." His smile widened even more as his brothers walked in. Then his expression dimmed and Kit knew why. There was no one behind them. His father hadn't come to opening night.

She watched, heart aching, as Tyler reassembled his smile and walked toward Miles and Parker for high fives and manly, backslapping hugs. Fury sent her pulse thrumming. Why couldn't his father see all that his son had to offer? She glanced around. Everything was running smoothly. People had drinks in their hands, smiles on their faces. She made her way through the crowd and grabbed her purse and coat from the office. With one last glance to make sure Tyler didn't see her, she ducked through the front door and out into the night.

THE BLUE GLOW of the television lit the living room of the Ellis family's big ranch house. The anger that had propelled Kit over the dark roads raced even hotter in her veins. She parked in front of the house and ran up the porch steps, knocking loudly on the door.

When Tyler's dad opened it, she let him have it. "I can't believe you'd rather watch TV than attend the opening night of your son's business."

"What are you doing here?" Ken looked older, more tired than she'd ever seen him. Or maybe it was the blue bedroom slippers he wore on his feet.

For a brief horrified moment, she wondered if he'd stayed home because he was ill. Then her anger kicked in again. "You should be at the Dusty Saddle. To congratulate Tyler on his new business."

"I'm not fond of bars. And I'd appreciate it if you'd let me get back to my show."

He went to close the door, but she blocked it with her hand. "I'd appreciate it if you'd get dressed and get down to your son's bar to say congratulations. Do you have any idea how hard he's worked? What he's had to overcome to learn to run a bar?"

"I'm sure Tyler makes a very good bartender." Ken's face was pinched like he smelled something bad. "He doesn't need me to tell him that."

"But that's the thing. He does need you. He needs you to *see* him. To accept him and appreciate him for who he is. You don't need to stay long. Walk around the place once, then leave. That's all my dad did, but it meant a lot to me."

At the mention of her father, Ken's eyes narrowed. "Well, I'm sure if your father came by, then Tyler's just fine."

It hit her, what this might be about. "You're upset because my dad and Tyler are friends?"

"I'm not upset about anything," Ken said. "Except I'm tired of you coming by here and getting involved in my life."

"Well, I wouldn't get involved in your life if you weren't always hurting the people I love." She felt the truth of her words, weighing warm and heavy in her heart. She loved Tyler.

Everything suddenly felt a little off. Like the world had tipped and she was having trouble getting her balance. "Just come by, Mr. Ellis. Maybe you're upset because you weren't very involved in Tyler's life. Or maybe you're upset because my dad was. Either way, it doesn't mean you can't be there for your son now."

She ran for her Jeep and drove toward the Saddle, her thoughts whirling and circling. She loved Tyler. She'd tried not to think about her feelings for the past few weeks. She was leaving, so she couldn't let their relationship mean more than simply time spent with an amazing man. But here she was. She loved him.

And she had no idea how she would walk into the bar and pretend everything was fine. Because even if she loved him, she couldn't let love keep her in Benson like it had before. She still had to get on that plane and leave, no matter what.

TYLER TRIED TO focus on what the mayor was saying. Something about what a great place the Dusty Saddle was and how happy he was that Tyler had invested in the community. But the whole time the mayor talked, Tyler looked for Kit. This was his bar, but it was their achievement. Without her by his side, it didn't feel quite as exciting.

Then he saw her, wrapped in her black coat, stepping quietly through the door and heading for the office. A moment later she came out, minus her coat, and walked over to the bar.

He excused himself and made his way over to her. "Everything okay?" he asked, startled when she jumped.

"Oh, hi! Everything is fine." Her voice had a shrill note he'd never heard before. "I needed to take care of something really quick. I'm back now. Hard at work. Yours for the rest of the evening."

Her sunny tone rang false. Something was bothering her, but it was clear that she wouldn't tell him what it was.

"I'm going to make the rounds," she said. "Make sure everyone is doing okay."

"I thought I'd do the same." He wanted to walk the bar with her. To celebrate all they'd achieved working together.

"Great idea." She gave him a light shove toward the restaurant. "I think Billy wanted to talk to you. Go see him in the kitchen and I'll check on the sports bar."

And she was gone, her heels clicking briskly on the wood floor, her tight dress accentuating every sway of her hips.

If Billy needed to speak with him, he'd better get going. But he sure would like to know what was bothering Kit.

When he ran into her again, ten minutes later, she was leaning on the wall at the entrance to the room with the mechanical bull. The contraption bucked and lunged while a young guy in a flannel shirt clung to its back.

"You were right," Kit said as he approached. "It's a huge success."

The bull swung to the left and the man went flying off, crash-landing in the padding below. "And you were wise to talk me into that huge insurance policy," Tyler said, wincing. He gave a thumbs-up to Ernie, who'd decided that operating the bull was more fun than being a bouncer.

"It's going to be a big hit." Kit pointed to the next wannabe bull rider—a young woman whose friends were in fits of laughter, snapping photos with their phones as she scrambled on.

"Hmm... How was it first described to me?" he teased. "What was that word? Oh yes...*tacky.*"

The look she gave him promised retribution, but he was glad to see her spirit back. Whatever had made her so anxious when she returned from her mysterious errand seemed to have been taken care of. "It's still tacky," she shot back. "But what can you do? There's no accounting for some people's taste."

"You tried it. Did pretty well on it, if I remember right."

"Oh, I'll try anything once." The husky tone

he loved laced her words with extra meaning. Or maybe it was just him reading things into every word with her, because she had his mind wandering, always, to what they did in bed together.

"You're giving me a lot to think about."

She flushed and didn't deliver the sexy comeback he'd expected. "I'd better go. I told Tim I'd help him restock the bar in here. Our guests are drinking a ton. Maybe we should have offered some kind of shuttle home after."

It was a good idea. "We still might be able to. Rob from the Mountain Shop has a van he uses to take folks on tours. He's here somewhere tonight and he's been sober for years."

"I'll ask him," Kit said. "Go walk around and be charming, so all these guests will become regular paying customers tomorrow."

He grinned. "That's all I am to you, huh? Just a piece of arm candy?"

She flashed him a sardonic smile. "You know it. Now get to work."

He watched her weave gracefully through the crowd, stopping to say hello to a few people. She was riveting. Everything he wanted. The image of the plane ticket he'd seen sticking out of her bag haunted him. He shoved his anxiety down. He still had time. She might decide to stay.

As he watched, she stopped walking suddenly and turned toward him, beckoning with her hand.

When he was by her side, she nudged him. "Look." He glanced in the direction she indicated and froze. His father was walking toward them, dressed in jeans and a sport coat, looking uncomfortable and stepping awkwardly past the people in his way.

"Dad?" Tyler knew he must be gaping like a landed trout. "You came."

His dad held out a hand and Tyler shook it, still confused. "I didn't think you were coming."

His dad glanced at Kit for some reason and gave her a quick nod. "I may not be much for bars, but I realized this is a big night for you. That I should stop by and say congratulations in person."

Tyler had been disappointed to see his brothers without his dad. But he hadn't known how much his father's words would mean. He cleared his throat. "I appreciate that, Dad. I really do."

There was an awkward silence, but Kit was there to guide him through, as always. "Tyler, why don't you walk your dad around? He might like to see the barbecue area. Or even the barn. I can make sure everything's going well here."

He tried to convey his gratitude in a look. "That would be great."

"That's kind of you, Kit," his father said, though the look he fixed on her didn't seem appreciative. "But I can't stay. I'm already up past my bedtime. Just wanted to see the place and congratulate Tyler on his new business venture." His eyebrows raised as an especially loud whoop came from the mechanical bull arena. "You've obviously worked really hard on it."

He clapped Tyler once on the arm and nodded to Kit. And headed for the sports bar and the exit there.

They stood side by side, watching him go. Tyler glanced at Kit and saw a small, satisfied smile playing on her lips. And it hit him what her errand had been. "Did you...?" He was unsure whether to suggest that she'd go to such lengths for him.

Her smile was unreadable and she shrugged. "I'm just glad he realized that he should stop by tonight."

"I don't think he realized it on his own."

"I think he cares about you a lot. He just has trouble showing it." With that, she headed toward the bar, ducking behind it. He watched her slip right into bartending mode, taking a drink order and filling a pint while she listened to whatever Tim said. Working her usual magic behind the bar.

Magic he was pretty sure she'd used to get his dad to show up here tonight.

KIT CLOSED THE door on the last of their customers, then turned the key in the lock. She leaned against the door and let out a breath. It had been a great night. People had loved the food, the different bars, the dancing. Tyler had been smart to close early. It had left everyone wanting more. Tomorrow night would be busy. And many nights after that.

Tyler strode toward her, beaming. "What do you say, Kit Hayes? Do we know how to run a bar or what?" His hand went up for a high five, and she gave it to him, surprised when he scooped her off her feet and twirled her around in a hug. "We did it," he said, setting her down. "We opened and people liked it and it went great!"

"It was amazing," she agreed. "Can you believe five months ago you walked in here with a dream, and now it's all happening?"

He laughed and tucked her elbow through his arm, and they walked through the sports bar to the dance floor. "Can you believe that five months ago you threw me out and dumped me in the parking lot?"

She laughed. "Now that I can believe." But their teasing didn't feel as lighthearted as usual. She'd learned so much since that night. And fallen in love with Tyler in the process. And now that the renovations were finished and the bar had reopened, it was time for her to move on. She just wished the thought didn't hurt quite so much.

THE STAFF PARTY was held in the back bar by the dance floor. Tyler kicked it off with a short speech thanking the staff. He was tired and so were they, but they'd created something great and he wanted them to know it. Then he set them loose to party.

And what a party it was. The kitchen staff had made tons of food and that's where everyone went first, filling their plates, hungry after rushing around to make opening night run smoothly.

Kit stepped behind the bar and yelled, "Come get your drinks. I challenge you to request a cocktail I don't know."

And for the past hour, no one had been able to stump her.

He'd stayed away, finding opportunities to chat with everyone and congratulate them on their work tonight. But he was also aware of Kit, watching her work, listening to the banter she traded with whoever was at the bar. But now everyone had a drink in hand, and most of them were on the dance floor, bopping around as the DJ spun eighties music.

He couldn't stay away anymore.

"What can I do for you, boss?" Her smile was warm, a little shy. "I hope you're celebrating, too. You deserve to cut loose."

He held out his hand. "How about you let me take you around the dance floor?"

Her dark eyes widened. "Really? Is that a normal boss-employee activity?"

He laughed outright. "Since when have we had

a normal boss-employee relationship?" He pretended to think for a moment. "Let's see…almost never. And certainly not last night. Or the night before."

Her cheeks went bright pink. "Shush. Okay, I'll dance. For a moment."

"Good. Because we both deserve to cut loose and celebrate." She came around the bar, wiping her hands on a towel. He tucked her arm in his as they crossed the room. Maybe it was weird to ask her to dance so formally, but he didn't really care. Their agreement was over. The bar was open and it was clear to him already that it would be a success. So he'd enjoy this night with her and try to make it another one she couldn't forget. Hoping that all of their unforgettable nights would add up to something she couldn't leave behind.

The staff let out a cheer when they stepped onto the dance floor. "Right on, Tyler and Kit," Loomis shouted, drinking a beer and bobbing up and down to the music, like a huge dancing bear. "To our awesome bosses," he yelled, and everyone joined in the toast.

It was amazing to remember that they'd all hated him at that first meeting. One more thing he had Kit to thank for. She'd taught him how to listen, how to be flexible. How to keep an eye on his vision but make it work for everyone else, too. He took her hand and spun her around. Then pulled her closer. He wasn't much of a dancer, but there was something about her that made him want to dance.

She twirled, laughing, into his arms, and her gaze met his. And he saw it then. The thing she kept so guarded, the thing she kept hidden behind all her teasing. Love. She felt it, too. He could see it in the shy warmth in her eyes. In the way she bit her lower lip when she looked at him. And he wanted a chance to tell her that he felt it, too.

He lowered his head to hers, just a little, and caught the sharp intake of her breath. "Kit…" he murmured.

"Not here."

"I don't want to wait another minute for you," he murmured.

"Your staff—"

"Can think whatever the hell they want." He wasn't hiding how he felt anymore. Not from her or from anyone.

She laughed low. "Okay then."

So he kissed her, right there on the dance floor, his hands in her hair, his mouth over hers, to the cheers and catcalls of the Dusty Saddle staff.

Then he had the best hour of his life. Because now they weren't hiding how they felt. She beat him at pool, he beat her at darts, the entire staff danced in a circle to "YMCA," and he felt like a fool but at least he had plenty of company. He took a spin on the mechanical bull and rode out eight seconds on the highest setting, Kit rewarding him with a passionate kiss at the end.

Then it was time to clean up. Everyone helped stack chairs, then Kit sent them home, and it was just them washing the glasses and wiping down the bar. "We did good, didn't we?" he said.

"I'm so glad we threw them this party. It was great for morale. And now the new people know everybody and it will make work so much more fun for all of them."

"It *is* fun, isn't it? Working at this bar. I like it."

"It's been really, really fun," she said quietly.

And he tried, really hard, to ignore the way she'd just spoken in past tense.

CHAPTER SIXTEEN

KIT WATCHED TYLER jump out of his truck in front of her house. So much about him was familiar now. The way his fingers fidgeted with his car keys as he walked up. The excitement in his smile and the searching way he looked at her.

"You're not too tired? I mean, we did open a bar and restaurant tonight."

"Oh, I'm tired," she told him. "But you promised to make sure I stayed wide awake." She shot him a teasing look. "Or was that all talk?"

His laugh rang out. He put his mouth to hers, weakening her knees with a long, slow kiss. "Not just talk," he said against her mouth. "Definitely some action, too."

"Then come in." She tugged at his hand. "Sleep with me." She kissed him again and he wrapped his arms around her, kissing her as he walked her through her front door and down the hall to her bedroom, shedding clothes as they went.

She clung to the solid strength of him, while his kisses moved to her neck as he laid her on the bed, to her breasts as he lowered himself next to her, to her waist and thighs as he chased away all rational thought.

He slayed her when he was like this, loving with no hesitation, no doubt, going after loving her with the same intensity he had when he pursued every other thing he wanted. He was hands, mouth, whispered words...every part of him showing her how much he wanted her. Every move he made pushing her toward her peak again and again.

They slept, but sometime in the night she woke and worried, desolation creeping over her. The black-hole knowledge that this relationship would be over soon and her heart would break. He must have sensed her mood even in sleep, because he woke, his hands seeking her, warming her, lulling her fears with the heat he brought, stoking that heat to incinerate her worry, at least for now.

After, he wrapped himself around her and snuggled them under the covers. "Let's get some rest."

She was already boneless, lost deep in the contentment he'd wrought. "I love you, Tyler. So much," she said, only half conscious.

There was a pause, then she felt his lips, soft on her shoulder. "I love you, too, Kit. So much."

Then exhaustion caught up with her and she slept.

KIT STARED AT her suitcase, waiting so quietly by the door. Looking so innocent. Just a simple piece of luggage. Except it was so much more. When she'd bought it, it had been a symbol of hope. A sign that she was finally doing something different with her life. That she was going to have adventures and see new things.

But this morning it looked different.

It looked like sadness, because she was leaving. It looked like cowardice, because she was leaving without a goodbye.

But how could she say it? She'd take one look at Tyler's beautiful face, his warm eyes, and she'd unpack in a heartbeat. And never know a life outside of Benson.

The very thought of that made the walls of her rental cottage feel smaller, as if they were inching in on her to crush her forever.

But she loved him. This past month had surpassed any fantasies she'd had, gone beyond any of her wishful thinking about what love could feel like.

When they'd finally rolled out of bed today, it had been late morning, and Tyler had to get to the bar. He'd had a fast shower, then they'd shared a quick kiss. He'd asked her if he could see her tonight, and she'd nodded yes. He'd caught her hands in his, looked into her eyes and told her he loved her. *I love you, Kit, with all my heart. I just want you to know that.* It was one thing to whisper it in the dark. But to say it out loud, in the bright light of day… She'd always remember his sweetness and the way she could see the love in his eyes. She'd also remember the way she hadn't found the courage to say the words back.

When she'd shut the door behind him, she'd slid to the floor, letting the tears she'd been holding back slide down her face.

Their timing was just so bad.

Her sobs had slowed as resolve kicked in. She'd told herself that love was only a feeling, and feelings could be managed. That bad timing happened all the time.

She'd pushed herself up and gone to her computer, tapping her fingers restlessly until the screen lit up and she could access her email account. And her plane ticket.

She was supposed to leave next week, but she read the fine print. For a hundred-dollar fee she could change her flight and leave tonight. She logged into the airline site, hesitating only a fraction of a second before changing her ticket. It was better this way. Better for both of them.

So here she was. A note for Tyler clutched in her hand. Her suitcase, so innocent-looking, so full of turmoil, waiting by the door. She walked toward it slowly. Hefted its weight. Took one last look around her shuttered cottage then wrenched open her front door. So what if her insides churned like a blender? So what if her heart hurt with every beat? Her new life started now, before old patterns could get in the way. Before she gave up everything for love one more time.

She glanced at the note in her hand. She'd drop it in his mailbox on the way out of town. That way he could read it after work this evening. She'd be in Mexico by then, and that was for the best.

TYLER PRIDED HIMSELF on his stamina. He'd always been able to push himself harder than the next guy. Hang in there, just a little longer, when the clock was ticking. But opening the bar yesterday, and his night with Kit afterward, had worn him out. So much that he'd left the bar in Lila's care to head home for a nap.

A nap. He must be getting old. Or soft. But sleep blurred his brain as he pulled his truck up to his rental house. He was surprised to see Kit on his doorstep, tucking something into his mailbox.

"Hey, beautiful," he called softly from the sidewalk. "Is that a love note?"

She faced him and he noticed her skin was paler than usual. That her eyes were shadowed underneath. "Are you okay? Is something wrong?" He went to her.

She stepped back, keeping space between them. "I'm fine," she said quietly. "But I'm leaving."

"What?" He grabbed the envelope from the mailbox and yanked the letter out of it, skimming the contents. She hadn't said much. Just goodbye and good luck. And that she loved him. He stared at her, his heart pumping ice water through his veins. "You were sneaking away? And leaving me *this*?"

She nodded and started to back toward the sidewalk. "I'm sorry. I thought it would be best for both of us if I just went."

The hurt crushed him. That she'd even consider just walking out of his life. "You were wrong."

Her face was ghostly white. "I have to go."

He couldn't let her. Not without a fight. "I thought you were trying to be brave, to go out and face the world. But this—" he held up the note "—is a coward's move."

It was gratifying, in a twisted way, to see the hurt he felt inside mirrored in her expression. "This is the *only* thing I could do. Because it hurts to leave. It hurts so badly."

"So don't leave."

She shook her head, vehement in her refusal to see logic. "This…this thing between you and me? It was never possible. I was always leaving and I never lied about that." Her voice rose. "What am I supposed to do? I have to go."

"You don't have to go. You don't have to do anything that you don't want to. Look, I've traveled. I lived in hotel rooms for years. Trust me when I say it's overrated. What matters is right here. Building a home and a community. People." He swallowed hard. "Even love."

She looked away at the word. When she looked back at him her hands were clenched to fists, as if she was ready to fight him. "Can't you see that I need to find that out for myself? I can't possibly stay when I have this chance to go. What if I stuck around, but became just like my mom? She was always looking down the road, wishing she could drive away. I don't want to live my life like that."

He stared at the pavement, his jaw so tense it ached. There had to be a solution for them. "I'm in love with you," was all he could come up with. "And damn it, Kit, you're in love with me. This thing we have, this love, this friendship...we belong together."

"You can't do this to me." Misery coated her voice. "You knew, before we ever got involved, that I was leaving."

"But I thought that if it was right, if we fell in love, you wouldn't go. Kit..." He held out his hands to her in a primal plea. "I don't want you to leave."

She brushed a sleeve under her eyes. "I *have* to go. This has been incredible. I care about you so much. But no matter how tempting it might be to stay with you, I can't put my life on hold one more time because of a guy. No matter how amazing that guy is." She put out a hand as if to touch him, then drew it back, like she'd changed her mind. "I have to go," she said. "Or I'll miss my plane."

He could see the tears streaming down her face, a clear message that she was making a mistake. That they'd both regret this moment. "Don't go." It was pathetic, but all he had.

"I'm sorry, Tyler." She hurried to her Jeep, got in, slammed the door, then drove away.

He watched her until she got to the end of his street. Until she turned on the county road and disappeared from view.

CHAPTER SEVENTEEN

TYLER SHOVED THE last box into the storeroom. The delivery had arrived just in time. He had a bull-riding clinic starting at the barn in about ten minutes. A few guys from San Francisco were signed up. They weren't serious, just here for a weekend bachelor party. He'd have to make sure they understood that drinking and bull riding happened at very different times. And that he didn't allow strippers at the Dusty Saddle.

He was looking forward to it, really. His coaching was going well. A few local boys were making a lot of progress under his and Garth's guidance. A few rookie riders on the professional circuit had spent time in his new arena, trying to work out some kinks in their ride. Trying to take it to the next level.

While Tyler appreciated all of their ambition and dedication to the sport, it might be nice to spend the weekend with some guys who were looking only for some fun. Because maybe then he could actually have some fun himself.

He pulled on his coat as he stepped outside. The

end of November had ice in the air here against the mountains. His boots crunched on the gravel, loud in the silence. He relished the quiet out here. He'd been spending a lot of his free time on the land, schooling his horses in the arena or heading out for trail rides in the mountains. Once in a while his brothers joined him, but more often he liked to go alone and have the time to ride and think.

It had been nearly two months since Kit left. He'd learned, pretty quick, that there were two parts to someone leaving. Them getting on that plane, and you letting them go. He'd tried every day to master that second part. But so far, it hadn't worked so well.

So he'd finally followed Kit's example and got himself a self-help book. *The Guy's Guide to Heartbreak.* And he was doing what it said. He kept busy. He exercised. He went forward with his plans. He was working on hosting a small bull-riding competition in spring, a practice event for contestants who hoped to enter the town's annual summer rodeo.

He kept busy inside the Dusty Saddle, too. He'd hired instructors to teach line dance and Western swing lessons, filling the dance floor with a solid weeknight crowd. And the sports bar was packed almost every night. His ladies' night, featuring women's sports and open to women only, was especially popular. It had been Kit's idea, of course.

But his self-help book might be a dud, because keeping himself busy didn't keep him from thinking about Kit. In fact, it was the opposite. The more time and energy he put into the Dusty Saddle, the more he missed her. She was the heart and soul of the place. And it felt empty without her.

He tried to focus on being grateful, like his book said. Even when losing her felt like he had a hole blasted in his heart. He had no regrets. It had all been worth it.

Regret, no. Loss, sadness and just plain old missing her? He had those in spades.

Garth waited at the barn, warm coffee ready in the office, the chart of bull-riding basics up on the big easel. "How are you?" Tyler asked, giving him a clap on the shoulder.

"Doing good," Garth said, pulling his hat down a little lower against the chill. "Though not sure we'll get these guys riding in one weekend."

"That doesn't matter too much. We just need to make sure they have a good time."

"Still," Garth said, watching a black SUV approach, "I wish Kit were here. She'd make sure these guys get the celebration they're looking for."

"Believe me, I miss her, too."

"I know you do."

Tyler glanced at Garth, wondering how much

he knew. They rarely spoke about Kit. What was the point of enduring all the inevitable father-boyfriend awkwardness when Tyler didn't get to be her boyfriend?

Garth must have sensed his confusion. He burst into a wheezy laugh. "Son, I may be old, but I'm not blind. I've known the both of you your entire lives. I'm fully aware you're in love with my daughter."

"I don't—" Kit's father deserved better than his denial. "I do love her. Very much."

Garth nodded, watching the SUV park a few yards away.

"You don't mind? About me feeling that way?"

Garth shot him a craggy smile. "You're like a son to me. So no, I don't mind that you love her. But I will mind if you don't get your priorities straight and figure out what really matters to you." And he went to greet their guests.

Tyler hung back a moment, feeling the sting of Garth's words. It wasn't Tyler's fault that Kit had left. He'd begged her to stay. What else could he have done?

Last he'd heard she'd finished her language classes in Mexico, done some traveling there, then headed to Guatemala. He got his news from Lila. Kit never emailed or sent him a postcard. Nothing. And he'd given up hoping she would. If she thought of him at all, it was probably with relief that she'd finally put Benson firmly in her rear-view forever.

Enough. He couldn't stand around missing her like this. He had to accept her choice and keep his focus on running a great business. He shoved his hat farther down on his head and stepped out of the barn to greet the guests. "Anyone here up for a little bull riding?" he called, gratified by the cheers that greeted him. Yeah, this would be fun, and he sure as hell could use some fun right now.

KIT STEPPED OUT of her bungalow on the outskirts of San Pedro, a bustling Caribbean town on the island of Ambergris Caye. She'd arrived in Belize almost two weeks ago, planning to stay a few days. After a couple months of hard traveling in Mexico and Guatemala, she'd been ready for an English-speaking country, for warm sun, sandy beaches and fruity drinks.

It had been an incredible trip so far. She'd walked the beautiful streets of colonial cities, climbed an active volcano and explored the ancient temples at Tikal. She'd learned to speak Spanish and still felt thrilled every time she had a successful conversation, or asked for directions, or ordered food. She'd walked through jungles, overwhelmed by their lush and dangerous beauty.

But she'd also been bitten by slimy leeches and enormous mosquitoes, and been surrounded by a

group of angry, chattering monkeys. She'd been
lost more times than she could count and had a
run-in with a tour guide who put the moves on
a little too strong. She'd had to pull out her bartending martial arts skills to escape him and it
had shaken her, and made her far more cautious.

She'd come to Belize for rest and peace, and
two weeks later, she was still here. She loved her
little bungalow with the coconut palms all around
it. She loved the white sand beaches and the incredible aqua water. She'd been snorkeling every
morning, floating in the clear, still ocean and
marveling at all the surreal fish floating along
with her. She'd seen an advertisement for a scuba-
diving class, and she was thinking of trying it.

She, Kit Hayes, Benson bartender, might learn
to scuba dive. It was almost impossible to imagine.

As always, she imagined running the idea by
Tyler. What would he say? He'd tell her to go for
it, of course. He'd say it was her next adventure.
But he'd also want her to make sure she had a
great teacher. That she'd be safe.

They might be thousands of miles apart, but he
was always with her, in her mind and heart. She'd
had countless propositions from men since she left
Benson. Other travelers wanting a quick hookup.
Locals hoping to score. She'd turned down every
offer without a single thought. There was one man
she wanted. One man she loved. And maybe they

weren't meant to be, but he'd showed her what real love felt like. And until a guy came along who made her feel like Tyler did, she wasn't interested.

Which meant she was leading kind of a lonely life these days.

That was okay, because the beach was calling and she'd picked up a novel written in Spanish that she was eager to tackle.

She hefted her bag and started down the sandy path toward the shore, passing the Southern Cross, a beachside restaurant that had become her favorite. Rogelio, the owner, was about her age. A family man who had introduced her to his pretty wife, Angel, and their three adorable children. He served fresh-caught fish and used local ingredients in his drinks, and his brightly painted restaurant had a huge deck where she loved to sit and watch the sunset.

Rogelio glanced up as Kit walked by and waved vigorously. She waved back.

"Kit, wait," he called as he hurried down the steps of the deck.

"How are you?" When she saw the worried line between his eyebrows, the shadows under his normally smiling eyes, concern stirred. "Is everything okay?"

"My head bartender quit last night. He's in love with a mainland girl. Decided to move to Placencia—gave me no notice."

"I'm so sorry. That's terrible." She knew well the bind he was in. It had only happened once at the Dusty Saddle, and they'd been lucky they had other bar staff who could step in to cover.

"I remember you saying that you are a bartender." Rogelio wrung his hands. The poor guy looked really stressed.

"I *was*," she answered carefully.

"Well, naturally, I thought of you. I don't know if you'd consider staying in Belize, but I can tell you like it here in San Pedro. Would you join me on the deck for a drink? And let me talk you into taking this job?"

Twenty minutes later, Kit stumbled down the steps in a daze. Rogelio was persuasive. He'd offered her a decent salary that would easily cover her living expenses. He'd understood that she couldn't stay forever. He wanted her for as long as she could spare.

So she'd said yes. She was the new head bartender at the Southern Cross, in San Pedro, Ambergris Caye, Belize. It was a pretty exotic address.

The opportunity was perfect, really. She'd still have plenty of time for her morning snorkel adventures. She could learn to scuba dive on her days off. And bartending on an island full of diverse people—locals and tourists and expats all mixed together—would be unforgettable. This had been her plan. To hit the road and see where life took her. And today life had deposited her in a beachside bar.

There was another reason she was thrilled to work. She'd never realized how much time traveling gave you to think. Hours and hours, days and days of time to think. And when she thought, she thought about Tyler.

About how he'd worked so hard to transform the Dusty Saddle into a bar that would make money. How he treated everyone with the same openminded, cheerful respect. How he made her laugh. How he'd given her father a new sense of purpose. How his kisses had transported her to another place, without her ever leaving home.

The memories were under her skin, making it hard to settle into her new life. She read books to distract herself. She practiced her Spanish. She wrote in a journal, making lists of countries she wanted to see. New experiences she wanted to have. Because no matter how much she missed Tyler, she knew that if she went home, she'd always regret not pursuing this dream to see the world.

She would start work this afternoon, so she headed to the beach, wanting some time with the sun and her book before she jumped into this next adventure.

TYLER WAS COVERING the original bar while Mario took his break. It was a busy Thursday night. Most of the crowd was on the dance floor, where the lessons had just ended and the DJ had everyone on their feet, trying out their new moves.

Stan was in tonight, though usually he didn't show up until Friday. With the cold weather starting, Tyler had noticed a bunch of the regulars coming in on Thursdays as well. They caught the early-bird menu in the restaurant, then spent a few hours nursing their drinks at the bar. Lately they'd been drifting over to the sports bar as well.

It was early December and snow was on the ground. Maybe that was another reason these guys were coming in earlier and more often. An old trailer out in the desert must feel mighty cold at this time of year.

Tyler was glad they were here, but it worried him, too. Crater, Stan, all the guys were getting older, and sometimes it felt like the Dusty Saddle was the only real home they had. Who was going to take care of them when they were too old to prospect? Too old to eke out their meager livings?

For the millionth time, he wished Kit was here. Not just because he missed her, but because he'd love to talk this through with her. Get her ideas. Though knowing her, she'd want Tyler to build homes for all these guys. Find jobs for them.

He made a mental note to talk with Gray and figure out what it would cost if some of these guys wanted to do odd jobs on his property for room and board and a little spending money. Because evidently, Kit's good-hearted generosity had worn off on him and he couldn't stand to think of a bleak future for his most loyal customers. For Kit's favorites.

The door burst open, bringing a blast of cold air. Tyler was surprised to see Miles stride toward him. "What's going on?"

Miles flopped down heavily on a bar stool. "Dad's sick. Dr. Miller says it's his heart. Parker is taking him to a specialist in Reno."

Tyler felt his own heartbeat get a little uneven. "Is he going to be okay?"

"They think they caught it early enough. He'll probably need some surgery, but they have to do some more tests first."

"Okay, what can I do to help?"

Miles shrugged. "Nothing. At least, not now. Later on, maybe go visit him."

"Of course." He studied his brother, noting the shadows under his eyes, the sallowness to his skin. "Are you running the ranch on your own?"

"I have the ranch hands there."

"Yeah, but you have winter calves coming soon. No offense, but you look beat."

"Are you saying you want to give me a hand on the ranch?"

Tyler looked around the bar. Everything was running smoothly. His staff was well-trained, and they hadn't had any major trouble since they'd opened. He didn't have anything scheduled at the arena, and Garth was perfectly able to handle the day-to-day care of the animals. "I can help out," he said. "I'll promote a couple of my senior staff to management. It's about time I did that anyway."

Miles grinned. A tired smile, but Tyler saw the relief there. "Okay, then. Welcome back to the family ranch."

It would be a welcome distraction from worrying about their dad. And from missing Kit. "I'll need a day or two to get things set up around here. After that, you can count on me."

"All right then," Miles said. "And now I need a beer."

"It's on the house," Tyler told him, and reached for a glass.

TWO WEEKS LATER, Tyler was questioning his decision. He put his truck in Park in front of the ranch house, but just sat, too tired to move. He and Miles had been up all night with a cow who'd calved early. Really early. The poor calf hadn't made it, and even though Tyler knew that this kind of stuff happened on a ranch, it still felt emotional. Like maybe they should have done more, or realized sooner that the birth was going badly.

The rest of the day hadn't gone much better. A cold front had come in, colder than a normal

December, and they'd decided to move the cattle into the long barns for the night. It was freezing work, rounding them up, and he'd fallen, somehow *fallen*, off his horse.

Miles had laughed long and hard about that. Would probably be telling that story for years to come. How his bull-riding champ of a brother couldn't sit a quarter horse in a routine cattle roundup.

Tyler rubbed his tired eyes with the sleeve of his heavy parka. Then reached into the chest pocket and pulled out the thing that was probably unsettling him the most. The postcard that had arrived a couple days ago. It was the first one Kit had addressed directly to him. The photo was of a colorful restaurant—the Southern Cross—in Belize. She'd written that she worked there, that she was sorry she hadn't written, that she figured they'd both needed some space. It wasn't much, nothing romantic. But she'd reached out to him and that was something.

He wondered why she'd written now. He suspected she was letting him know that she was settling down somewhere far away, to make sure he knew she wasn't coming back.

The light was fading from the day, afternoon turning to evening so fast in these winter months. Just like this postcard was sucking any last hope out of his heart. She had a job. She'd be living in Belize.

A horn sounded, startling him. He turned and was surprised to see Parker and his dad pull up. They were due home tomorrow. His dad had needed a double bypass and insisted that Miles and Tyler stay home to run the ranch while he had the surgery. This would be the first time he'd seen his dad since he'd moved here to help Miles.

Parker climbed out of the driver's side and Tyler went to meet him. And got the breath knocked out of him by Parker's strong hug. The guy must be desperate for the company of his brothers, or of anyone remotely sane, after two weeks of trying to look out for their mulish dad.

Tyler grabbed the suitcases from the back of the truck while Parker went to help their father. His efforts were rewarded by a "Back off, I'm fine." Yep, that was Dad. Maybe they should have asked the cardiac surgeon to inject a little patience and compassion into Dad's heart while he was under.

"Tyler." His dad leaned on a cane and Tyler was struck by this proof that his dad was getting older. A lot older. They were lucky Dr. Miller had caught the heart problem before his dad had a heart attack all alone in some remote corner of the ranch.

"Dad, great to see you," he said. "Come on. Let's get in out of the cold."

Inside, his dad sat heavily in his favorite arm-chair by the fire. Miles came in to say hello, then returned to the kitchen to finish making dinner. He was the best cook among them by far. Parker, looking beat, disappeared somewhere. Probably to go see his horses. That's usually where he went when he was frustrated, and spending two weeks in a hospital with their dad would have tested a saint.

Tyler took the suitcases into his father's room. "Can I get you something to drink?" he asked when he came down.

"Nah." His father stared at the flames crackling in the fireplace. "Sit down, son."

Tyler sat warily in the opposite chair.

"Tell me how things have been around here while I was gone."

Tyler told him about how they were dealing with the sudden cold weather, about the calf, about the hay delivery he'd refused because he could smell the mold in the bales.

As he talked he realized that it had been a great two weeks, being on the ranch, working so closely with the cattle. Working alongside his brother.

And the surprising thing was the Dusty Saddle did fine without him. Tim and Lila had everything in control. They checked in with him about big decisions, but every time he'd stopped by, the place was immaculate, the customers were having a great time and everything was running smoothly. It was strange to realize that he and Kit had created something so organized and well-thought-out that it barely needed them anymore.

When Tyler ran out of things to say, there was a short silence. He went through what he'd said, wondering which part his dad was upset about. Because he always said the wrong thing when it came to his dad. Always.

His father cleared his throat and Tyler braced himself for the criticism. Instead he got gratitude. "I appreciate you pitching in around here. I know you have your own business to run."

"I'm glad I could help out."

"While I was in the hospital, Parker showed me a bunch of videos. Of you riding bulls and winning all those titles. Of your world-championship ride."

"You watched them?" His brain could barely take it in. "You never watched me ride. Not once."

His father's expression was almost sheepish. "I couldn't stand to. It was a lot easier to watch it now when I know the outcome."

The meaning in the words trickled through Tyler's confusion. Gelled until he understood. "You never watched me because you were worried?"

"You're my son. And I didn't want to witness you getting killed or destroyed by one of those bulls."

"I had no idea." Tyler slumped in his chair. Years of perceived rejection and misunderstanding evaporated, leaving him crumpled. "Why didn't you tell me? I thought you were pissed because I wasn't ranching. Or that you just didn't like me."

His dad straightened in his chair at that. Then clutched his chest.

Tyler was by his side in an instant. "Are you okay?"

Looking pale, his father leaned back in the chair. "I'm fine. Just too much too quickly."

"We can talk about this another time," Tyler said. "Why don't you let me take you upstairs and get some rest?"

His dad gave a wheezy chuckle. "If there is one thing I learned the past couple weeks, it's that there might not be another time. So let's finish the conversation."

Reluctantly, Tyler sat.

"Of course I like you, son. But I'll admit, I never understood you very well. Maybe because your mom passed when you were young, so I wasn't paying close enough attention to getting to know you. Maybe because we're different. I was always real studious in school. I toed the line, you know? Did what I was told. I'm not what you'd call a risk taker."

It was strange to hear his father's perceptions of

himself. Tyler had always thought of him as strict. Unwavering. Could some of those behaviors come from fear? Aversion to risk. It explained a lot.

"Then I got a kid like you. And you were climbing the tallest trees and riding the biggest horses before you even went to kindergarten. You hated school and you loved adventure. And maybe I should have tried to do a better job understanding you, instead of just trying to keep you safe all the time. Because what you taught me when you joined the army, then took up bull riding, was that there was no way I was ever going to keep you safe. No matter what I tried."

His dad's eyes glistened in the firelight. Tyler was sure of it. His rigid, unemotional dad was almost crying. It was disorienting, as if everything in life was out of order. "But I *was* safe."

"I know that now. But I didn't know it then and I felt guilty. Like a failure. When your mom was dying, she made me promise I'd look after all three of you boys. That I'd guide you into being solid, stable men. It was easy with your brothers. They were so much like me. But you… I couldn't figure out how to get you there."

His brothers were solid and stable. He was the problem child. He'd known it forever, but it still hurt to hear it said so bluntly aloud. "So that's how you see me? As a failure?" The defensive note in his voice betrayed him.

"I saw myself as a failure because I couldn't get you to choose a career, and a lifestyle, that would keep you safe. I'd broken the promise I made to your mom."

Tyler sat, elbows on knees, staring at the fire. His dad had just been worried this whole time? Blaming himself?

"I watched those videos of you and I was so damn proud. You earned the title of champion, son. No one else rode the way you did."

"Thanks, Dad," Tyler said weakly, wondering if maybe the surgeon had done something a little different to his father's heart after all. Or maybe swapped it with someone else's.

His dad paused for a long moment. "It's ironic, isn't it? I was so scared I'd lose you that I pushed you away, and I lost you anyway."

"You didn't lose me." Tyler swallowed the emotion. "I'm still here." They sat in silence, then Tyler asked what was still on his mind. "And me owning the bar? Why is that so hard for you?"

His dad sighed. "I guess I wanted you to come home. To lean on me, just a little, for once. But I know I lost my right to have that a long time ago. And now here I am, all sewn back together, leaning on you to keep the ranch up."

"You'll be back on your horse in no time," Tyler assured him. "The doctors all said so."

"I sure hope so."

Tyler wondered if he should try one more time to get him to go to bed. But then his dad started to speak. "But I'll tell you, I was glad that Kit talked me into going to the bar that night. You took that old bar and turned it into something special. And I realized that you've grown yourself into that solid, stable guy your mama wished for. You just did it in your own way."

The praise meant everything coming from his dad. Through the emotion, Tyler registered what his dad had said about Kit. "She talked you into coming that night? I thought maybe she had, but she wouldn't say."

His dad smiled slightly. Which for him was a lot. "She didn't let on, huh? I can see that. She's got fire, that woman. She came out here and laid it all out for me, clear as day." His voice went creaky. "She loves you, son."

"Well, I love her, too. But she's gone now. She's in Belize."

His dad regarded him silently for a moment. "Huh," he said. And that was it.

"What?"

"I'm just wondering why you're sitting here. If you love her, you should go after her. The same as you'd do with anything else you want in life."

"She was pretty clear that she doesn't want me going after her."

"Well, all I can say is that she sure as hell went to bat for you. So maybe you should do the same for her. Why do you think she came out here that night? Because she enjoys my company? I'm not exactly her favorite person after the way I treated her dad."

"Garth works for me now, by the way. He's doing a fine job."

His dad ran his palm over his face. "I messed that one up real bad, too. I was taught to play by the rules. To stick to 'em like they were gospel. I should have bent them for Garth. He deserved that from me."

"I got him covered. His finances are just fine now."

His dad shook his head. "You shouldn't have to clean up my mess. If I write a check, will you take it to him?"

"I think it would mean a hell of a lot more to him if it came straight from you. It wasn't just the money, Dad. Your ranch was his life's work. The way you let him go, it knocked his pride right out of him. It's taken him a while to get it back. I think you should take that check to him personally. With an apology."

"I'm not very good at all this heart-to-heart stuff."

Tyler walked over and put a hand on his father's shoulder. "Seems to me like you're doing it just fine. Now, come on. You need to get to bed. One of us will bring your dinner up." He helped his dad out of the chair, startled when his father pulled him in for a quick hug and a clap on the back.

"You're a good man, Tyler. I'm proud to be your dad."

It was hard to get the words out, but no way was he going to bawl like a baby. "Thanks, Dad. I appreciate that."

"Just don't go riding too many more of those bulls."

"I was thinking of breeding some. I was hoping to get your advice on it."

He watched his dad's eyes light up at the thought. He rested his arm across Tyler's shoulders as they made their way slowly upstairs. "Now that's something I can help you with. You get me the bloodlines you're thinking of. Let me check them out. You don't want to buy from any rancher who's gone in for too much of that inbreeding."

"I'd appreciate your help," Tyler said, trying to take in this moment, so perfect, such a relief, that it almost felt surreal. "I really would."

His dad kicked him out at the bedroom door and Tyler headed down the stairs, trying to absorb their conversation. Trying to let the information settle in. All his life he'd believed his dad thought he was nothing but trouble. But it hadn't been quite that simple. Mostly, his dad had been scared. Scared he'd lose another person he loved.

Tyler went to where his coat hung on a hook. He pulled Kit's postcard out of the pocket. The white sand, the palm trees, were so exotic they looked unreal. He'd never been anywhere like that. But it seemed like a pretty good time to give it a try. Especially because the woman he loved was working there. And if his dad was right, there was a chance she might love him enough to let him back in her life.

She might tell him no, she might send him back home, but he had to try again. He'd missed out on decades with his dad due to misunderstandings and fear. He wouldn't let those same problems ruin what he might possibly have with Kit.

CHAPTER EIGHTEEN

KIT SWIPED AT the bar with a clean rag. The sun had gone down, the dinner guests had cleared out and the late-night crowd at the Southern Cross was growing. This was her favorite time of night. When the locals showed up. She loved the cheerful crowds, the stories they told of growing up on the island. Tonight some of Rogelio's friends had brought their instruments and were playing the traditional punta music of Belize. Its African-sounding rhythms had her swaying behind the bar.

She'd never lived anywhere like San Pedro. The camaraderie reminded her of working at the Dusty Saddle. Locals looked out for each other. They danced and sang together. And thanks to Rogelio's and Angel's friendship, they were welcoming her and making her feel a part of their community.

A young American couple who'd had lunch here today threaded their way through the dancing crowd to the bar.

"Hey!" Kit shouted over the music. "You made it back!"

"You were right!" the girl shouted back. "This is amazing. What great music!"

"Isn't it incredible?" Kit often tried to get tourists to come by for the late-night music. She was no expert on Belize culture, but to her nothing seemed more essential to what she knew of this island than these impromptu parties at Rogelio's bar.

Kit made them their drinks, glancing nervously at the growing crowd waiting for her help. Usually Rogelio helped her bartend at these parties, but she hadn't seen him in several hours.

A movement at the end of the bar caught her eye. A man stood there, quite still. He was tall and broad, and wearing a cowboy hat. "You need a little help back there?" he called, and his voice went straight to her heart.

"Tyler?" She slid the drinks across the bar and ran to him on instinct. But stopped before she reached him, remembering their fight, the harsh words. "What are you doing here?"

"Helping you, I think. You're swamped. Permission to come aboard, Captain?"

"I can't afford to pay you," she told him, her heart taking happy leaps in her chest. "But I could use the help. Work for tips?"

"Deal." He grinned and stepped behind the bar. "Who's thirsty?" he yelled to the crowd, and picked up a pint glass, flipping and catching it in his best Tom-Cruise-in-*Cocktail* style.

Kit laughed and took her next order, snapping the tops off of a few bottles of the local Belikin beer. Tyler caught her eye and flashed her that wide smile she'd first fallen for.

"Why are you in Belize?" she asked when they stood near each other for a moment.

"To see you. Nice place you've got."

"Well, it's not mine. But thanks." Her words were stilted but there was no way to be fluent when her mind was busy trying to comprehend that he was here. "Is everything okay at home? What about the Dusty Saddle?"

"Everything is good. Your dad is happy running the barn, and Tim and Lila are managing the bar now. Hey, these folks want rum punch. How do I make it?"

"It's the local specialty. Watch and learn, grasshopper."

He laughed. "Just like old times."

She showed him the measurements of white and coconut rum and added orange juice, pineapple juice, a spritz of lime and a dollop of grenadine. She decorated the glasses with a tropical garnish and put them on a tray. "There's your rum punch," she said, sliding the tray to him. "You should try one later on. They're delicious."

"Maybe, but it looks pink. And fruity."

"You're in the Caribbean now," she reminded him. "And you're sort of an expert at pink drinks back home, if I remember right."

He grinned. "I might have to take this recipe back to the Dusty Saddle and start a new trend. I could use a break from making cosmopolitans." He took an order for beer and reached in the big cooler below the bar for bottles. "Maybe we could name it after you. Kit's Island Elixir."

She laughed. No matter how they'd left things between them, it was so good to joke with him again. "My own memorial cocktail. I'm honored."

They separated for a while, but when a few more orders for rum punch came in, they were back side by side, with Tyler trying his hand at the cocktail with Kit observing. She couldn't help asking another question while he poured rum into the shaker. "When did you arrive?"

"Yesterday evening. I stopped by here, but they told me you had the day off. I found a great place to stay not too far from here. It felt incredible to wake up this morning and just jump right in the ocean. I've never been anywhere tropical like this. It's another world."

"A really great world." She sliced a few wedges of pineapple for the garnish and impaled them on toothpicks. Added a cherry.

"You love it here, then?"

"It's thirty degrees at home. This is a nice change."

They worked together for another hour or so. The music pulsed and even Tyler couldn't resist the driving rhythms, busting a few moves behind the bar. He was funny and gorgeous and everything that she was in love with, and he was here. Which meant he must have missed her, a lot.

Which was thrilling, but scary, too, because her heart was still raw from missing him these past couple months. And now, when he left again, she'd miss him even more.

Finally Rogelio showed up at the bar, rushed and apologetic. "Angel's mother is ill and needed her help. I had to run home to be with the kids. It took me a long time to find someone to watch them." Then he caught sight of Tyler. "You have a coworker." He looked at Kit, puzzled.

"Rogelio, meet Tyler. From California. He owns the bar I worked at for years. He showed up tonight and I put him to work. For tips only, of course."

Rogelio strode over and shook Tyler's hand. "Nice to meet you, Tyler. Welcome to Belize. Thank you for stepping up tonight." He surveyed the crowd. People weren't drinking nearly as much now, just dancing to the music outside under the tropical stars. "Why don't you two go enjoy yourselves? I can handle it from here on out." He reached into the cooler and pulled out two beers, popping the tops off and sliding the bottles toward them. "Go. Dance. Enjoy the night."

"Thanks, Rogelio," Kit said, leaning over and giving her boss a kiss on the cheek. "Tell Angel I hope her mother feels better soon. And that I'll make sure to tell her all about it in the morning."

Rogelio gave a booming laugh at the inside joke. "My wife, Angel, loves to gossip," he explained to Tyler. "If I tell her I gave Kit the night off to see a boy, and I don't have more information, she won't let me sleep, asking questions I can't answer."

"Sounds like our hometown," Tyler said, laughing. "Gossip is a hobby for a lot of folks."

Rogelio grinned. "It is the same here in San Pedro. It's universal, I guess."

They thanked Rogelio, took their beer and left the bar. Kit couldn't help dancing a little as they made their way through the crowd. "Isn't that music incredible? I love working here. Come on, let's go walk out on the beach and you can tell me why you're really here."

As THEY THREADED their way through the dancing crowd, Tyler tried to absorb this new version of Kit. He'd managed to steal a few glances while behind the bar, but it had been really busy. Now he had a moment to study her, lit up by the nearly full moon. She wore no makeup. Her hair was pulled back in a simple ponytail, revealing thin silver hoop earrings. A loose cotton sundress, patterned in pale reds and golds, clung to her skin, but not in the tight way she'd worn her clothes at home. Her dress showed her tattoos, the rattlesnake on her arm reminding him of the mountains and desert back home, the exotic flower on her shoulder matching her current location perfectly. As if she'd somehow known she'd end up loving both places.

She was beautiful in such a natural, comfortable way that something tugged at his stomach. A longing so sharp it ached. This was the Kit he loved.

No matter what happened between them, he was glad he'd come. Glad he'd seen her this way. "Rogelio seems like a great guy," he said, as they emerged from the palm trees and out onto the white sand beach.

"He and his wife have been so good to me. And they have three kids, Carlos, Lucia and Gabriella. They're adorable."

"It's good to see you happy," he said. "You *are* happy, right?"

"I'm happy," she said mildly.

But there was something else there, too. He didn't pry. Instead they walked on the beach, drinking their beer while she told him about Mexico and Guatemala. And he told her about his father, and working on the ranch. And how his dad finally watched his rodeos on video. "He said he's stayed away all these years because he couldn't deal with losing me. He couldn't handle seeing me compete because it is so unsafe."

"He loves you. I could tell when he showed up at opening night."

"He told me what you did. How the only reason he came that night was because you went out there and yelled at him."

"Oh, that." She smiled faintly. "Well, someone had to. Might as well have been me."

He laughed. "Well, you worked some kind of magic on him. He's different now. Or trying to be." The beach ended in a rocky point a few yards in front of them. "Want to sit? You might need a seat for what I'm about to tell you."

"Good news, I hope?"

"I think so."

She folded her legs and sank into the sand. He plopped down beside her and told her how his dad had shown up at his barn the other day, when Tyler and Garth were in the office making plans for next spring. How his dad had astounded them both with a heartfelt apology to Garth.

"No way." Kit shook her head. "I never thought that would happen."

"Believe me, neither did I. But there's more. After my dad apologized, he handed your father a big check to cover the loan he took against his pension."

"No way!" Her eyes were wide in the moonlight. "That is a miracle."

"But your dad flat-out refused to accept it. So I mentioned this idea I've been playing with, of providing housing for some of the old-timers at the bar. You know, Crater, Stan, some of those guys? They're getting older and I've been worried that maybe they can't stay way out in the desert anymore."

She stopped him. "You want to provide housing for my regulars?"

"Don't get all sappy on me." He could feel his face growing warmer even in the cool night air. "They're my regulars now, too. But yes, I'm thinking about it. I mean, it seemed like kind of a crazy idea at first. But they've been coming into the bar more often. I can't help but think that they're lonely and uncomfortable the way they're living. A few of them have got to be pushing eighty. And who else is going to help them if we don't?"

"It's a great idea," she said. "I love it."

It warmed him to hear her praise, but he had to be honest. "I don't know if it'll work. I need to find out what's really going on. I wish you could talk with them."

"Me, too. Maybe we can video conference me in."

Tyler laughed. "It's hard to picture those guys

in a video conference. Stan would spend his whole time asking how the whole thing worked." He imitated the old miner's voice. "'Now tell me a little more about this contraption, Tyler.'"

She giggled. "They sure are characters, aren't they? I miss them."

"They miss you."

Kit was silent a moment, sipping her beer and staring at the ocean. Maybe it was selfish, but Tyler hoped she was homesick. That she was thinking of coming home. But she just said, "So how is this connected to your dad's apology?"

He'd forgotten to finish the story. Just the memory made him smile. "So my dad offered this big check and your dad refused. But when I mentioned my plans for our older regulars, your dad yanked that check right out of my father's fingers and handed it to me. And told me to use it toward making my idea a reality."

"That's amazing!" Kit's face was lit with her smile. "It's like that money is coming full circle. To help other older guys in need, now that my dad's okay."

"It seems like justice," Tyler said.

They sat for a few minutes, watching the waves, sipping their beer in awkward silence because he was sure Kit was wondering what the hell he was doing here. It was time to stop hedging his bets. He'd flown all this way to make sure they didn't lose their chance together because of pride and misunderstanding. He had to go for it.

He glanced at her. She was staring out over the ocean, her beer forgotten beside her. He bumped her gently with his shoulder to pull her attention back from the moonlight glinting on the waves.

"I've missed you so much."

Still watching the water, she nodded slowly. "I miss you, too," she said softly.

"I've been working hard, pushing myself, to try to let you go. But I can't. You're all I think about—all I want. Nothing's the same without you." He paused, took a deep breath and went for it. "You're my adrenaline rush, Kit. Without you everything feels flat. I love you. More than I thought possible to love anyone."

She leaned her head on his shoulder, so he put his arm around her and pulled her against him. It felt incredible to have her so close again. Like an essential piece of a puzzle that fit perfectly under his arm. He waited for her to say something. Anything.

"I love you, too. Tyler, I love you so much it hurts not to be with you."

The relief he felt was soul deep. He'd been desperate to hear it. He planted a grateful kiss on her soft hair. She looked up at him with wide eyes and parted lips, and he kissed her sweet mouth, feeling like he was home after being lost for months. "We're meant to be together," he said between kisses. "Please, Kit, spend your life with me." With his free hand he reached into his jeans pocket and pulled out a blue velvet box. He flipped it open to show her the diamond and ruby ring inside, his heart smashing into his rib cage because he needed this. He needed her. "Please come home with me. Please say you'll marry me."

She gasped at the sight of the ring. And scooted a few feet away. It wasn't the reaction he'd hoped for. And he sure wasn't ready for the anger narrowing her dark eyes, or the way the moonlight glinted off the tears sliding down her cheeks. "I can't marry you. I love you, so much, but I don't want to go back and live in Benson. Not yet. Maybe not ever."

Desperation had him grasping for reasons why she *should*. "That doesn't make sense. We're perfect together. The moment I showed up tonight, we were in sync. Totally happy together. How can you walk away from something like that? From me?"

"Because I need to do this. I need to travel, try new things, see new places." Her voice rose and her hands balled to fists.

The solution was so clear to him. He just had to make her see it. "You can travel. I'll make sure we take a lot of vacations."

"That's not my dream. You're not listening to

me. I'm not your bar or your rodeo career. You can't keep trying, asking and pushing, and assume that eventually you'll get what you want!"

Her words hit him like a punch. "What's wrong with trying hard for something that we both know is right? Why can't you trust me?" he countered. "Why can't you trust in our love?"

"I keep trying to explain. This isn't about love. I do love you. I *want* to be with you. We *are* perfect together. Except that you want to run a bar and rodeo school in Benson, and I can't spend my whole life there. I have gone around this in my head about a million times since I left home. We want different things. I don't see how we can be together."

"There has to be a way. You could travel for a little longer. Then come home to me. I'll wait for you, as long as you need."

"No!" Her raised voice startled them both. "Can't you see? This is my dream! *You* had a dream for the Dusty Saddle. And I supported it, even when it worried me. I stepped up for you to help make that dream happen, over and over. And, yes, you were paying me, but I could have just done the minimum. But I didn't. I put my ideas, my creativity, all of my energy into your dream!" She paused as if catching her breath. "Why can't you do the same for me?"

"I'm trying." He stared at the ring, a bitter feeling pooling in his stomach. She was right. He was selfish. But it was a part of him, a stubborn, bull-headed part of him, that drove him to reach for what he wanted. "I'm trying to support it. But I need you, Kit. I need to know you'll come home to me. Eventually."

She shook her head. "I can't promise that. There's still so much I want to see and do. If I went back to Benson anytime soon, I'd just feel like my whole life had been one big stretch of the same old thing. I can't handle that. I just can't."

His heart was thumping in an uneven rhythm, like it couldn't find its way in the face of her refusal. "There has to be a solution for us."

She swiped at the tear that spilled down her cheek. "I can't see it. And it breaks my heart. Because I love you so much, and I've missed you every minute that I've been gone. But you belong in Benson. And I can't go back right now."

She pushed herself up from the sand, tears streaming down her cheeks, and he stood to face her, shutting the ring box and shoving it back into his pocket.

Her voice sounded broken. "I wish you hadn't come here. Because I was just starting to accept losing you. I was just thinking that I might learn to live with the pain. And now it's back. All of it." She started walking away, her arms wrapped around her chest as if she was holding herself upright.

He ran after her. "Let me walk you home."

"I'm fine," she insisted, but she was sobbing, and when he put an arm around her she leaned into his chest and he could feel her shaking. He held her close and together they crossed the beach and made their way along quiet streets to her bungalow.

He'd planned to say good-night at the door, to let her go no matter how much it tore at him. But she clung to him and he couldn't leave her alone with her heartache. So when she reached up, teary-eyed, to trail her fingers down his jaw, he gave in to what felt right in every part of him. He kissed her. Gently. Slowly. Savoring every blissful second of her mouth under his. And when she pulled back to look at him, stunned, he kissed her again.

And he kept kissing her, reminding her of what they were together, reveling in the heat of her mouth, the satin of her skin, the fullness of her hips under his hands, as she pulled them through the door of her bungalow and over to the bed.

And maybe it was just a funky beach bungalow in Belize, but with her there, it felt like home. He felt it even as she tore at his clothing, as if she could tear down the things that kept them apart in the process. Even as she ran fevered hands over his skin, and his body roared to life in response.

It felt so good to throw off the doubt and worry.

To shove aside the burden of the future, to stop thinking about what couldn't happen and focus on what could. This fiery want that seared away everything but her body, her skin, her hair, wound like a rope in his hand, anchoring him to her as she shoved down his jeans, as her hand closed around him and almost sent him over the edge right then and there.

"Wait," he managed to gasp out, and he set her away, kicked at his jeans to get them all the way off and pulled her dress over her head.

She didn't wait. She yanked back the covers and slid onto the bed. She unhooked her bra and tossed it aside, never taking her dark eyes from his face.

And no way would he look away. Because her eyes held a promise that went deeper than any he could have made with that ring. That no matter where she went or what she did, she'd love him like this.

He could see it. Feel it in the way her breath matched his when he lay on the bed, as they filled their hands with each other, filled their souls with everything they'd missed while apart. And when he entered her, he buried his face in the scent of her neck, and whispered over and over that he loved her. And that they would find a way. That he'd think of something. Hoping that if he said it enough, the tears that ran down his own face would dry. Hoping that his words would come true if he repeated them enough.

TYLER SAT ON a narrow dock, built out over a shallow bay. Kit was working the day shift, so he'd rented a bicycle and brought his snorkel gear to this quiet place outside of town, where he could float with the fish and try to relax.

He'd seen some great fish. The sun beat warm on his skin. The whisper of water was soothing. But he wasn't relaxed.

There was no escaping the voice in his mind that reminded him that days were going by. That he couldn't stay in Belize, making love to Kit in every free second she had. It was paradise, but he had responsibilities to get back to. He'd checked in town before he rode out here. There were seats available on a flight to Belize City tomorrow morning. From there he could catch a plane home. But he wasn't sure he could get on that plane without knowing that he'd see Kit again, very soon.

Maybe for now, all they could do was this. She'd travel somewhere and he'd hop a plane and meet up with her, whenever and wherever he could. As long as he had Lila and Tim managing the bar, and he didn't overschedule the rodeo school, he could take a fair amount of vacation.

But it didn't solve their problem. Him showing up for brief vacations, but not really experiencing the world with her, would end them eventually. He'd had days to see how she lived here. How she'd gotten to know so many people on the island, and how much she enjoyed learning their culture. Traveling was her dream. And she was glowing and content, living that dream here in Belize for now.

Plus he didn't want visits. He wanted life with her. Real, everyday life. He wanted kids. Gorgeous, dark-haired, pale-skinned babies that they'd take on adventures every chance they got.

Regardless, he still didn't have a solution, so he got on his bike and headed back to San Pedro. Along the way he tried to psych himself up for the trip home. He'd brought his laptop, so on the flight back he'd go through the calendar he and Garth had drafted before he left. Maybe make some adjustments so he'd have time to visit Kit again soon. Again, not a solution, but at least it was something to look forward to.

He dropped his bike and gear off at the rental shop and went to find her. Her shift was ending soon and they'd talked about walking through town and grabbing dinner. Maybe he'd wait until after they ate to tell her he needed to leave. Not that he had an appetite for food.

Kɪᴛ ᴛᴏᴏᴋ ᴀ sɪᴘ from her beer and studied the menu. They'd picked a local restaurant on a side street in town, and the big open windows and bright tropical colors on the walls should have made for a cheery meal. But Tyler had been quiet when he picked her up, and most of her attempts at conversation had failed.

A waiter came to take their order. When he'd finished, Kit reached across the table for Tyler's hand. It was tanned from his days in the sun here. Island life suited him. Cargo shorts and flip-flops actually went pretty well with his rodeo T-shirts. She loved having him in Belize with her these last couple weeks. And despite the unresolved issue between them, she was glad they'd moved beyond their epic fight his first night here and been able to enjoy each other.

She'd become remarkably adept at ignoring the future these past few days. She'd conjured up some kind of mental blinders that had her seeing only what was directly in front of her. Because when she looked ahead, to life without Tyler, it felt like she was heading into some kind of abyss. "What's going on?" she asked.

"I need to get back home. There's a flight tomorrow. I think I should be on it."

And there it was. The abyss. Looming and

lonely. "Oh?" She tried to hide the quaver in her voice by taking a sip of her beer.

"It's time." His voice sounded like a burden that he was tired of carrying. "I've got events planned at the bar that I can't delegate."

"Okay." She took a deep breath, hoping it would stabilize her. But instead her lungs filled with tears and she had to stare hard at the label of her bottle to keep them from rising up to her eyes.

Tyler stared out the window at the palm-tree view, his jaw a set line of resolve.

Kit didn't try to fill the silence between them. And into it crept a conversation from a nearby table. American voices, discussing the menu.

"I like Belize," a man was saying. "But I wish I could get a decent steak. Or a burger. Or anything."

"I know, honey," a woman's voice agreed. "The meat here is terrible. Everyone says so. Their cattle are just so lean. But fish is better for you, anyway."

Their voices darted back and forth as they discussed the pros and cons of each menu item. Kit peeled the label off her beer, wishing the couple would find something that appealed to them and be done with it. But slowly, the tourists' debate over plantains, beans and types of fish sank deeper into her mind and an idea started forming, growing...

Tyler turned to face her suddenly, a determined expression on his face. "I'm staying here," he told her.

"What?" she gasped out. "You can't—"

"Just listen," he said. "Please?"

She stared at him, her heart pulsing in her throat. Not believing what she'd just heard.

"I keep thinking about what you were saying that first night. That this is your dream. That traveling, living in new places, is what you need."

She nodded, trying to remember to breathe.

"Well, I've had my dreams. A bunch of them." He smiled a little sheepishly. "Hell, I'm a world champion bull rider. Most guys would be satisfied with that."

She couldn't help but smile. It was so true. "You've always been driven. I get that."

"Well, maybe I've been too driven. So busy pushing forward with this bar, with this rodeo school, that I've lost sight of other stuff that matters. Being here, in Belize, and just hanging out, swimming, snorkeling, being with you, it's taught me something. That there's more to life than chasing after a goal. There's also plain old living."

Kit inhaled a shaky breath. She'd dreamed of hearing words like this from him. But she never thought she would. "I don't know if you'd be happy just living," she said gently. "I always figured that your drive to turn the Dusty Saddle into something so big was part of that adrenaline rush you told me you need. That working so hard to make that place a success was your new eight seconds on the bull."

His slow-building grin warmed better than the tropical sun streaming in the restaurant window. "You're probably right," he said. "But there're other ways to get that rush. And the best way I know of is spending time with you."

She was smiling so wide it ached. How was this possible? Life hadn't delivered much of what she'd dreamed of, but now it was handing her this. "Are you saying that I'm your eight seconds?"

He laughed. "I want a hell of a lot more time than that. I want to be with you. Have kids with you. Have a life with you. I could see it all so clearly today, on my bike ride, but I was still scared to throw away what I've been working for. Sitting here with you, I realized I don't want that anymore. At least, I don't want it the way I want you."

He reached for something below the table. And brought out the ring he'd had on that first night, on the beach. "I shoved this in my pocket tonight. Just in case I could convince you to come home with me. But I *am* home. Wherever you are is home for me."

She took the ring with shaking fingers, studying it, giving herself a moment to take this all in.

Fiery rubies and cool diamonds clustered into a flower. The dark and the light combining to make something incredibly precious and unexpected, just like them.

This miracle. This happy ending. Over everything else, he was choosing her as his dream, as his goal.

He was beside her suddenly, on one knee. "Marry me." His voice was rough with so much emotion behind it. "Marry me and I promise you, I will fill your life with love and adventure."

She nodded, and he took the ring and slid it onto her finger, where it sparkled like a beacon in the sunlight. She threw her arms around his neck and kissed him through the tears that had spilled over now.

And when they'd toasted with rum punch, and thanked the waiters and their fellow diners for the congratulations, she leaned across the table, trying not to be too distracted by the beautiful ring on her finger. Because there was one piece missing from this life he'd just offered. But she thought she might have a way to fix it.

"What about the Dusty Saddle?" she asked.

He looked a little uncomfortable. "Well, we can keep it, for now, and pay Lila and Tim to run it."

"I don't want you to give up everything for me. I know you say you want to, but it doesn't feel right. We would need to go home to check on the bar. Maybe we could go in the summer, and you could still do some of your rodeo clinics."

He brightened. "I'd like that. And your dad and Gray can run the classes when I'm gone. I bet I know some other ex-rodeo cowboys who need a purpose in life. I can hire them, too."

"So you'd still have your rodeo school," Kit said, relieved. "And we can see our families and friends and have some time in Benson."

"And we could still house our old timers," Tyler added. "If Crater and Stan and the other regulars decide to move onto the property, they can do general maintenance. The place would do well with all of them helping."

"And I had another idea," she told him. "What if we took the Dusty Saddle on the road with us?"

"What do you mean?" He gave a nod toward her rum punch. "Do I need to cut you off?"

She giggled. "No! I was listening to these tourists earlier, complaining that they couldn't get decent beef here. It made me think…what if we opened a chain of Western bars around the world? Then we could live in a different place each time we opened one. And we'd have a purpose, because as much as I love traveling, I've realized that without work, it can feel kind of aimless. That's why I was so happy to take the job at Rogelio's bar. But what if, instead, we opened bars of our own?"

He leaned forward in his chair and she could

see the excitement in his eyes. "We're an amazing team," he said. "And I love working with you."

"Just picture it," she said. "We'd travel the world, building new versions of the Dusty Saddle."

"A Dusty Saddle empire." He threw back his head and laughed. "I like it."

"Let's say we opened a Dusty Saddle right here in San Pedro. A nice bar, done Caribbean style, but maybe with a few Western touches to the decor, too. They have ranchers in Central America. We can honor their traditions. Put their photos on the wall. Their lariats, their saddles."

Tyler's green eyes had a familiar spark to them. "And a restaurant. We could find local beef that's raised well. Maybe some of our menu could reflect local ingredients, and some choices would taste just like home."

"We'd play country music, so people could hear something familiar. And we'd make awesome cocktails, of course." Kit wasn't sure it was possible to be any happier. She picked up her glass of punch and raised it. "To the Dusty Saddle," she said.

He lifted his glass to meet hers. "To us. Together. Wherever life takes us."

"Together. Wherever. Forever." Kit took a sip of her punch.

"Sounds like you just wrote our wedding

vows," Tyler said, and he was out of his seat, pulling her up and into his arms to kiss her right there in the middle of the restaurant. "I love you, Kit. I think I always have. I know I always will. I came back to Benson, looking for home. And I found you. Thank you for showing me where home really lies."

Kit wrapped her arms around him, knowing with a sudden fierce certainty that there was nothing else she needed more than this. "Thank you, so much, for coming home, to me."

EPILOGUE

KIT CHECKED THE buckle on her harness, even though the employee at the Rain Forest Canopy Tour had already checked as well. She looked up to see Tyler doing the same. "Ethan would be proud of us," she teased, then made her voice deep and gruff, like their friend's. *"You, and only you, are responsible for your safety."*

"And that means you check every piece of gear personally." Tyler adopted the same voice.

And then they both laughed and said their favorite Ethan quote in unison. *"Trust your feet."*

Kit glanced down at the rickety wooden platform that made it a little hard to trust her feet. Memories of their friend made her wistful. "I wish he could see us now."

Tyler pulled his phone from his pocket. "He can." They took a selfie with the canopy behind them. "I can email it to him once we have some Wi-Fi."

They'd been in the jungles of Costa Rica for a week. Taking a break from supervising the construction of their new bar in Belize. Taking time for some fun before they started planning their wedding, which would take place at the Dusty Saddle back home.

The man in charge of the platform turned to them. "Are you ready?"

"Ready to slide along this cable suspended seventy feet in the air?" Kit's heart started hammering so hard it was almost hard to hear. "Um... sure?"

Tyler laughed and pulled her close to kiss her hair. "You'll be fine. More adventure, remember?"

More adventure. Their motto these days. "More adventure," she agreed.

Before they zip-lined side by side through the rain forest, their host gave them a few last-minute instructions. "Now, to go together, count to three, then jump," he told them. "And most importantly, have fun."

Kit tried to avoid looking down, but her eyes were drawn to the forest floor so far below. She bit her lip, her nerves threatening to overtake her sense of adventure.

"We've got this," Tyler said quietly. "Just look at me."

So she watched him and he held her gaze, the look in his eyes a mix of excitement and comfort. "There's no one I'd rather jump with," he told her.

"Ready?" The man looked a little impatient.

He probably had another band of tourists waiting below.

She could do this. She could do anything with Tyler at her side. She nodded, "Ready."

The man counted off for them. "One...two... three..."

And they jumped.

She was flying. She was airborne. It was terrifying except the harness held her firmly to the line and the handlebar gave her something to grip, and Tyler was flying beside her, laughing like a maniac and making her laugh, too. They sailed down and into the trees past a flock of parrots sitting on a high branch, past the vines and tangled branches of the rain forest canopy.

"Look!" Tyler took a hand off his bar, to point at something ahead of them.

Kit, white knuckling it all the way, looked in that direction and yelped, "Monkeys." Howler monkeys, lounging on branches, gazing at them with sleepy eyes as they flew by.

Then they were at the next platform, and the worker there unhooked them and attached them to the next line. This time, when they jumped in unison, Kit looked around at the green blur of the trees, at the bright blue of the sky. She'd never felt more alive. It was almost scary to think that if she'd never left Benson, she might never have felt this.

Then she glanced at Tyler and he gave her a wink that warmed her with love and gratitude. That he'd come home and bought the Dusty Saddle. That he'd given her the chance to see the world—that he loved her enough to uproot his life and see it with her. Most of all, she was grateful that he made her feel, every day, the way she did right now. Completely loved. And like every moment, every experience, was a new and perfect adventure.

* * * * *

Get 2 Free Books,
Plus 2 Free Gifts—
just for trying the Reader Service!

Get 2 Free Books,
Plus 2 Free Gifts—
just for trying the Reader Service!

HARLEQUIN *Presents*

Get 2 Free Books,
Plus 2 Free Gifts—
just for trying the
Reader Service!

YES! Please send me 2 FREE Harlequin® Heartwarming™ Larger-Print novels and my 2 FREE mystery gifts (gifts worth about $10 retail). After receiving them, if I don't wish to receive any more books, I can return the shipping statement marked "cancel." If I don't cancel, I will receive 4 brand new larger-print novels every month and be billed just $5.49 per book in the U.S. or $6.24 per book in Canada. That's a savings of at least 19% off the cover price. It's quite a bargain! Shipping and handling is just 50¢ per book in the U.S. and 75¢ per book in Canada.* I understand that accepting the 2 free books and gifts places me under no obligation to buy anything. I can always return a shipment and cancel at any time. Even if I never buy another book, the 2 free books and gifts are mine to keep forever.

161/361 IDN GLQL

Name	(PLEASE PRINT)	
Address		Apt. #
City	State/Prov.	Zip/Postal Code

Signature (if under 18, a parent or guardian must sign)

Mail to the **Reader Service**:
IN U.S.A.: P.O. Box 1867, Buffalo, NY 14240-1867
IN CANADA: P.O. Box 611, Fort Erie, Ontario L2A 9Z9

Want to try two free books from another line?
Call 1-800-873-8635 today or visit www.ReaderService.com

* Terms and prices subject to change without notice. Prices do not include applicable taxes. Sales tax applicable in N.Y. Canadian residents will be charged applicable taxes. Offer not valid in Quebec. This offer is limited to one order per household. Books received may not be as shown. Not valid for current subscribers to Harlequin Heartwarming Larger-Print books. All orders subject to credit approval. Credit or debit balances in a customer's account(s) may be offset by any other outstanding balance owed by or to the customer. Please allow 4 to 6 weeks for delivery. Offer available while quantities last.

READERSERVICE.COM

Manage your account online!
- Review your order history
- Manage your payments
- Update your address

> ### We've designed the Reader Service website just for you.

Enjoy all the features!
- Discover new series available to you, and read excerpts from any series.
- Respond to mailings and special monthly offers.
- Browse the Bonus Bucks catalog and online-only exculsives.
- Share your feedback.

Visit us at:

ReaderService.com

RS16F